DON'T BE AFRAID

ALSO BY STEVEN HAYWARD

BUDDHA STEVENS AND OTHER STORIES

THE SECRET MITZVAH OF LUCIO BURKE

STEVEN HAYWARD

DON'T BE AFRAID

ALFRED A. KNOPF CANADA

for Katherine, again

PUBLISHED BY ALFRED A. KNOPF CANADA

 Published in 2011 by Alfred A. Knopf Canada, a division of Random House of Canada Limited. Distributed by Random House of Canada Limited, Toronto.

Knopf Canada and colophon are trademarks.

www.randomhouse.ca

The first stanza of A.A. Milne's "Disobedience" on page 16 is taken from *The Complete Poems of Winnie-the-Pooh* by A.A. Milne. The William Bligh passage on page 106 can be found in *A voyage to the South Sea, undertaken by command of His Majesty, for the purpose of conveying the bread-fruit tree to the West Indies, in His Majesty's ship the bounty, commanded by Lieutenant William Bligh.* "My Grandmother's Love Letters" on page 292 by Hart Crane is from *The Complete Poems and Selected Letters of Hart Crane.*

Library and Archives Canada Cataloguing in Publication

Hayward, Steven
Don't be afraid / Steven Hayward.

Issued also in electronic format.

ISBN 978-0-676-97736-3

I. Title.

PS8565.A984D66 2011 C813.'6 C2010-902045-6

First Edition

Printed and bound in the United States of America

10 9 8 7 6 5 4 3 2 1

JAMES FORTITUDE MORRISON

My full name is James Fortitude Morrison, but nobody calls me that. Instead, I'm Jimmy or Jim. And so this is what I tell people: "I'm Jim Morrison of Cleveland Heights, Ohio." It's a sort of joke, like saying I'm no one at all.

I tell people that because the other Jim Morrison—the one everyone's heard of, the legendary lead singer of the Doors—was found dead in a hotel bathtub three days before I was born, on July 3rd, 1971. If news of his death wasn't on the front page of every newspaper, it was close. It was on the radio everywhere, for sure. There was even one radio station in Tampa, Florida, that played "Light My Fire" over and over again for seventy-two hours. It wasn't a planned thing. The disc jockey who happened to be there in the middle of the night when the news came in from Paris put on the song. When it was over, he put it on again. Then a third time, and a fourth. Soon other radio stations were doing the same thing. Three days later—when there was no choice but to accept that Jim Morrison had died and wasn't coming back—they took it off. Changed the record.

Some stations played "The End," which is another Doors song, but most played nothing at all. Just let the silence hang in the dead air. People started crying because it meant he was really gone. One of the nurses at the hospital when I was born told my mother James Morrison was the most beautiful name she had ever heard. "You can call him Jim," she told my mother, and burst into tears. She was a Doors fan, probably.

I throw in the Ohio part because that's what you do when you're from Ohio. Watch the next time you see a kid from Ohio on TV. He'll come out with it. Like there'd be some confusion. Like anyone cares. He'll also maybe say USA, but that's understandable. It's one thing to come from a country that's basically conquered the world; it's another to come from some nowhere place in the middle of that country. If you're from Ohio, you know the last thing you expect to see on TV is someone from Ohio. Except Paul Newman or Bob Hope. Or Steven Spielberg. Most of the time though, ordinary Ohio people have no business being on television and everyone from Ohio knows it.

Three days after the library exploded I was on television myself. Asking people if they'd seen my dead brother, Mike, if they knew where he was—that's what I was supposed to say, anyway. There was a big cue card in front of me that had the whole thing written out in thick black letters. I found out later that it was already too late. But that was later. Right then I was supposed to be talking to Mike, too, telling him that if he was out there watching, he should just come home, to not be afraid, that if he wanted to come back it would be okay.

Maybe you saw me that night on television.

Maybe you even remember what I look like: seventeen, ordinary eyes and ordinary hair, a little on the heavy side. Not obese exactly, not the kind of kid who has to be air-lifted out of his parents' basement every time he goes to the dentist, but if some guy were to show you a picture of me and my dead brother Mike and say, "That's him, the fat brother," you'd know exactly which one of us he was talking about.

I call Mike my dead brother because he is, and so there won't be any weirdness later. Otherwise there'd be this awkward moment when you'd have to nod and say how sorry you are, just like you'd have done if you'd been at the funeral home and had to stand there with me in front of Mike's casket. I'd thank you for being sorry, and maybe you'd say it again, say how really sorry you were, but eventually you'd walk away, leaving me there while you took off somewhere else, anywhere else, relieved it's not you in the middle of this, that it's my dead brother in that coffin, not yours.

The library blew up all at once: a flaming geyser shooting up into a dark night. First there was a flash, followed by a blossom of flame, and then everything from inside the library—the tables and the chairs, the microfilm rolls of defunct newspapers, the old 16 mm films, the computers, the green carpet in the children's section, the cassette tapes and the video cassettes, the Devhan Starway books, the old and the new record albums, the framed pictures of Pete Seeger and John F. Kennedy, the typewriters, the card catalogue, the telephones and paper clips, the due date stamps, the unused blank library cards, the staplers, the staples, the overdue notices in their stamped envelopes—all of it shot up into the night air.

Three days later the guy at the television station told me: "First say who you are, then get into the whole missing person thing."

I told him fine, and then he counted down.

The cops had given me a picture of my brother to hold up in front of the camera, a blown-up version of his yearbook photo. The weird thing about the photo was that the photographer had altered it, the way they do to take out zits and moles and anything strange. Except that instead of taking out a zit, the guy who touched up the picture took out the dimple in Mike's chin, airbrushed it smooth, as if it were some kind of defect and not part of his bone structure. It wasn't the first time I'd seen that picture, but I hadn't noticed the airbrushing until I stood beside the magnified version of it in the super-bright light of the television studio. It made it seem like I was there to talk about a Mike who had changed in some mysterious way, a version of my brother who'd already crossed over to the other side, or a replicant, like in *Blade Runner,* some robot who looked a lot like him but who wasn't him, and who I'd eventually have to kill. And the fact is at the time I sort of did want to kill him. I didn't know what he was doing or why he was doing it—or why I was in the dark about it. But I said none of that. Instead, I held that photo up and started to talk.

"Ohio" was as far as I got. It aired that night anyway. You can't hear what I'm saying but you can see my lips moving. "I'm Jim Morrison," I'm telling people, "from Cleveland Heights, Ohio." Then I passed out, fell face first onto the floor of the television studio.

A NICE PLACE

Mike and I—along with our younger sister, Vivian—had jobs at the public library because of our mother, who ran the reference desk. She was the one who did the hiring, and she hired us. Whether or not we wanted to work there was beside the point.

If you'd ever been to Cleveland Heights—before the explosion, that is—you'd probably remember seeing the library. Cleveland Heights is just east of Cleveland itself, one of the first places where people moved when the city began to go broke in the 1960s, around the time the Cuyahoga River caught fire. It's a nice place. Anyone will tell you that, and, for a while, Cleveland Heights *itself* told people that. According to my father the city ran a campaign that was supposed to make people want to move here. They put up signs and handed out T-shirts, even had a bunch of coffee cups made, all of which had printed on them the same incredibly lame slogan in bright green letters: "Cleveland Heights, a *nicer* place to live."

What that means is it's a suburb like any other, an ordinary nowhere. It isn't the sort of place you've ever seen in any movie because it's been designed so that nothing tragic or overly ironic ever happens here. You can still see where the library used to be, the collapsed concrete walls, a few stray pages in the wind, the whole of it fenced in so kids won't get hurt or killed by all the wires and rubble that's still there.

Because our mother wrote up the library schedule each week, she saw to it we worked at the library whenever we could, on weekends and after school, and every single day of our summer vacation. My sister Vivian—she's sixteen, a year and a half younger than me—worked on the main floor and she did normal library things: stood behind the circulation desk, typed up library cards and catalogued the new books by stamping them with the Cleveland Heights Library stamp and covering them with the plastic that shielded their covers from the ravages of time.

Saying that plastic would shield anything from the ravages of time was something our mother liked to do; it was her idea of a joke. Before she'd met our father, she'd been a nun and lived in a convent on Cleveland's West Side. This was something we knew, which she had sat us down to tell us in the same tone of voice with which she might have revealed we were adopted, or that our father was actually a robot. And we'd seen pictures of her in her nun's habit, her standing saintly and unsmiling outside a church on Easter Sunday with my grandparents, or beside a small, incredibly sick child in a wheelchair on Chester Avenue outside University Hospital. In each of those photos she is wearing the same heavy-rimmed black glasses they gave her in the convent, the ones she still wears today. Mike used to say there were two ways you knew my mother had been a nun, the first being those glasses, and the other being how much she liked jokes about things shielding other things from the ravages of time. "There," Mike said once, after putting some leftover meatballs in a Tupperware container, "safe from the ravages of time." You wouldn't believe how that cracked up my mother.

Perched on her stool behind the reference desk, our mother was usually the first person anyone saw upon coming into the library; Mike and I, on the other hand, led a shadowy, subterranean existence in the basement, away from most of the patrons. We were supposed to run the children's section as well, but our library had fewer than a hundred kids' books, all of which were decades old. Whenever a kid or a parent came downstairs we would suggest going to one of the two other libraries in town. If that didn't work, Mike would say something about lead paint.

Instead of signing out or shelving books, most of our time was spent cleaning and repairing the library's collection of 16 mm films. Originally, each of the Cleveland Heights libraries had had its own film collection, but videos came along, and not long after that actual films began to go the way of the dinosaur. There were good reasons for this, as Mike and I found out not long after we started working with the films. When you put a video in a video player, it works. You know it's going to play. Actual films, on the other hand, break down constantly; if it isn't the film itself that's tearing and crumbling, if it's not the sprockets that have become so frayed they can't make it through the machine, it's the projector itself that won't run. By the time Mike and I got hired by our mother, all that was left were films librarians had deemed irreplaceable in one way or another—footage of endangered species, documentaries about vanished African tribes, or antiques like *The Big Sleep* and *Mutiny on the Bounty.* They'd all been brought into a single collection that ended up being housed in the basement of our library. Mike and I had the job of making sure the films still worked: we'd splice them back together when they broke, and we'd clean the fading frames using a grey machine that sat in the rear corner of the library basement. It weighed about five hundred pounds, and Mike called it the Beast.

As endless and tedious as the job was, I didn't mind it. There were even some people who still used our films, couples having a retro movie night or a mom wanting to give her kids the experience of seeing a real roll of film pass through a real projector, unwinding at one end and winding up at the other. One man we knew liked the sound of the sprockets ticking along; he'd turn down the volume so he couldn't hear the movie and just listen to the projector.

Though our mother always saw to it that Mike and I worked the same shifts—part of my job, it seems to me now, was to make sure Mike showed up and to make sure he stayed in the library—I was the one who did the actual work. And while I did it, Mike would talk. Since about the fourth grade he'd been an ardent believer in the mysteries of the unknown, in ghosts and ESP and aliens and robots. These were the kinds of things we would discuss during those empty, otherwise silent hours in the library basement: whether the Egyptians could really have built the pyramids, if Mike could move a pencil with his mind (attempted, unsuccessfully, over a thousand times with me standing by as an objective witness), if you could come back from the dead, if you could know the future, if you could come back from the future, how much he hated Cleveland Heights, how much he hated almost everything, how it would suck to be thirty, if you could still wear a fedora the way Bogart did, and, of course, we talked about the movie that we ourselves would make, the film about our life and times and which told the truth about us, the one that would win an Academy Award and get us out of Cleveland Heights forever.

"We already have the technical side of it down," Mike said to me one afternoon, after school. This was near the end, when he had just a few weeks to live. What I remember is that he was sick of it all, of Cleveland Heights, of our parents, and maybe of me as well. I knew this—that something between us had changed, or was about to. Though sometimes he let me think differently—that we were in it together. This was one of those times.

"I don't know if that's true," I told him. "There's more to making movies than splicing, and that's all I know how to do."

"Sean Penn would play me," he said.

"And me?"

"That would be up to you," he said.

I hated it that Mike never gave this question much thought, but there was nothing I could do about it. It didn't matter how many times I asked him. I even suggested Chris Penn, thinking he'd like the famous-brother connection and that he'd still be the skinny cooler Penn brother. He said sure, whatever, but never mentioned it again. One of the things I came to understand was that the problem of who would play me was one of the things my brother didn't care much about.

Vivian, on the other hand, had made it clear she wanted herself to be played by either Molly Ringwald, from *The Breakfast Club,* or the version of Audrey Hepburn who existed around the time of *Breakfast at Tiffany's.* Whenever we were repairing an Audrey Hepburn movie and had to watch it afterwards to be sure it worked, she would come down and watch it with us. "Actually, I don't care who plays me," she told us. "So long as she's pretty in a sneaky way, the kind of girl who's really smart, but you don't know it until halfway through the movie."

"Audrey Hepburn's too old now," I said. "She's, like, seventy."

"She's old," Mike said, "but she's been covered in plastic the whole time, shielded from the ravages of time."

We all cracked up when he said that. We were our mother's children, all of us. No matter how hard some of us tried not to be.

FRANK DeSILVA

The projectors broke down almost as frequently as the movies themselves, and when they did it was Frank DeSilva who fixed them. Frank was an inspector for the Cleveland Office of Public Safety, which meant he spent his days looking at accidents, deciding if they were random occurrences or the sort of serious problems the government would have to do something about. At least once a week Frank would visit the library basement and work on broken projectors, sometimes taking them home with him at night. He was a conservationist in a way, a technological version of those Greenpeace guys who hurl themselves onto whaling boats because they love whales so much, as if the sound of clicking sprockets might one day disappear from the face of the earth if he didn't do something.

Frank was married to Mary DeSilva, the older woman who ran the library with our mother and who had worked there even longer than she had. Like Frank, Mary was in her sixties—her late sixties—though where he was thin, she was fat, with short, thick fingers and billowing cheeks. The two of them lived in the big house directly behind the library, and when you saw them walking together in the mornings they were like a couple who had defected from a nursery rhyme, one eating no fat and the other no lean, whatever that could possibly mean. You imagined a first date when Frank reached out his spindly fingers to take the measure of Mary's plump arm, like the witch in Hansel and Gretel reaching between the bars of the cage next to the stove. You could almost see Frank, licking his lips as the jeweller sized Mary's finger, saying yes, that will do nicely. Mary's actual job was running the circulation desk on the main floor, but during the hours when we were in school, it was Mary who took our place in the basement, just in case a child looking for a book or someone wanting a film wandered in.

"I was beginning to think you'd never get here," Mary would say when we showed up for our shift.

After that she would make her way upstairs, though never before trying to press on us whatever Devhan Starway novel she happened to be rereading at the time. As everyone from Cleveland Heights knows, Devhan Starway is an old-time science fiction writer, like Isaac Asimov or Arthur C. Clarke. Most of his novels have to do with robots, and, in particular, a robot named Hart Crane, which is also the name of a famous poet who was born in Cleveland. In almost every Devhan Starway book the existence of the poet Hart Crane is something someone else reminds him about. He's the other Hart Crane, he has to say, he's the robot. It's always pretty sad when that happens.

While it wouldn't be true to say Devhan Starway is the most famous person ever from Cleveland Heights—that's Bob Hope, who used to live on East Derbyshire Road in what is now a completely rundown house where the people never mow their lawn—Devhan Starway is the most famous *writer* to come from Cleveland Heights. Which isn't saying much. The house where Devhan Starway lived is a house like any other, a couple of streets away from the library, and thanks to the efforts of the Devhan Starway Appreciation Society it's on the National Register of Historic Places.

That means if you're a student at Cleveland Heights High School you get marched out each year by your English teacher to look at it, the ordinary house where Devhan Starway lived until he was eighteen. Actually, he was born somewhere else and only moved into that house when he was four years old. And it wasn't until after he moved away that he wrote any of those books he's famous for. The important thing is that he spent his formative years in Cleveland Heights, those years when his mind was being *forged*—that's the word Mrs. Long, my freshman English teacher, used for it, forged, like metal heated up in a furnace and hammered into shape—and all the while that was happening, he was sitting in English class next to Mary DeSilva. She would turn out to be his greatest fan, his official bibliographer, as she liked to say—which basically meant that she was the only person she knew of who had read every one of his books. Even though she went on to marry Frank DeSilva, the truth was that Mary never really stopped loving Devhan Starway.

Mary's dead now too. Killed in the same explosion that killed my brother.

I remember the last book she recommended to us was *My Brother, My Robot,* a ratty Devhan Starway paperback from the 1950s with a cover showing a half-naked woman being harassed by a demure robot.

I remember her telling us: "Don't judge a book by its cover."

"Too bad," said Mike. "The cover looks pretty good."

"It does, doesn't it," she said wistfully.

"That's a pretty demure robot."

"Devhan's robots were always demure," Mary said. "They were nothing if not demure."

There was something about the way she said this that made me think she wasn't talking about the robots at all. "So what happened?" I asked. "How come you're not Mrs. Devhan Starway now?"

"He was demure," she told us, "but he was no Frank."

Frank was sitting beside me, fiddling with some invisible projector part, acting like he couldn't hear a thing. Mary was, I decided, flirting with him. Frank seemed to understand this and acted accordingly—like an oblivious, disinterested robot who had been specifically programmed to resist her advances.

"I was eighteen," said Mary, "and Frankie put a spell on me."

"Not a real spell," said Frank, suddenly able to hear again.

Mary said, "But if it was, I'm still under it."

"There's really no magic involved," Frank said.

"But it *feels* like there is," said Mary.

"Does it really?" Mike said. I couldn't tell if he was really asking her or not.

Frank said, "Mary thought I was cute."

"Cute's always how it starts," said Mary.

"You *call* it a spell," said Frank, talking to us but looking at Mary, "because that's what it feels like to be in love."

"And also," said Mary, "you say it's a spell because it's something that can vanish in an instant. That's the way it goes. One day the sun rises and sets on him and the next day you can't stand the sight of him. One minute you're in love and the next it's gone." And here Mary snapped her fingers for effect, to show us how quick it can happen, how all at once you can wake up to find the world wrecked, not at all the way you remembered it.

What I think is that Mary was the last person Mike spoke to that night, seconds before the two of them were wiped off the face of the earth, though I don't know that for sure. That's four months ago now. Ancient history for everyone else in the world.

According to my father, after about a year they took down the signs saying that Cleveland Heights was a nicer place. My father said he never knew who changed his mind or why. But it makes sense. Because as nice as it is, it's only *nicer.* It's not the nic*est,* or completely nice. Cleveland Heights is like Ivory Soap, which is 99.8% pure; however pure—however *nice*—you make it, there's only so much you can do. No one really knows what that .2 percent is, maybe tears, or blood, or some unnameable industrial waste, something radioactive that you wouldn't give to a rat, but it's there all the same. It got in.

JAMES JAMES MORRISON MORRISON

Mostly people call me Jim or Jimmy.

But not my mother.

What my mother calls me is James James or J.J. because it reminds her of a poem she read to us when we were kids by the same guy who wrote those *Winnie-the-Pooh* books. Up until the day she found out about the existence of the dead rock star Jim Morrison—this happened because she saw Mike with a copy of *No One Here Gets Out Alive*, the biography of Jim Morrison and the Doors—she was under the mistaken impression that it was that kid in the poem, a good boy, as my mother would say, who other people thought of *first* when I told them my name was Jim Morrison.

Just in case you didn't used to have a job in an outdated children's section at the Cleveland Heights Public Library, this is how that old poem starts:

James James Morrison Morrison Weatherby George DuPree
Took great care of his mother though he was only three.
James James said to his mother:
"Mother," he said, said he
"You must never go down to the end of the town,
if you don't go down with me.

Don't ever go down to the end of the town,
if you don't go down with me."

"Now *that* James Morrison," said my mother as she turned around the book in her hands, "was a *nice* boy. Not like this other Jim Morrison, this singer, the one so worried about getting out alive."

"It's 'no one here gets out alive,'" Mike told her. "It means we're all going to die."

"Well, that's true," said my father. He's an engineer and, as such, he—like Mary's husband Frank—believes it's his duty to regard all things with scientific objectivity.

"Besides," said Mike, "that poem about James James is weird."

"What kind of name is James James?" asked Vivian. "Is James his middle name *and* his first name?"

"There are two apostles named James," said my mother. "Maybe he's named after both of them."

"There are other apostles," observed my father.

"They preferred James," said my mother. "It's been known to happen."

"It's what I'd call an unusually strong preference for James," said my father, as if he were trying to find some sensible middle ground on the issue. "All the same," he said, turning to my mother, "you have to admit it's a bit strange to give someone the same name twice."

"These are the kinds of things that Catholics do," my mother observed.

"What I want to know," said my father, "is where Mr. Morrison is for all of this. Why is the boy taking great care of his mother, though he's only three? All that going down to the end of the town, I'd like to know what the father thought about it. I'd like to know where he is."

"Maybe they divorced," said Vivian, who had just broken up with a boy named Grant who lives on Berkshire Road. The two of them would get back together in less than two weeks' time, but right then she was in the midst of a tragedy, and she liked reminding everyone of it.

"Now that wouldn't be nice," said my mother.

"It's the sort of thing that happens," pointed out my father.

"There's nothing you can do about it," said Vivian. "You can't make another person fall in love with you."

"Do unto others," said my mother, "as you would have them do unto you."

"What about masturbation?" asked Mike. "Jimmy does that to himself—should he do it to his neighbour? That seems like it should be against the rules, but maybe it isn't."

"Shut up, Mike," I said.

"Don't try to say you don't."

"Masturbation," said my father, "is perfectly normal."

"There you are, Jimmy," said Mike, "you can relax."

"Please," said my mother, "Petey is listening."

(Petey—little Petey as we call him—is my younger brother, the baby of the family. There are four of us, or at least there were once upon a time—Mike, me, our younger sister Vivian and little Petey. I was born fifteen months after Mike and my sister Vivian fourteen months after me. "Like birds on a wire," my mother liked to tell people. "Which is to say," my father would interject, as if he were about to turn it into a math lesson, "almost equidistant." Petey is four, more than eleven years younger than Vivian, born when my mother was forty-five years old. "An accident," my father would tell people, as if he's barely able to restrain himself from saying something X-rated. "And," my mother would immediately add, always in a way that made you think she was suggesting Petey's had been the sort of virgin birth that catches *everyone* off guard, "a most unlooked-for blessing." At the time of this discussion about James James Morrison Morrison, Petey was sitting next to me at the table. He was eating pasta with his fingers and not really listening to anything, in that utterly tuned-out, completely oblivious way that four-year-olds have. This was a Sunday, and pasta was what my mother always made on Sundays, a remnant of her own childhood and her own mother. Before Mike died, that is. You might think that, by now, we'd have gone back to having Sunday dinners the way we always did, but we haven't, and maybe we won't. The fact is, I don't know. For a while I thought my mother—along with the rest of us—was going to be turning a corner in the near future, but I don't know now. I don't know what that corner would look like, if I would see it coming even if it was right in front of me.)

"Petey," said my father, "don't listen."

"What?" said Petey.

To change the subject, Vivian said Grant—who she intended not to speak to, no matter how often he called—had a cousin who did this thing where he put out cigarettes on his own arm. "And every time he did," Vivian told us, "he got, you know—"

"A hard-on?" cut in Mike.

"Michael," snapped my mother. "Petey is here."

"What?" said Petey.

My mother told Mike: "You have to set an example."

"I wonder why that would be," said my father, as if he was inquiring into the hydraulics of the guy.

"But what if the guy likes it?" asked Mike. "What if he *begged* you to put a cigarette out on his arm?"

"I hope you would never associate with people like that," said my mother.

"I wonder what's down at the end of the town," said Mike. "James James says she can't go down to the end of the town unless it's with him."

"It must be something," said my father. "I can tell you that."

"It must be good," said my mother.

"Or else bad," said Mike.

"James James doesn't think much of it," pointed out my father.

"It could be she was addicted to crack," said Vivian. "Grant had this other cousin, or maybe it was his second cousin—and if he does call, tell him I'm not here—who was addicted to crack and he's in jail now."

"*There's* something that you'd get at the end of the town," said my father.

"They didn't have crack back then," I said.

"I don't want to hear any more discussion of crack," said my mother. Then she turned to me. "How do you know so much about the subject?"

"It must be a party that James James's mother is on her way to," said my father. "No kids allowed, a real formal affair."

"It's because she's a hooker," said Mike.

"A what?" said my mother.

"A prostitute," translated my father.

"That is a terrible thing to say about the mother of James

James," said my mother. "A mean thing. I'm sorry I ever told you about the poem."

"Everybody knows that poem," I pointed out. "You didn't tell us about it."

"Why else wouldn't she want her kid around?" asked Mike. "The golden gown? In the middle of the week?"

"Where does it say 'middle of the week?'" My mother shook her head.

"Then she disappears," said Mike.

"You know," admitted my father, "I never thought about it that way."

"That's because Mike is making it up," said my mother.

"What am I making up?" said Mike.

At which point my mother stopped talking. It's a common enough thing for mothers to give their teenagers the silent treatment, but more times than not, the mother can't keep it up. Most mothers will forget they've taken a vow of silence, and will tell you to pick up your shoes or call you down to dinner. Not our mother, who not only had been a nun in her twenties but *also* had been the kind of nun who took a vow of silence and kept it for two years. She gave it up abruptly on her twenty-fourth birthday, after blowing out the candles (one of the few indulgences, according to my mother, that it was easy for nuns to get their hands on) on the icing-less cake her fellow nuns had baked for her. She hadn't planned it in advance, but as the other nuns sang to her she felt it was time to talk again, and did. When the rest of the nuns asked her what had happened, she said: "Heaven is not a newspaper."

The question of how this moment—our mother's exit from the nunnery—was going to fit into the movie Mike and

I would one day make was a real problem. We decided that what we needed was a really great scene, a moment of decision where our mother walks out of the convent and into the rest of her life. Maybe it would be something simple and fleeting, like a close-up of her face as she catches sight of my father's eyes. Like Julie Andrews in *The Sound of Music,* who's never the same after she sees Christopher Plummer. Or something else, a starving or sick child who died in her arms, frozen in the Cleveland winter, that shook her faith. What was needed, we decided, was a serious pivotal incident that would lead to an epiphany, the kind of thing you'd read in the sort of book they give you in school that's supposed to make you cry and be a better person. A transitional moment, like the nearly fatal case of pneumonia my mother survived just before she left the convent. In the movie she'd get sick from selflessly nursing another of the nuns or maybe some leper who'd collapsed on the doorstep. A scowling priest would refuse to call in a doctor and, after she recovered, our mother would storm out of the convent in a rage and never look back. After that sickness she wouldn't believe in any of it. Not in being a nun, not in the communion of saints, not in the forgiveness of sins and definitely not in the resurrection of the body. But that's not what happened—when she got sick, she told us, she'd been happy. She'd deteriorated quickly and suffered horribly, and all the while she'd been so happy because she had always wanted to understand Christ on the cross and she'd even *prayed* for a terrible illness to come to her and nearly kill her but not quite, so she could feel how afraid, how helpless Christ must have felt when the sword pierced his side. When Mike got killed in the explosion she tried to do the same thing. To understand it as a great blessing that had come her way. As we sat there at the kitchen table, talking about James James Morrison Morrison, Mike had less than two weeks to live.

According to the police report, this happened on Sunday, November 5, 1989, a little before two in the morning. 1:56 a.m., to be exact. The night after the night after the Friday Halloween parties.

There were two casualties: Mike, and Mary DeSilva. But you know that already.

In the days right after the explosion there were pages in eavestroughs, and the upper branches of trees were an eerie white, like they alone were covered in snow. And when it did start to snow, the snow came down black. You'd be walking along and all of a sudden you'd find yourself standing on half a John Donne sonnet, or a recipe for scallops. Or a page offering sound advice about how to balance your chequebook or where to find the best restaurants in Buffalo. As I walked out of the house on the morning of Mike's funeral, there blew up into my face a tattered, burnt page of *The Runaway Bunny,* a kids' book our mother used to read to us. It was a grey day in Cleveland Heights that morning. The leaves were off the trees and a cold, damp wind blew in from Lake Erie, somewhere in the distance. It was the beginning of winter in earnest. In a few weeks there would be snow everywhere.

My father and I were on our way to be pallbearers, which meant we needed to get to the funeral home early to assist in the carrying of the casket. As he put on his shoes he was talking to my mother, telling her she had to hold herself together as though the parts of herself could be picked up and smashed into each other. I didn't want to listen, so I went out and stood in the driveway.

That's when the soggy and charred page from that book flew up into my face. I recognized it right away. And so would you, probably. *The Runaway Bunny* is one of those kids' books everyone reads, whether they remember it or not. What happens in the book is a baby bunny tells his mother he's going to run away and the mother bunny replies by saying she's going to follow him. Which is what happens. He turns into a trout and she fishes for him. Then he turns into a crocus in a hidden garden and she becomes the gardener. Later, he turns into a sailboat, and she turns into the wind so she can blow him where she wants him to go. That's the page—where the bunny is the boat and the mother is the wind—that attached itself to me, and when I saw what it was, a hopeful feeling surged through me, all at once—like a patch of warm in a swimming pool. But then my father came out of the house, and it went away. I thought about telling him, even showing him the page. But I knew what he'd say, and so I let it go into the wind. I resolved then to do what he would do, to regard the wind as he would, from the scientific perspective of a man who had been trained as an engineer. The kind of father who will tell you, even if you don't ask, that engineering is the study of the world as it really is. That's how I tried to look at it. As if the wind was just the wind, and nothing else. Just the movement of air across the surface of the earth.

GRIEF THERAPY

After Mike's funeral our family began going to grief therapy. This was my father's idea.

There's the individual sessions we each have with a shrink named Dr. Kasoff once a week whether we need it or not, and then we have group therapy sessions with Dr. Kasoff and a bunch of other families who have also had a kid killed in one way or another.

At the group sessions there are ten families in all. There's the couple with the sixteen-year-old kid who was killed in a jet-ski accident, and the couple with the four-year-old kid who was killed by an unnamed viral infection. And there's the man whose wife and ten-year-old kid were killed one snowy day when a tractor-trailer veered out of control on I-270 and crushed their station wagon against a guardrail, and the woman whose twelve-year-old disappeared one day and is only attending these sessions because Dr. Kasoff has asked her to. Though as far as she's concerned there's still a pretty good chance her daughter is going to show up again. And there's a pregnant woman who already knows there's something wrong with her baby, that it's got a rare genetic defect that means it's going to breathe for half an hour and then die. Maybe half an hour, she's been told, if everything goes perfectly with the birth. She's carrying the baby to full term because it's the best thing, according to the doctors at the Cleveland Clinic, if she wants to have children in the future. Her husband, she's told everyone, is refusing to attend the sessions.

At one of the sessions there was a woman whose daughter was raped and killed by a distant relative who buried her in his backyard. When she said this, Dr. Kasoff stood up and said he was sorry, but she had come to the wrong room, the session she was looking for was down the hall, past the men's washroom. This was the *accidental* death group. Right at the end of the hall, he told her, if you see the water fountain, you've missed it.

And there are the parents of the three-year-old who fell off her tricycle. It happened one afternoon in their concrete driveway and it was the kind of thing three-year-olds do all the time without the slightest consequence. There are the parents of the baby who died one night in her sleep for no reason. Sometimes the siblings of the dead kids are there, and sometimes they aren't. Little Petey never comes, and neither does my sister Vivian, who stays home and babysits him. That means it's me and my parents. Every Thursday, we get in my father's station wagon and go to grief therapy whether we feel like it or not.

It's probably for the best that Petey stays at home, because one time, the mother of the four-year-old kid who was killed by an unnamed viral infection brought her *other* kid, a ten-month-old who did things like coo and sit in the middle of the floor and play with red and green blocks. But looking at that baby started making the woman who is carrying her defective baby to full term cry. She started off by sniffling a bit and tried to look cheerful, but soon she hid her face in her hands and then her shoulders were heaving. Eventually, Dr. Kasoff stood up and said something to the woman who'd brought the baby that I couldn't hear. He must have told her to leave because that's what happened next. She started gathering her things—the baby's coat, the bag that held the baby's diapers and bottles—grabbed all of it and lurched toward the door, dropping her bag at the last minute so that the blocks spilled out of it, all red and green, like a patch of alien blood on the rug. The woman didn't seem to care. That's how pissed off she was. Dr. Kasoff got down on one knee and started putting the blocks back into the diaper bag, but she pulled away and went out the door. Dr. Kasoff stood there for a moment with the blocks in his hand, then went and picked up the rest of them, stowing them away in the pockets of his corduroy jacket.

Dr. Kasoff sat down and, after a moment, the woman with the defective baby inside her started to talk, saying how the week before, she'd felt her baby kick. It was a miracle, she told us, and it made her think—made her believe—that maybe those doctors, the ones who'd located the baby's chromosomal defect in the first place, had been wrong and the baby was going to live happily ever after, after all. She had even called her husband at work, and he came home to feel it. Only by the time he got there, the kicking had stopped. Still, she told us, he'd knelt down in front of her. It was like he was proposing all over again, or praying. If *we* prayed, she told us, all of us together, it would make a difference. Maybe it would.

I put my hands together and bowed my head, and as I did, I looked over at my mother, who wasn't moving. Not even to lift her hands. This was my mother, who used to never leave the house without a rosary. There's nothing wrong with saying the rosary, she'd tell us, if you have a spare minute. If you find yourself just sitting somewhere, say the rosary. You don't need an actual rosary. You can use anything to count out the prayers. Use whatever's handy, she'd say, in the same practical tone with which other kids' mothers reminded them to take vitamins. Be joyful always, she would tell us, pray continually. That's Paul to whom? she'd ask. Thessalonians, I'd say. Because I knew—I always knew. You're a good boy, James James, she'd tell me. This is the sort of thing she'd ask so often that we ended up knowing the Bible whether we wanted to or not. Or I did anyway. The way of the wicked is darkness, she would say, they know not at what they stumble. That's from Proverbs.

"Hail Mary," began the woman, "full of grace."

I said the words along with her because maybe she was right, maybe it would do something. And as I did, I looked again over at my mother, at her closed, unmoving lips. It made me wonder what had happened to her. But I had no idea where to begin. The morning after the explosion, she saw Mike. That's what she told me, when I spoke to her on the phone. That Mike was sitting at the kitchen table, right there with her. And even after the coroner had determined Mike had been inside the library at the time of the explosion, she went on thinking it. What she thought—what she maybe still thinks—is that Mike will walk back into our house, and that life will pick up where it left off, the way it always has.

I know my father, by making us all go to grief therapy, is trying to get her to do the opposite, to accept the idea that things end and don't start up again. That a person can die.

Dr. Kasoff says that the important thing to do during the group therapy sessions is ask questions, even if you don't have any answers, and even if no one knows you're doing the asking. And as I sit there with the group looking like I'm praying, the questions I ask are these: What was Mike doing in the library that night? Was my mother lying? Could it have been my brother at the kitchen table?

And, if it was, why was it *her* Mike came back to see?

I should say these things out loud, but I don't. Sometimes, though, as I sit there with the rest of the group, I imagine myself looking straight at my mother, can almost hear the words coming out of my mouth. Not actually, but almost.

Everyone else has their own stories and their own things to say, and Dr. Kasoff is really big on letting them all talk. The whole point of the group sessions is that kids die every day. There's nothing strange about it. It's nothing to be ashamed of. Dying is one of the things that kids do, like teething or smoking dope. As far as I can tell, the only thing our stories have in common is that it's a beautiful day when it happens. It's a warm afternoon in August, sunny and eighty, when the jet ski crashes into the rocks, breaking open the skull of the fourteen-year-old whose name was Bruce. It's another perfect day when Campbell, the three-year-old girl on the tricycle, hits her head on the pavement which, nine times out of ten, is nothing to worry about. A beautiful day in an ordinary time. The sun is shining and the sky is blue. You can smell the grass, the snow beginning to fall.

FORT MORRISON

Unlike my mother, who never gets into a car unless there's a St. Christopher medal attached to the rear-view mirror, my father believes in truth. And not just that truth exists, but that you can touch it. That it has a length and breadth and if you multiply the two the result will be its volume. His name is the same as mine—James Fortitude Morrison—but I'm not James Fortitude Jr. or James III or IV. This is the way it's done in our family. My grandfather was named James Fortitude Morrison, and so was my grandfather's grandfather. One James Fortitude Morrison after another, as far back as anyone—and by anyone, I mean my father—can remember. It's like we're photocopies of each other, exact reproductions, or are supposed to end up that way. As if it's only a matter of time.

Which is exactly what's going to happen. That's the truth. It is, as my father would say, a pure fact, true whether you want it to be or not. According to R. M. Evitt's *Manual of Forensic Anthropology*—this is the sort of thing you can look up when you work in a library—it takes approximately a year for the skin of a human body to disappear. There are exceptions, special circumstances and climates where the skin can last for a decade, but most of the time it's a year before everybody—not just those of us named James Fortitude

Morrison—starts looking like everybody else. The eyes and the skin are the first things to go. In my own case it's started already. I have more hair than my father, but that's it. And that's not forever.

My father works now as a forensic engineer. What that means is that instead of building bridges or designing aerodynamic cars—which is what he started off doing and would still be doing if he was a normal engineer—his job is to inspect accident sites and figure out what happened and why. It's not as thrilling as it sounds. By the time he gets to the scene of an accident everything you'd see in the movie version of the explosion—the dead people, their weeping relatives, the cocktail waitresses and their low-cut dresses, the millionaires with open chequebooks—are gone. All that's left are broken and burned parts of whatever it is that's caught fire or crashed. There's a lot of sifting through ash and looking at frayed wires. There's a certain amount of measuring tire markings, of getting down on concrete with a ruler and a camera. What my father's interested in are the immutable laws of the universe, in everything you can't change no matter who you are. Gravity, and the facts about bursting into flame.

He and Frank DeSilva—Mary's husband, who was so often downstairs with us at the library, keeping those old projectors running—are, or at least were, in essentially the same line of work. More than once, they found themselves working on the same cases. But where Frank worked for the government, our father worked for our mother's brother, my uncle Marco, a personal injury lawyer. This was one of the reasons why, no matter how much Frank and my father saw each other at the library, the two of them would never be friends. They were on opposite teams; most of the time the people my father and uncle represented sued Frank's office. It wasn't *only* the Office of Public Safety that got sued, but almost always they were part of it.

"The one thing you can say about your father," Frank would tell us, "he knows his right from his left." I knew that what Frank meant was what really mattered were the laws of the universe, that the truth was still the truth, no matter who uncovered it.

Officially, my uncle Marco and my father are partners. It's Marco who finds the injured and maimed and mournful people who have had horrible things happen to them; my father runs the investigative side of things, piecing the past together and figuring out what happened, and why. Sometimes it turns out to be the fault of the person who's been hurt, but not always. Marco's specialty—where the real money is, he'll tell you—is cases where people are injured because of a mistake a company has made, a manufacturing defect resulting in catastrophe, class action suits where a large group of people sue a big corporation together and get a settlement, of which sometimes as much as 30 percent goes to my uncle and father.

"When bad things happen to good people," my uncle likes to say, "the good people should at least get paid."

Last summer—Mike's last—my uncle and father got famous for a case they won against a big car company. Maybe *famous* is the wrong word. They were on television. I'm not going to get into the technical details of the case or any of that. I'm not even going to tell you the name of the company, in case one of their lawyers reads this and decides to sue me, just to get back at my father. Maybe that's paranoid, but maybe not. My uncle Marco agreed that I should keep names out, preferably everybody's name, which he almost always thinks is a good idea. Say "car company," he's advised me, let them figure it out. So I'm leaving the car company name out. It's a big one though, make no mistake. Let's just say odds are there's probably at least one of their cars in your driveway right now. If you think for even a second you know all about it. The case had to do with pickup trucks that would catch fire when you turned off the engine and then restarted it a few seconds later. You know the story. How one of the people called my uncle about how his truck caught fire, and how almost a year passed before someone else did the same. How my father studied the blueprints and came to the conclusion the explosions were a result of an airtight fuel-injection system. There was no circulation of air, which meant gas vapours would collect; turning the car on and off in rapid succession could, under certain conditions, blow the truck up.

Once my father had figured this out, my uncle started running TV ads and full-page spreads across the country, telling people that if they had a truck like that, they should contact him because they might be eligible to receive some form of compensation from the company. In those commercials my uncle sat behind an oceanic wood desk in a dark suit and made clear to the viewing public that they could trust in my father's engineering ingenuity. That he knew what had happened, and why. What he said was this: "You can try, but you can't get around Fort Morrison."

Soon the calls were coming in. There were a group of people—ten of them—who'd actually had their trucks explode and had been injured in some way. But that wasn't the end of it. There was a second group of people, represented by

Marco too, who sued the car company for having sold them the truck at all. A third group, also represented by Marco, sued the company for making it so they couldn't get into a truck ever again without wondering if it might blow up. But it all started with my father—Fort Morrison—getting to the bottom of it, figuring out what was really happening with those trucks, and why.

Even though he named me after himself, I've never once heard anyone call my father Jimmy or Jim. Or even James for that matter. Definitely not Jimmy. You take one look at my father and you know right away he's not a Jimmy. Instead, he's a Fort. Which is actually what he looks like, a squarish military installation constructed out in the middle of nowhere—a squat building you can't knock over even if you tried. He isn't what you would call handsome. You might say stocky. Or stout, as in tubby. The impression you get as you watch him walk is that he's evolved for the sole purpose of pushing something heavy up a hill. His eyes are a little too close together, which gives people the feeling he's squinting all the time, as if when he speaks to you he's only half speaking to you because he's located a piece of lint on your shirt he intends to remove. He's bald, though in an uncertain way, as if his hair might change its mind and return at any time.

My father began calling himself Fort when he was a teenager, growing up in the wilds of Canada. Which is how he likes to put it, how he *still* puts it, despite having lived here in Cleveland for longer than he ever lived in Canada—as if at any moment he might be overcome by the urge to go snowshoeing or drink maple syrup. He was born in South Porcupine, Ontario, a small town near Timmins. Even in its heyday—the 1930s—South Porcupine wasn't much more than a hockey arena and a gold mine where my grandfather worked as a dynamiter.

That mine is closed now. Boarded up, like the elementary school my father attended, but the hockey arena isn't. Kids practise there on weeknights, and an old-timers league uses it on weekends. At the start of last summer, about a week after my father and uncle won their case against the car company, my father made up his mind it was time for us to see it for ourselves. So we all got into our station wagon for the seventeen-hour drive. There wasn't much to see, but we saw it anyway. We looked at our reflections on the surface of Porcupine Lake where he fished for walleye and peered into the darkness of the abandoned mine where my father's brother—our dead uncle Michael, after whom my dead brother Mike was named—was killed in a mining accident. Then we went to the town graveyard and looked at the gravestones, at the one that belonged to my grandfather, James Fortitude Morrison again, and the one that belonged to my father's brother, which had Mike's name on it.

Technically speaking it was Mike—not me—who should have been named after my father. From a purely chronological perspective, he was Cain, the first-born son, and I was Abel, not the other way around. He's the one who should have got my father's name. Only he didn't, because he'd been born weighing just over three pounds, a premature baby born when my mother was just five months pregnant. There's a photo of our parents in the hospital, a black-and-white 1960s photo that's slightly out of focus the way all my parents' photos are from those days, as if they didn't quite know how to use cameras back then. In it, my mother's hair is pulled back and she's wearing those nun glasses and my father is wearing a short-sleeved white shirt with a nondescript black tie. In the picture my father is reaching toward the camera, which makes it seem like the tiny baby in his hand is not a baby at all but a small bird he's intent on replacing in its nest. This is the first picture that was ever taken of Mike, one week after he was born. If you look closely you can see his face, see the tiny black marks on his forehead from the ashes, after he got the last rites from the priest. In the first two months of his life Mike got the last rites five times. And because neither of my parents thought he had very long to live, they named him Mike, after my father's dead brother. It was a dead kid's name for a kid they thought would die.

The rest of us—even little Petey who came along so long after the rest of us—were all ordinary babies, born weighing ordinary amounts after what seems to have been ordinary labours. It was only Mike who came out looking like he was going to die. I don't know if everything that happened after Mike died—the way both my parents fell apart—can be chalked up to those first couple of months. It didn't help. It's not like our parents don't care about the rest of us, but I also think that neither spent nearly as much time willing any of us to live as they did my brother.

NANNY

I'm now into my third month of looking after little Petey. I'm his nanny or babysitter or whatever you want to call it. It's a job I've had ever since Dr. Kasoff got my father to let me drop out of school and my mother made it clear she'd turned into the kind of basket case who can't look after herself, much less a four-year-old whose idea of a good time is to put on a Jacques Cousteau video and roll around on the carpet with his stuffed sharks pretending to be a scuba diver.

"While baleen whales eat lots of small animals with each mouthful of water," little Petey will say, for no apparent reason, "toothed whales eat them one at a time."

It's that kind of thing that makes my mother lock herself in the bathroom.

I thought that after Mike's funeral, Petey would forget about the diver's mask and his obsession with sharks. That it would just go away. But it hasn't—if anything, it's gotten worse. That morning of Mike's funeral my father tried to get him to leave the mask behind, but Petey threw a fit and in the end he let him bring it. Though Petey didn't put it on he kept it right there on the pew beside him, like he thought that at any moment the church might start filling with water. Now Petey never goes anywhere without that mask, including his preschool. I can't say if it's normal or not, if he's lost it completely or he's the kind of four-year-old who'd have worn a diver's mask everywhere even if a member of his immediate family hadn't been killed in some freak explosion.

One time I brought it up with Dr. Kasoff. Instead of answering my question about Petey he asked if I ever thought about putting on a diver's mask myself.

Then we just sat there for a bit.

That happens a lot in my sessions with Dr. Kasoff. I say something and he says something back and then we sit there. It's like he's interrogating me, like it's a spy movie and he's trying to get me to say where the plans are stashed. But I have no idea where the plans are hidden, or why. Or even if there are plans. Still, Dr. Kasoff gives me that look which makes me think that he knows what I know. One time I said: "I know nothing about these plans." This seemed to make sense to him, though at the same time he looked back at me as though it was only a matter of time before I cracked.

"Do you think it's important that you were named James Morrison instead of your brother?" Dr. Kasoff asked me at our last session.

"I don't know."

"I'm not asking if you know, I'm asking what you *think.*"

"Actually," I tell him, "there are a lot of other Jim Morrisons. It's not like it's just me, my father, that kid in that poem and the lead singer of the Doors."

Dr. Kasoff nodded, but only a little. I wasn't telling him anything and he knew it. I went on talking anyway and told him about the James Morrison who lived near the end of the eighteenth century and was a boatswain's mate on the *Bounty,* one of the mutineers who broke into Captain Bligh's cabin and forced him out on deck, in his nightshirt.

I told him about the James Morrison who played third base for the Chicago White Sox.

And the James Morrison who was a bishop in Nova Scotia.

I told him about the James Morrison who's a professional wrestler, though no one knows it because he changed his name so people wouldn't confuse him with the Jim Morrison the rock star.

"That's all very interesting," said Dr. Kasoff, though by the way he said it I could tell he thought the opposite. "But does it matter?"

What I said was this: "It's a strange and haunting world, reminiscent of a new wild west." That's a pretty cool thing to say, and the fact is that it was said by the dead rock star Jim Morrison to a reporter from *Rolling Stone.*

"Is that a quote from somewhere?" Dr. Kasoff asked me.

I had to say it was. "It was like he knew," I said. "Like he was telling the reporter that he wasn't going to be around for very much longer."

Dr. Kasoff kept his face completely still after I said that.

"Do you think that's possible?" I asked him.

"What would it change?" he asked. "How would it make it different?"

"If you knew?"

"Knowing and acting aren't the same—you can know everything and still do nothing."

"I guess, though, you'd at least have your lines down, say something cool, you know."

"Is that what you'd want?" he asked me. "To say something cool?"

"I didn't mean it like that," I told him lamely, and then I stopped talking. Dr. Kasoff stared back at me for a long moment and said he was sorry, that our time was up for today.

Dr. Kasoff is in his fifties or something, and completely bald. He looks like Captain Picard from *Star Trek,* only taller and without the cool accent. He's six and a half feet tall, in fact, and he grew up thinking that he was going to be in the NBA, even played for Ohio State. But then somewhere along the line he made up his mind that what he really wanted to do was help people. The story of how he woke up having decided to be a shrink is something you get told during your first session with him. How he knew he had to put basketball aside if he wanted to shape people's lives. He has a way of saying *shape* with his big basketball hands out in front of him. It's supposed to be comforting, the shrink equivalent of that insurance ad where the guy turns his palms up, to show you're in good hands, but Dr. Kasoff's hands move around like they aren't really listening to what he's saying, like they're thinking of detaching themselves at the wrist and crushing or swallowing you whole.

It was Dr. Kasoff who recommended I stop going to Heights High. Drop out and take a leave of absence, he said. I hated the idea, but I went along with it. I'm going to finish the second half of my senior year in September.

It's not like I didn't try to go back. The school, which is just down the street from the library, reopened the week after the explosion, after the windows that had been knocked out by the force of it had been replaced and the shards of shattered glass swept up. On the sidewalk outside and in the old trees next to the library there was paper everywhere. Lee

Road was still blocked off, but things were starting to get back to normal. This was something I could feel—other kids were starting to talk about Christmas and who the cops had busted for drinking that weekend. There was going to be a memorial service for Mike the next week, but for now it was business as usual. I tried to be normal, like everyone, tried to go to homeroom like I would have done on any other day.

But I got stopped on my way there by the vice-principal, who said how sorry he was about my brother and said to be sure I conveyed to my father how sorry he was. I told him I'd convey it for sure. To my mother as well, he said. Absolutely, I said, your being sorry will be conveyed to both of my parents. He gave me a look and I watched him decide not to give me a lecture. Instead, he told me a sad story about how, when he was my age, a friend of his was killed in a boating accident. This was his best friend, the vice-principal told me, they even had the same name. He was the blond Stan and the other kid was the other Stan. It had been a sunny day and the two of them had been out fishing. On the way back to the cottage some speedboat came out of nowhere and smashed into them. The other Stan never had a chance. I said I was sorry to hear about the other Stan. He thanked me for being sorry, and then he reminded me to pass along to both my mother and father how sorry he was for the loss of my brother.

Which is why I got to homeroom late and ended up stepping into the classroom at the very moment the national anthem came on, which meant I had to freeze at the front of the room where everyone could see me. For once I did what I was supposed to, and stared up at the flag with my hand on my heart like I was really just unbelievably happy to be American. But it was at that moment I noticed Jennifer

McKellar—Mike's girlfriend, or ex-girlfriend, or widow, or whatever—hadn't come to school that day.

Part of me was relieved because I'd spent the night before worrying about what I was going to say to her, and the other part of me was hugely crushed. I hadn't seen her since before the explosion. She didn't even come to Mike's funeral, or at least I didn't see her there. Though, I was willing to leave open the possibility she'd been there in disguise, or that she had walked right past me and I didn't know it. I knew for a fact that she'd been questioned by the police after the explosion like me and my mother and everyone else. They sent a squad car over and walked around in the house for a bit to make sure Mike wasn't hiding out there. I know this because it was in the police report. And I know what's in the police report because my father has a copy of it. He also has a copy of the missing person report I filled out at the police station on the third day after the explosion, after the police started figuring out that the only one who'd seen Mike after the explosion was my mother, and that she'd only seen him for a few seconds which she didn't remember that clearly. That she only really remembered the sound of his voice. "Where did Mike sit?" the detective asked her, pulling a chair out from the table. "Was it here?" She couldn't remember that either—couldn't say with absolute certainty where my brother had sat that morning.

I know Jennifer McKellar told the cops something, but I don't know what. Whatever it was, it's not in the report. The specifics just aren't there, nothing really, except the fact of her being interviewed by them. I'd like to know if it was a matter of Mike keeping a lookout so that he could let her in or if she'd already been there and already left. It was something like this, some secret piece of info she gave them. This is the kind of thing Bogart does all the time in movies where he plays a detective. He'll be in the middle of an investigation and find out something about a girl, some really key thing, and even though it helps him solve the case it's only him that knows it because Bogart is a gentleman and never damages a girl's reputation. That's the kind of thing the Cleveland Heights cops did for Jennifer, maybe because her father's a lawyer. Maybe she was on her way there and she saw the explosion in the distance, then turned around and ran back home. Maybe they'd done it already and Mike had fallen asleep afterwards in the silence of the library with the books all above him, thinking he was safe. Or maybe Jennifer passed Mary on her way out of the library. Maybe Mike was going to tell me about it all in the morning. Maybe not.

THAT BANNER

All of that went through my mind as I stood there at the front of the class, while the anthem played and I stared at Jennifer McKellar's abandoned desk.

I made it almost to the end, to the part where it asks if that banner still waves, after all the bombs and the red glare of the rockets. Then I broke down. Mr. Atkinson, our old Geography teacher, came and helped me out into the hall, and then the school nurse drove me home. The next day it was the same, only this time Atkinson was talking about tectonic plates, about how all the landforms in the world had originally been a single land mass, then broken apart forever. Finally I ended up in Dr. Kasoff's office and he was telling me I should take a leave of absence. *Sit this one out* is how he put it, like he was my basketball coach. Everyone understood, particularly my father—which was the worst part of it.

What I expected was that my father would say no way, then tell Dr. Kasoff the story of how his own brother had been killed in Canada just two weeks before he came to Cleveland. How he went on with his life after that. And that he expected the same of me. That he expected no *less* of me. To buckle up or knuckle down or whatever you're supposed to do in a circumstance like that. Apparently, if he didn't show up in Cleveland for the start of school, Case Western would give his scholarship to someone else. And he'd end up getting stuck working in a mine just like all the other James Fortitude Morrisons had ever done, getting killed in some random mine collapse or coughing himself to death like my grandfather. I don't know if that's true, if Case would actually not have cared about his brother being killed, but that's the way he made it sound. The point is, my father got on the train that day. That was the story I figured my father was going to tell when Dr. Kasoff called him up and put him on speakerphone so I could hear. I was ready for him to chew Dr. Kasoff out, but he didn't. Instead he said Dr. Kasoff was right. "James can only handle so much," said Kasoff. My father agreed completely.

After that I got depressed—if your idea of being depressed is not going to school and instead lying on your dead brother's bed for eight to ten hours a day listening to your dead brother's tapes on your dead brother's Walkman. Refusing to change the tape or the batteries, even when the tape starts slowing all the way down, turning everything into the same blurry mess. One day turned into two, and soon three weeks had passed. Little kids from Fairfax Elementary, the grade school down the street from the library, could be seen walking up and down Lee Road, picking up stray pages from wrecked books and stuffing them into black garbage bags. Other than the massive fenced-in area around where the library had been, the street started looking like a normal street again.

I knew I should be doing something productive now that I didn't have to go to school; hitchhiking to California, or learning judo, or working on a model ship inside a bottle which I'd destroy the day I went to college by throwing it into Lake Erie. People would cheer as they watched it float away and understand it was a way of saying I was ready to get on with the rest of my life.

I considered getting a job. This was to have been the summer when Mike and I would quit our library jobs and work instead for the Cleveland Heights Parks and Recreation Department. Everyone said this was the best job you could get because it was a total breeze. Mike had heard from a friend of his who had been on the grass crew that it was a matter of maybe having to cut one or two municipal lawns and then spend the rest of the day sitting in a truck behind Cumberland Pool, smoking dope and drinking Mountain Dew. I even went so far as to fill out an application and got a call from a girl asking me to come in for an interview. I thought about it, then said no. She told me she was sorry to hear it and I could tell she knew who I was. That she knew about Mike dying at least, and maybe the rest of it. There was a long silence on the phone in which I guess I was supposed to say something, like ask her name or maybe if she'd like to have sympathy sex with me in the back of my dead brother's Gremlin. But I said nothing. Finally she said that if I changed my mind, I could give her a call. I told her thanks but before she could give me the number, I'd hung up.

Eventually, my father told me I'd be looking after Petey. He did this one night after dinner when Vivian was putting dishes in the dishwasher and my mother was upstairs with Petey.

"You mean, like, be his nanny?"

"Is that the word for it?"

"What would you call it?"

"I'd call it getting him to his preschool in the morning and home afterwards," he told me. "Then after that, thinking of something for the two of you to do until dinner."

"Be his nanny, in other words."

"If you want to call it that."

"What does Mom say?"

"She says it's a good idea."

"She said that?"

"No," he admitted. "She doesn't know."

"Why not Vivian?"

"Your sister has to go to school, and besides, she's doing the cooking."

"What do you mean I'm doing the cooking?" Vivian came over and stood in front of him. "You think I have time for that?" Vivian has the same dark hair as my mother and gave my father the same kind of look my mother gives him when he says, again, that he's not coming to church with us. "What about my social life?" At the time, she was dressed in a David Bowie T-shirt that was three sizes too big for her.

"You can use the microwave," my father told her. "That's what I bought it for."

Our microwave is a Litton Minute Master, a two-foot-wide stainless steel box weighing approximately two hundred and fifty pounds. When my father bought it in 1976 for $479—an actual retail price he often repeated in connection with the observation that my mother refused to touch it—it had been near the top of the line. Like most things he did in his life, my father's purchase of the microwave had been carried out in the name of science, an attempt to bring my mother over to his way of thinking, to show her that there was more to cooking than cooking. Before Vivian could object, he handed her a paperback entitled *Mastering Microwave Cooking.*

She looked at the book but didn't touch it. "'The greatest invention since fire,'" she said, reading from the cover. "They're kidding, right?"

Then I went upstairs with my father and told Petey and my mother. Petey was in the bath and my mother was watching him, sitting on the toilet seat, as if it were all going on at great distance from her actual location.

"It'll be fun," my father told Petey, "you and Jimmy."

"Bonnie and Clyde," said my mother.

My father ignored that.

"So," my father asked Petey, "what do you say?"

Petey burst into tears.

"Petey," said my father, "be a good boy."

"Don't cry, Petey," said my mother. It didn't even look like she could hear us but I guess she might have caught on to the fact that what was happening was the mothering equivalent of having her driver's licence revoked.

ROUTINES

Looking after Petey is a matter of not messing with his routines. At six thirty every morning he appears at my bedside with his diver's mask on and a stuffed shark in his hand. I take him downstairs, give him a glass of milk in his Cleveland Browns commemorative plastic cup and then watch *Sesame Street* with him. When it's over, he gets up and presses the off button on the set as if it's a task he's been contracted by the Pentagon to perform. Next, I make him breakfast: a blueberry Eggo waffle with syrup, but no margarine. If I get any part of this wrong—if I forget and even touch his waffle with margarine—he will just sit there and stare at it no matter how hungry he is, like it's a plate of radioactive waste. When that's done, I take him upstairs, dress him, and by eight forty-five he's in his stroller and we're on our way to his preschool.

I could drive—I mean, I have my licence—but the car I'd use is Mike's old light green Gremlin. It still smells like him, like the whole time he's been living in the back seat smoking and making out with Jennifer McKellar, and it doesn't start half the time.

My father said that I can have it, though there's something wrong with the ignition that has to be fixed. It won't start. It's not a big repair, but it involves calling a tow truck and getting it to the garage. Even the thought of it seems monumental, like making the bed Mike slept in or changing the batteries in my dead brother's Walkman. Until I can manage any of that, it's the stroller for Petey.

At four, the truth is that Petey is old enough to walk on his own, and probably if he's going to end up normal he should be made to walk. I know that. I've actually read that exact thing in *Growing Toddlers,* one of those parenting books my father gave me after I took over from my mother. But the couple of times I let him, we almost didn't make it. He'd stop to look closely at a crack in the pavement or get really interested in a bunch of ants or start touching cigarette butts. Each time, I had to pick him up and run the rest of the way to get him there on time. The last time I did that, I was sweating so hard when I got there that Petey's teacher asked if I needed her to call a doctor.

So now he doesn't have a choice—I put him into his stroller no matter how much he kicks and screams. He'll probably grow up into a lunatic and blame it on me, call me late at night, wrapped up in a straitjacket, to let me know.

The route we take is always the same: we walk to Lee Road, turn right, and then it's straight down Lee past my old high school, past Amy Joy Donuts, past the vacuum store and Simon's Photography, and finally past the vacant lot where the library once stood. There are other ways to get there, side streets I could walk down, but I don't. I don't have to walk by the library every day I suppose, but I do.

According to my uncle Marco the ten-foot fence that now surrounds the ruins of the library was put there for insurance reasons, to make sure no one gets into it and hurts themselves before hiring someone like him to sue the town. As expensive as that fence was, as much as it looked like a prison camp in the centre of town, my uncle says it's cheaper than paying the lawsuits.

It's a sort of game that I play with myself when I walk by in the morning, to see how long I can avoid looking at the remains of the library. Today as I walk by, I see Frank DeSilva standing there, looking even thinner than he did before the explosion. He's peering in at the rubble and I cross the street. I tell myself I'll stop if Frank turns and looks at me. He's standing there with his fingers curled around the links of the fence and when I pass, he gives the fence a pull, and above him the chain-links rattle, like tiny church bells. He doesn't turn and I keep walking. When I go by later, he's gone.

The problem my father had with Frank and the Office of Public Safety had to do with the fact that it always took the government so long to do anything. Most of the time it would come to light that someone in the Office of Public Safety knew something about whatever catastrophic event had occurred before it actually happened—there'd be preliminary reports of malfunctions, or reports of accidents that hadn't been serious—and had either decided to not do anything or were still getting around to it. So my uncle sued the government and the Office of Public Safety as well. It was about making money, but it was also about my father wanting to teach inspectors like Frank a lesson. Not Frank specifically maybe—though more than once my father had sent an accusatory letter to him personally—but my father maintained that the people who did Frank's job needed to *feel* the urgency of what they were doing. It was a sort of part-time job for my father. When he wasn't solving engineering problems for my uncle, he'd write letters to the Office of Public Safety which said that if something wasn't done about a particular issue, and if it wasn't done quickly, they would have to bear full responsibility. The letters my father sent were more or less the same in that they always contained the same phrase, the same threat, which was that the next time something happened, the blood would not be on my father's hands. There'd been a defective gas fireplace and a suburb of illegally wired bathrooms. There'd been an elevator shaft he'd called a death trap. There'd been flammable paint. There'd been a new kind of cheap fuse he'd shown would never blow no matter how hot it got. And, of course, there'd been the pickup trucks with the defective fuel-injection system. In the end the car company had to pay a settlement and recall several hundred thousands of their possibly defective pickup trucks. You don't have to know much about car companies to know that's the kind of thing that hardly ever happens. And would *never* have happened if it hadn't been for my father finding what was wrong with the trucks in the first place and sending all those letters out saying the next time one of those trucks explode the blood won't be on his hands.

Those words—*blood, hands, trucks*—were *actually* the ones my father used in his letters, and which the governor himself seemed to remember when he showed up that night at the state capitol after the hearing. Silver haired with those crazy blue eyes like the bad guys in *Dune,* the governor had a whole crowd with him—assistants, advisers, cameramen, reporters, burly guys who looked like they were packing heat. Gradually the scene took shape, and I saw a reporter with a microphone. Behind him were the technical guys, one with a camera and another with a light, holding it up over his head like a wayward star. The governor was reaching out to touch my father's shoulder. Turning him around like they were old friends. Then he faced the cameras and talked about it being an important day for public safety in the United States. That without concerned Ohioans like my father, this country would not be the fine country it is. And then, just when it seemed like the governor was about to leave, he didn't. Instead, he leaned in close to my father and said something that none of us could hear. And as he spoke, he turned the palms of his hands upward—they were white even in the new darkness—as if to show him they were empty. Or clean.

While this was going on, Frank DeSilva came out of the courthouse. Frank knew he had to admit that he and his office had made a mistake by not initiating the recall, that he was going to have to take responsibility, even if it wasn't all his fault. But not right away. Before he got into any of that, he had something else to say, and so, the first words he uttered in response to a reporter's request for a comment were: "Who do you think I am, the robot Hart Crane?"

"Could you please repeat that?" said the reporter.

Frank opened his mouth, as if he was planning to say each word again, this time with precision, smiling at the thought of it. You can see that in the videotape, the corners of Frank's mouth beginning to curl. But then he stops smiling and turns pale as his legs fold away underneath him and he crumples to the ground. Afterwards, the reporter who'd asked the question speculated that the only reason Frank had been talking about Hart Crane was that he'd been in the midst of having a heart attack, and that if oxygen was still making its way to his brain in a normal way, he'd never have said such a thing.

Maybe that's true, but what Mike thought—and when he said it, I believed it—was that Frank knew exactly what he was saying because he was quoting from Devhan Starway's novel *Scream of the Robot,* which was published in 1964, ten years after he moved away from Cleveland Heights. In that book there's a moment when the robot Hart Crane, instead of screaming, begins to weep. This happens on the third moon of a planet named Andromeda, during a murder trial, and it's the way you know for sure that the robot Hart Crane is innocent. It's also the first time in the history of the universe that a robot has been seen to weep, and it produces widespread panic. Just before the first tear edged its way out of his metallic eye, the robot Hart Crane looks into the faces of those interrogating him and asks: "Who do you think I am, the robot Hart Crane?"

It might have been that Frank would not have said what he did under normal circumstances when his brain was not beginning to suffer from oxygen deprivation. But what Mike thought was that as Frank was coming out of the courthouse, he began imagining Mary at home watching him on television and knew that she'd be feeling bad for him. And so, when he saw the reporter, he decided to cheer Mary up by saying something about Devhan Starway.

"He did it for love," said Mike. "He did it for Mary."

"I think it was deranged," was my father's opinion. "It makes me wonder if Frank's losing his mind."

"There are three things that last forever," said my mother. At the time we were watching *Nineteen Action News*, who were playing, then replaying, then replaying again the footage of Frank falling to the ground while they discussed the extent of the recall that would have to be initiated by the car company. "Faith, hope and love—but the greatest of them all is love."

"Paul to the Corinthians," I said, like a guest on some holy game show my mother was hosting.

"That's my James James," said my mother.

According to the paramedic who revived him, Frank DeSilva was dead for a full two minutes.

"But then I came back," Frank told us. "They brought me back."

"What was it like?" I asked him.

"It was like nothing," he said.

"Did you see anything? Anything at all?"

Frank shook his head.

"What did it feel like?"

"I don't know what you mean," said Frank. And he didn't. Frank was an engineer, like our father, and like him he believed it his duty to tell the truth, no matter who tried to get him to do otherwise.

When he got out of the hospital, Frank announced his retirement. It was something he had talked about for years, insisted Mary, and had nothing to do with Uncle Marco winning that case or how Frank was made to take the blame for it. It was time for Frank to enjoy the good life, and besides, he was getting close to seventy. If he had any regrets or harboured any animosity toward my father, he never showed it—except once. Mary threw a party for him at a restaurant in the Flats and we all went, including my father, who laughed along with everyone else when Frank made his speech, at his old joke about the telescopic ladder raised to the wrong window at the right time. Just as he was wrapping it up, though, Frank seemed bitter, pointing out that Eliot Ness had once been public safety director of Cleveland and Kevin Costner had played him on the silver screen. The same thing might be in store for him, even if he was only an inspector. "I do promise you one thing," he said, and he didn't quite smile when he said it, "Fort Morrison isn't going to have Frank DeSilva to kick around any longer."

It was sad seeing him up there, quoting Nixon. It made me think Frank thought he'd been impeached. And if that was true, the guy who'd done the impeaching was my father, who didn't feel bad about it. From my father's perspective, it was a victory. He'd blown the whistle, and people knew it. On the way home from the party Mike and my father got into a fight, the worst ever, or so I thought at the time, worse even than the time my father discovered a bag of weed in Mike's desk drawer. Mike said my father had ruined Frank's life, pointing out that Frank himself had done nothing to deserve it. My father replied he'd do it all again, and more. It didn't matter if Mike liked Frank, or if they all liked Frank; if Frank hadn't done his job, or if he'd been doing his job too slowly, that was that, case closed. If Frank had committed a crime, said my father, if his own son had done something wrong, he'd turn him in without a second thought. That really pissed off Mike, and soon they were screaming at each other. But the whole time they were fighting, I remember thinking that handing Mike over to the police wasn't something my father would really do. It was something he had to *say* he would do. In front of Mike he had to make a point of insisting he would be entirely and brutally truthful no matter what the circumstances.

After that, Mike refused to speak to my father, not even when he announced we were going on our trip to Canada.

Mike tried to get out of it, but my father put his foot down, and Mike had to sit in the back seat with Petey's extra scuba gear and all our rubber boots. He listened to his Walkman the whole way in desultory protest, and after four days of driving we were there in that old hockey arena, looking at the old picture of my father in his hockey uniform, down on one knee, left defence.

"Guys would try," said my father, looking at his younger self, "but even then there was no getting around Fort Morrison." This, he told us, was something he'd shout at forwards when they tried to stickhandle past him. It was strange to hear him say that, for some reason. The thought of my father on a team. But there he was, smiling, one of his front teeth chipped, even then.

After that we went out to the car, where Mike had remained, sitting in the back seat with the window down. When he saw my father walking back toward him, saw that nostalgic look still on his face, like the whole trip had been worth it, Mike sang out the chorus of "All You Need Is Love" in an uneven half-scream, not really singing at all. My father didn't reply, just told the rest of us to please get into the car so we could go back to Cleveland.

THE CO-OP

The preschool Petey goes to is in the basement of Church of the Saviour on Lee Road, near where the library used to be. The church is huge and gothic and the preschool is on the first floor, a bright and airy room with big windows. At one end of the classroom are nine wooden cubbies where the children hang their coats and hats; at the other end is a brown carpeted area where they sit in a circle each morning when they arrive. There are two hamsters named Rex and Gina, and a goldfish named Leon. Three tables sit at the back near the big window for arts and crafts and there are two easels in the corner near the door, back to back, for painting.

It's a co-op, which means that once a month I have to be a Parent Helper—bring a snack and help kids get their coats on when it's time to play outside, sit around in the circle and sing and count, that kind of thing. The school was founded in the sixties, back when hippies wanted their kids to grow up outside the machine. And it still has a power-to-the-people vibe to it: there's a big mural on one of the walls that was painted the same year as Woodstock with a lot of flowers and doves and peace signs. Looking up at it you imagine the parents and kids working on it together, all of them stoned out of their heads, sitting around with flowers in their hair, really digging each other.

I haven't been Parent Helper yet, but my turn is coming. It's there, on the calendar in the kitchen, in my mother's handwriting, put there back when she was thinking straight. Bright red, capital letters—PARENT HELPER—the date circled and starred. I should have had to do it already, in late January, but we got a pass given the unprecedented level of tragedy our family has had to endure. Soon enough, though, I'll be up.

Not including Petey there are seven children in his class: a blond girl named Megan, fraternal twins named Jane and Austin, a small boy with glasses called Cyril, his next-door neighbour Jonah, a boy named Alexander whose mother's Romanian, and a girl named Brittany who, no matter what her mother says, is not toilet trained.

I've come to think of the mothers of the other children as the Mothers, like they're a street gang with a ringleader, a bunch of henchmen and also a couple of loser sidekick characters who you know are going to end up being killed early in the movie because of a botched robbery. Looking at these women with their strollers and purses, their diaper bags, you don't automatically think of a gang. But if you sat around in that hallway waiting for that classroom door to open in the mornings, watching them mutter to each other plotting the overthrow of Petey's teacher, you'd know they're not to be messed with. They are looking for trouble and are going to find it.

At first I thought the Mothers didn't speak to me because they figured I was crazy or something, like if they said anything to me it'd remind me of my brother and I'd start bawling my eyes out. Of course, none of what happened to us is any secret, not to the Mothers and not to anyone else in

Cleveland Heights. They saw me that night with the weirdly altered photograph of my brother and probably also saw my father on the news, the footage of him going back to the explosion site, after he'd been told to stay away, the cops escorting him home. A clear conflict of interest, the Office of Public Safety had told him, he could not be a part of any investigation. At one point *Nineteen Action News* even sent a reporter to interview my father at our house. Probably all the Mothers saw that too, my father on his knees in his basement office, moving slowly across the photos he'd taken of the rubble after the explosion, looking for something he'd missed.

Eventually, though, the Mothers got sick of sitting there in silence and now they talk about everything in my presence. It's not so much that I'm one of them, but they've stopped worrying about it, the way you stop worrying about a security camera in a stereo place. You know it's there, but you pick your nose anyway. So long as you don't do anything illegal or involving nudity, it's cool. Today's topic when I'm dropping off Petey is the school-wide ban on peanut butter and any other food that has nuts in it (this includes all tree nuts, whatever those are). And, like the outlaw nonconformists they are, the Mothers have made up their minds to send their kids to school with peanut butter and jelly sandwiches no matter what anyone tells them.

The peanut butter ban was instituted about a month ago when a kid named Henry enrolled in the daycare downstairs. The daycare kids are there the whole day, from seven in the morning to six at night. Mostly they're from families where both parents have to work and can't afford to take the time off and be Parent Helper whenever your name happens to appear on the schedule. This Henry kid with the peanut allergy is one of them.

But that's all we've been told. That's it, and that's what is pissing the Mothers off. Other than the fact that this kid Henry is in daycare and allergic to peanut butter, the Mothers have none of the details. They've never been told a thing about the severity of the allergy: they don't know if it's a matter of Henry immediately dying or just getting a rash. Maybe not even a rash. Neither has there been any discussion about how unlikely it is that little Henry—a child the Mothers have never seen—may wander into our specific classroom at some point. All the same, the decision was made that peanut butter should be understood as a toxic substance, like asbestos, or a radioactive isotope that really should be kept a hundred miles under ground.

"I think it's completely ridiculous," says Jenna McLean, who I consider to be the ringleader of the Mothers. She's thirty or something and the mother of twins, which confers on her a kind of authority in the group. No matter how exhausted any of the other Mothers become, Jenna always points out it's nothing compared to what she's been through, often having no choice but to breastfeed her twins at the same time, which she did until just before they started preschool.

"I mean, it would be one thing if this Henry was in the class," says Ellen, who looks a little younger than Jenna. "But he's not. I think that's ironic."

Ellen is the mother of Megan. Her husband's a cop, and so is her brother, which makes her a sort of henchman amongst the Mothers. The one who can be called upon to do the really dirty work. If this were a movie about a hard-boiled detective trying to get to the bottom of things, Ellen would be out back with one of the slimeball guys who witnessed the murder, letting him know she'd break his arm if he didn't cough up the right names. Jenna would sit looking at her nails the whole time, saying in a sarcastic way what a shame it was that people have to be so stubborn. It's always Ellen who steps in when one of Jenna's twins has an accident, which is almost every day. She's the one with a spare set of clothes, and she'll also take whichever twin has had the accident into the washroom. It can get really disgusting sometimes, and I've seen Ellen wash the poop out of one of Jenna's kids' pants in the kind of unblinking, unsmiling way that makes me certain that at another time, in another life, in a Bogart movie, she'd have no qualms about gouging out the eye of an evil criminal mastermind with a rusty nail. I don't know exactly what she means by *ironic*, but I'm pretty sure it's not the standard definition. "I mean," she says, "I think it's pretty ironic we all have to suffer because of this Henry."

"We should *say* something," says Debbie, who seems a little younger than both Jenna and Ellen and is the prettiest of the bunch. She's the mother of the bespectacled Cyril and also the mother of a three-month-old who I think is a girl but can't say for sure.

Debbie has the most sensational breasts I've ever seen, and she's always moving them in and out of her loose-fitting blouses to breastfeed the baby. More than once I've been sitting there in the hallway and prayed for the kids to stay there a little longer because Debbie has just arrived and is about to start breastfeeding, moving herself around, feeling first her right breast and then her left as she tries to remember which one the baby fed from last. I don't know if it makes me a bad person that I've asked God to make the strap of her bra fall

all the way off or if it's the kind of thing God gets asked all the time and is willing to overlook. If I ever go to confession again, which is something my mother used to ask me to do all the time and now has completely forgotten about, I'll bring it up. But probably not before then.

"I'm ready to say something," says Karen, the mother of Brittany. She's the youngest and least attractive of the Mothers, with a half-grown-out perm that makes her head look triangular. She's the sort of person who, in the *Friday the 13th* movies, gets killed with maximum gruesomeness very early on, as a demonstration of the pitfalls of not taking the possibility of psychotic killers seriously enough, and of being unattractive in movies.

"In my old co-op this would never fly," adds Jonah's mother, Moira, who's a little older than the other Mothers. She grew up in New York, on the Upper West Side, which is where she met her husband, a banker who got transferred to Ohio. "You'd never get away with this kind of thing, there'd be people marching outside with signs. Maybe a guy in a Mr. Peanut costume."

"Who is this Henry?" says Ioana, in her somewhat sexy Romanian, James Bond–villain accent. She defected with her husband five years ago, when she was pregnant with Alexander.

"This is the first I've heard of him," says Jenna.

"Have we seen the Henry?" says Ioana.

"The thing is," says Debbie, manoeuvring a nipple into the mouth of her baby, "Cyril loves peanut butter."

"So does Megan," says Ellen. "It's the *only* thing she'll eat. The other night, I made spaghetti just for her, and she threw it on the ground. So I gave her peanut butter."

"Try it with twins," says Jenna.

"I can't imagine," says Ellen.

"What can you make for the lunch that isn't the peanut butter?" says Ioana. "Does she want me to wake up in the morning and cook the chicken to make the chicken salad sandwich?"

"Who has time to make the chicken salad?" says Ellen.

"I know I don't," says Jenna.

"Does she want me to make the sushi, to make the chef come to my house?" says Ioana. "Back in Romania, if you had the peanut butter, you'd have the big celebration. The whole of the kids ate it, and if someone died, they died."

"Well," says Ellen, "that's communism for you."

"I've never had sushi," says Karen. "It looks just awful."

"There was a great sushi place on the Upper West Side," says Moira. "Back east when I worked in advertising and we lived in the city, I went out with this guy—well, not really, I mean, he was probably gay—but whenever we had big clients in town, that was the place."

"The twins have their own word for peanut butter, you know," says Jenna. "It's *pee-bu*."

"For peanut butter?" says Karen.

"Now that is adorable," says Debbie, running a single finger down her left breast, absently, like nobody can see her.

"Jane will say to Austin, *pee-bu*, and he'll say it right back."

"Some twins have their own private language," says Karen.

"Not mine," says Jenna.

"That's good," says Karen.

"What I'm saying is it's normal," Jenna insists. "If they did have their own private language, it'd be completely normal. But they don't. They have a single word. And that's *it.* It's not the same as having a whole secret language."

"The whole peanut butter drama," says Debbie, "I could do without it."

"I'll tell you what," Jenna tells us. "I'm going to say something."

"I think you should," says Ellen.

"I mean," says Jenna, "it's too much."

"What're you going to say?" says Karen.

"Just tell her we've had enough," says Ellen.

"That if you crush the people for so long," says Ioana, "it's only so much time before they take it back."

"Maybe don't put it exactly like that," Ellen tells Jenna.

There's a noise from inside the classroom, and the Mothers stand up, calling out to their kids to stop running up and down the hall. Then the door opens, and instead of the confrontation I'm expecting, instead of Jenna taking a hamster hostage and issuing a set of demands, she kisses her twins and she's gone. The other Mothers do the same. I don't know where they all go for the two and a half hours they have until they have to pick up their kids, but they're out of there. I pretend to do the same.

JOHNNY WANG GOOD FOOD

The fact is, though, I don't have anywhere to go. Not really. I walk down Lee Road to Heights High and the Johnny Wang Good Food Truck, which is always parked at the curb near the gym doors at the back of the school. There are picnic tables on the lawn and that's where I sit while I wait for someone to come over and talk to me. This happened once or twice before it stopped altogether. It's like I'm invisible, or radioactive, one of those zombies in *Night of the Living Dead* you have to shoot down, because if you don't you'll catch whatever they've got.

Some days it seems like the only one who remembers me—the only one who can see me—is Johnny Wang, who runs the food truck. "Yes please, Mr. Jimmy," he still says to me, just the way he did before any of this happened. "What'll it be today?"

I order one of Johnny Wang's Bacon Specials with hash browns on the side. But just as Johnny is in the process of ringing it up on the cash register, I change my mind and order instead one of his Eggo Fiascos, which is really two Eggo waffles with eggs and bacon pressed between them like a big sandwich and covered in syrup. And that's when Johnny Wang stops me and says maybe I should take it easy, maybe not eat so much of Johnny Wang's good food. He smiles when he says it, then laughs like he's kidding, really, that I can eat as much as I like. I sort of give up after that, take my money and walk away. He calls after me but I keep going, don't even turn around. I'm not starving to death or anything.

It's depressing. I mean, I know that it's not physically possible to put on that much weight in the time it's been since I've been Petey's nanny or whatever you want to call it. That at most it's ten pounds. Absolutely not more than fifteen. But that's enough. When someone puts on fifteen or twenty pounds you see it right away. The fact of the matter is that there are some guys who can eat two or three of Johnny Wang's Eggo Fiascos every day of their lives and no one would even know—but I'm sort of fat to begin with.

Ever since ninth grade I've been on one kind of diet or another. Either I wouldn't be allowed to eat bread, or allowed to drink milk, or was supposed to eat only bananas, which was the kind of diet I was kind of on around the time the library exploded. If I ever left the house I had to carry my banana igloo with me, a red and white thing that looked like a big lunchbox but was really a container that prevented the bananas inside it from aging or bruising. I was supposed to have bananas with me at all times, in case I got hungry. The idea being that instead of heading over to the Johnny Wang Good Food Truck I'd open the banana igloo and take out as many bananas as I liked. That's the diet's big selling point, the thing that makes it different from other diets—you're never hungry because you can eat all the time, so long as you're eating bananas. As many as you want, whenever you want. I got the banana igloo as a present from my father out of the blue one Saturday when the two of us were supposed to be watching the hockey game. I didn't know what it was at first, and there was a moment before he told me what it was when I was really happy, thinking, as I pulled the wrapping off, it was some kind of exotic radio.

On the morning of the first day of visitation for Mike at the funeral home on Taylor, I had the banana igloo with me, though I didn't bring it inside. Instead, I kept it in the back of my father's station wagon and went out every so often for a banana, walking past the smokers outside, mostly kids from our high school. One of them, this really beautiful girl named Carla, saw me eating the bananas and came over and asked if I was quitting smoking. I told her yeah, it sucked. Then she walked away and I never saw her again. I felt good for about fifteen minutes, then went back to hating that banana igloo.

Maybe you know what it's like to have an inexplicable death in your family, maybe not, but when that happens all bets are off. It feels like you should take your time card and punch out and then rip it up because you'll never be punching back in again. I've never had that kind of job, never had a time card, but my father did, back when he worked in the mines up in Canada. In the morning he would punch in, and at the end of the day he'd punch out and go home. That was the way it worked in the mine. Either you are drilling into the rock or you aren't. You don't take any mining books home with you at night—though my father said he had a lot of mining dreams about the rock caving in. And then one day, around the time he got accepted into Case Western for engineering, he punched out for good and that was it. He never went back.

What I'm saying is that when you have some freak accidental death in the family, you're entirely off the hook. Or should be. The whole time I was at the funeral home, I kept thinking that somebody was going to tell me it would be a good idea if I forgot about the diet for a while. That really the best thing for me would be to go back to eating whatever I wanted. I was ready to say no, at least at first. But then they'd insist, and we'd go out for pizza or maybe to McDonald's or maybe even to Kentucky Fried Chicken, which is just across the street from the funeral home. But no one did. And I kept thinking about that Kentucky Fried smell and I wondered if it meant I was a bad person, to be wanting fried chicken so badly while everyone was shaking my hand, saying how sorry they were for our loss. One after another. Saying that it was just unbelievable such a thing could happen. Or that they'd taken books out of that library the day before it exploded, that very same library.

Thanks for coming, I'd say.

Or, we're doing the best we can.

Or, it's hard to believe.

My father and I stood to the left of the casket and to the right was that big picture of Mike that I'd been given that day at the television studio with his airbrushed chin. People came up and shook my hand and the whole time my mother knelt at the casket saying the rosary. Or pretending to say it. Maybe she was just kneeling there, letting the beads slip through her fingers, not saying anything.

It's not that different from high school, hanging out with the Mothers, except instead of complaining about how their last class sucked or talking about who they think is a loser they talk about what a hassle their kids are and how they never have time to do anything. It's like it's an all-girl school and I've snuck in somehow. Which isn't the worst thing. One time, Ellen told me she liked a shirt I was wearing. It was light green, a nothing shirt from Wal-Mart that my mother bought me. That's the kind of thing that happens. I'll just be sitting there, and then one of the Mothers will come out with something like that and I'll feel like one of them, like a fully fledged human being.

If we lived in some third world country, there'd be nothing weird at all about me having to look after Petey. No one would think twice when they saw me pushing that stroller in the morning, sitting out in that hallway waiting to take him home. It's the sort of lesson about cultural differences—or whatever—I'd be learning in Geography, if I was still going to school. There'd be a film showing Petey following me to the well in Africa each day, him squatting down beside me and holding a huge pot still while I worked the pump. After it was filled with water, he'd help lift that big pot to my head. We'd walk back to our camp, me with the pot balanced expertly and Petey following along behind uncomplainingly. I suppose the whole thing would be more plausible if I was a girl and maybe if Petey was my own kid rather than my brother. There are a lot of places where girls have their first kid around my age. And sometimes I let myself think exactly that, act as if I got a girl pregnant and now have to raise our illegitimate child on my own. I can't imagine this—the part where a girl actually sleeps with me, that is—but it does make me wonder what kind of father I'd be. If I'd be tough like my own father, tell my kid that I'd turn him in to the cops if he ever did the wrong thing, or let him figure that out on his own.

One time, about a week ago, Jenna's husband, a tallish, almost fat guy in a suit, dropped off her twins in the morning. I watched him come into the classroom and take off their coats and shoes and I tried to think of Jenna and him meeting and deciding to get married. How do things like that happen? It occurred to me that being a father would mean I'd have to be a husband first, and hanging out with those mothers, I find myself thinking about who I'm going to marry, and which of the Mothers I'd marry if it was up to me. Before I was Petey's nanny, I hadn't given it much thought except that I'd probably end up with a really smart and funny swimsuit model who didn't mind the way I cry sometimes for no reason. But the Mothers are real mothers, who have had actual weddings and turned out to be normal people. It makes me wonder if they're normal *because* they had weddings. No matter what they flunked in high school, or the stupid things they might have said when they were my age, they got to be mothers and lived happily ever after. I know there's going to be a day, someday, when I can walk around and no one will know anything about my brother, or the library, or any of this. I don't know if I want that to happen, or even if there's anything I can do about it. Some days when I'm sitting there with them, I feel it building inside me, the urge to say something about how I had a brother once upon a time, how in the morning I'd hear him brushing his teeth and now I don't. Just tell them, whether they want to hear it or not.

After preschool is over I put Petey into the stroller where he usually passes out and naps for about an hour. Sometimes it's longer, but mostly not. There are days when he wakes up after just five minutes feeling really refreshed and that's when I want to kill him most. Once he's awake it's my responsibility to keep him occupied until my mother takes over, if it's one of her good days. It's not hard to tell my mother's good days from the rest—you only have to look at her. On the good days she plays with Petey like a normal mother, maybe takes him grocery shopping with her, maybe folds some laundry, and on her bad days she'll walk around the house in a daze, or sit for hours at the kitchen table looking really carefully at a pencil that has Mike's very own teeth marks on it.

On her bad days I have to entertain Petey until dinner, which means reading him his favourite book, *Sharks and Whales of the Ocean,* or else pretending to be whatever kind of sea creature he decides I should be.

"Jimmy," he'll ask, "do sharks eat coral?"

"I don't think so."

"Okay, I'll be the shark and you be the coral."

Or else, he'll say, "The giant grouper eats Volkswagens."

"*Could* eat one," I'll tell him. "There's no evidence of that ever actually happening."

"Okay," he'll reply, "I'll be the grouper and you be the Volkswagen."

If anything goes wrong with Petey's day, it's a major catastrophe. You think he'll drink his milk out of a normal glass like a normal person, but he won't. Maybe you think he'll eat peanut butter on toast for once in his life, but he won't. Maybe you think you'll get him out the door without his diver's mask on and his ratty stuffed shark that Mike bought him at a garage sale for a quarter, but you can't. You can't even get that shark out of his hands for long enough to wash it so that it doesn't smell like waffle syrup and piss. You can try but he'll throw the milk at you, or burst into tears, tell you he hates you.

He's a lot like the rock star Jim Morrison when he was at the height of his fame, when both "Light My Fire" and "Break on Through" were at the top of the charts and he couldn't walk down the street without some girl asking to sleep with him. Everything was going so perfectly for him that he freaked out and starting acting Petey's age, starting having these massive temper tantrums when he'd throw TV sets out of windows and not leave his hotel room for days at a time. Petey's a lot like that, like the most temperamental lead singer in the most temperamental band. He's too small to lift the TV, but that doesn't mean he wouldn't if he could.

SISTER MARY DAMIAN OF THE INFANT JESUS

Cleaning the library was something we did on Sundays. There was a janitor, of course, but as far as my mother was concerned the work the janitor did was just the beginning. He didn't do the kind of scrubbing and polishing, the dutiful and thorough shaking out of rugs she'd grown accustomed to during her time as a nun. Our father claimed to find the whole thing incomprehensible; he would wonder how someone as devout as our mother could make her children work on Sundays. But even he seemed to understand that for our mother, cleaning the library was a form of prayer, a natural extension of whatever it was we were supposed to be doing when we were down on our knees at Mass.

And so our Sundays were all the same: we'd drive into downtown Cleveland to St. Claire's Church for Mass in the morning, at the same parish that had been my mother's when she'd been a nun, and after that we'd drive back to the library in Cleveland Heights and start cleaning. Only after we finished cleaning—it was usually three or four in the afternoon—would we have Sunday lunch. Sometimes it would be the floor she would make us scour and sometimes it would be the walls. Or the bookshelves, which meant stacking the books carefully on the carpet before washing the shelves with a damp rag. Or else she would make my father bring the ladder from our garage so we could wipe down window ledges no one had ever seen, and which no one except us would ever see.

Most Sundays our mother cleaned with us, and it was then that she would talk to us about what her life had been like in the convent, as if the act of scrubbing itself teleported her back to that earlier part of her life. All kids have a hard time believing their mothers are real people, she'd say, can't quite believe that their mothers didn't fall from the sky, perfectly formed and maternal. But what we had to understand is that all mothers are other people—all mothers are several people, and this was literally the case with her, who'd been not one but *two* other people before turning into our mother. She'd been Filomena Ricci before meeting our father, she said, but in between she'd been Sister Mary Damian of the Infant Jesus, a nun who'd entered the convent on her eighteenth birthday. She'd expected to be given a teaching job, but instead the nuns had sent her to the diocesan archives, to catalogue the voluminous and scattered correspondence of a bishop named Cooper who had gone on a polar expedition. So it was that most of her twenties—at a time when the rest of the world was hanging out at Woodstock and listening to Jim Morrison and zoning out on acid—was spent in a small cubicle in a windowless library on Cleveland's West Side. She told us she resented not being assigned to teaching, but only at first, because by sending her to the library the nuns had assured her salvation. It's libraries, she maintained, that show us what heaven will be like. Look at these books, she'd say, how can there be so many books and no eternity in which to read them?

Despite all of that religious indoctrination—that's what Mike called it—it wasn't long after our trip to Canada that

Mike declared himself an atheist. He told me about it, how he had made up his mind, one night in the bedroom we shared. The lights were out and we'd both been pretending to sleep. "Jimmy," he said, and then he told me—he'd stopped believing in God.

"You mean like Dad?"

It wasn't the response he wanted. "What's there to believe in? Seriously, think about it."

I tried to do that, to imagine an empty, godless universe. "Don't you think there must be something up there?"

"*Out* there maybe," he said. "But up there, no way. I'm sick of it, the way Mom shoves it all down our throats. I can't take it anymore."

"Yeah," I said, though I didn't remember our mother shoving anything down our throats.

"It's only logical," he went on. "When you die, you're gone forever." He'd made up his mind, he said, after Frank DeSilva had seen nothing after being dead. When Frank had fallen to the ground, Mike had run to him, had felt Frank's un-pulsing wrist himself. Frank had seen the other side, according to Mike, and had come back to tell us there was nothing there.

"Mom is going to freak," I told him.

"I'll tell her tomorrow, before church."

"Maybe you should do it after dinner," I said. "I mean, it's not like it's an emergency."

For a moment he said nothing and it seemed like he was thinking it over, changing his mind. But then his breathing began to change and I knew he was falling asleep. I tried to sleep too but couldn't. I could picture our mother, staring at Mike with tears in her eyes, asking how could he do this to her. Mike not knowing what to say, for once.

The next morning, though, after Mike sat down at the kitchen table and dropped his bombshell, our mother was almost happy. At the library, if one of the patrons ever spoke above a whisper she had a way of turning in her chair so that it creaked loudly and scared the offender into silence. Only rarely did she get up and actually hush someone, and when she did, she had a way of putting a single finger across her parted lips that let the offender know he or she had already been forgiven. What she did with Mike was like that. When he finished telling her, she said that was fine, and as far as she was concerned, he could still come to church with us and still clean the library afterwards.

"God loveth the clean," she told him. "Even atheists like you."

"There is no God," Mike said.

"How can you be sure?" she asked him.

"But that's what I'm saying, I've thought about it."

"And you should go on thinking about it—it's a good thing to think about God, Michael."

Mike appealed to our father, who, as we all knew, believed in nothing but the physical laws of the universe. "Do I have to go?" he asked, his voice petulant and thin, like he was nine years old again. "I mean you don't, why do I have to?"

My father almost said something, then didn't. He made a small, nearly imperceptible movement with his eyebrows as if to say it was out of his control.

Mike turned back to my mother, trying to make her angry now. "I know that you think being in the library with all those books will change my mind in some kind of magical way," he told her. "But it won't. The books are just books, just paper."

"Thank you for telling me what you think," she replied. "Now please get ready."

"Aren't you going to cry or something?" I interrupted. This confrontation was going in a different direction than I'd imagined: she hadn't threatened once to disown my brother and didn't seem about to fall to her knees and pray for divine intercession to save him. What she was saying was that his being an atheist wasn't going to change anything.

"Heaven is not a newspaper," she reminded me. "People wish it was, but it isn't."

"I seriously don't get what that's supposed to mean," Mike said. "You always say it and I have no idea what you're talking about."

"It means believing in God isn't something you can subscribe to," she said. "You can call the paper and pay your money, and the paper arrives. But not faith. You don't just open your door in the morning and the headlines are there."

"What headlines?" Mike asked. "There aren't *any* headlines—there's not even a newspaper. That's what I'm trying to tell you. I can't subscribe because there's no such paper."

At this our mother shrugged in the enigmatic way she shrugged when she had been talking about her time in the convent, and afterwards we all—Vivian, me, little Petey, my atheist brother Mike—went to Mass, and then came back so Mike and I could clean the library as usual. Vivian and Petey were getting the day off from cleaning so they could go with my mother and take lunch to Frank DeSilva, who was back in the hospital for some kind of heart procedure. This was my mother's way of telling Frank she was sorry for my father nearly killing him with that case about the exploding pickup trucks. As we were driving to the library she informed Mike and me that our task would be to thoroughly clean the green rug in the AV section in the basement where we worked. Our mother was a great believer in shaking rugs—if it was possible, we'd been taught that the right thing to do was to take a rug outside and shake it or beat it with your fist until all the dust was out of it. There was only so much good that a vacuum could do, she maintained, and so we both knew what she was really saying was that we had to move everything off of it, roll it up, then carry it all the way outside. It was difficult and dirty job. The carpet my mother was talking about was one that had never been moved. It sat in the back corner of the basement under the heavy metal film shelves and was a disgusting dark shade of green, like it had been woven out of ancient green pubic hairs. Mike saw the job our mother had given us for what it was, her way of getting him to back down—as if she was daring Mike to refuse, so she could understand and go on loving him with the same saintly composure with which she always had. And because he knew this was what she wanted, Mike resolved to suffer through it, to be obedient and make it clear that it wasn't long before he would start to hate her.

"Any questions?" she said as we were getting out of the car.

"We'll have to move all the films, just to get at it," I said.

"I don't care how long it takes," she said. "I care that it's done. And before you put the carpet back in, I want the floors mopped as well, thoroughly."

"This is stupid," said Mike. "I get it, okay?"

"Michael," said my mother, "I know you're good, even when you try to make me think the opposite."

"Maybe you're wrong," he said. "Maybe one day I'll do something evil, some really awful shit, and you'll have to disown me." He had a serious look on his face, and he was breathing quickly. I could tell he was trying not to cry.

"Try me," she told him.

Mike looked away.

"I hope you do," she said. "And then you'll know that I'd never disown you."

Then she drove away and left us there. Mike took out a pack of Marlboros and began to smoke. He lit one cigarette after another, taking long drags, smoking each one down to the filter as quickly as he could. I went inside and got to work. There was nothing else to do, and I didn't want my mother to come back and see me standing there outside with him. I had the sickening feeling that I had been an accomplice in it all, a bystander who could have intervened but didn't. I started off by taking the 16 mm films off the shelves and stacking them up in the children's section, then moving the shelves, a few of which had to be disassembled to get them out of the way. After a bit, Mike came down into the basement but just sat there. When it was time to lift the shelves though, he stood up and lifted the opposite end, helping me. Then we vacuumed the carpet, and once that was done, he helped me roll it up so we could carry it outside to shake it.

And that's when we found it.

We rolled up the carpet and there it was, a large rectangle carved into the basement floor with a handle in the top of it.

"It's a door," said Mike. He hadn't spoken for a long time before that, and his voice came out hoarse and brittle.

"Leave it," I told him.

Mike took hold of the handle and tried to open it. But it stuck.

"Seriously," I said.

Mike gave the trap door a second and then a third tug, and it was on the third tug that it made a small popping sound and gave way. As he pulled it open the old air that had been trapped inside wafted into the room.

"There's stairs, I think," he said, and started walking down them.

I called out to him to stop, but I don't know if he heard me. I don't know what happened next, not exactly, because I fainted. Passed out cold.

Just like I would do that day in the television studio when I was supposed to be telling Mike he could just come home.

When I woke up, he was still down in it. "It's a bomb shelter," he was saying.

I called out to him.

"This is so cool," I heard him say. And I realized he wasn't talking to me at all.

There's a name for what's wrong with me: vasovagal syncope. That's the medical term for it. It means ordinary fainting. There are three other kinds of fainting, two of which have to do with serious neurological or cardiac problems and a third that has to do with standing up for too long. Then there's my kind. Which happens if you're nervous or angry or freaked out. This is the kind of fainting I do—the lamest kind of fainting there is.

It's not that I faint all the time. But it happens. It *can* happen. Once or twice a year, maybe more, depending on the year. Here is a list of things Mike told me I sounded like when I fainted: a ton of bricks, a bag of cement, a bag of hammers, a six-pack, a bag of six-packs, a dead bird, a loaf of bread, a hunk of lead, a brick, the sound of the word *boom.*

God, I miss my brother.

SNOW QUEEN

"So, Jim," Jenna is asking me, "how old are you anyway?"

"Seventeen, I guess."

"You guess?"

"Almost eighteen," I tell her. "Eighteen in July."

"When I was eighteen," she says, "I was so hot."

"I bet you were," says Debbie, encouragingly.

"Seriously, I mean," says Jenna. "I was Snow Queen."

"You were what?" says Moira. "They don't have that in New York."

"I bet they do," says Karen.

"Maybe it's a Cleveland thing."

"Like hockey," says Debbie.

"They play hockey in New York," says Moira. "But they don't have a Snow Queen, or whatever."

"In Romania," says Ioana, "they would have the big parades for Ceauşescu. Always for Ceauşescu. You go out and you stand for the hours to wait, and then he comes and you go crazy with the waving."

"I can't imagine that," says Karen.

"Anyway," says Jenna, "they have a Snow Queen here, and it was me when I was eighteen. That's how hot I was."

"It's part of the winter carnival," says Ellen. "They do it every year."

"Do they still?" asks Moira.

They do, I tell her, and the winner gets named Snow Queen. The way they decide on a winner is that the girls all get asked questions, like their favourite book, or what kind of vegetable they most resemble. Or else, if they could change one thing about the world, what it would be.

"I'd say world peace," says Karen.

"Everyone says world peace," says Ellen.

"In Romania, if they would have a thing like this, everyone would give the same answer. If you don't, you go to jail."

"When I was a junior, I was runner-up for Snow Queen," says Debbie, "and one of the other girls—I forget her name—she said world peace, and had to move away. Right out of town. People would walk by her and laugh."

"It's true, that's how bad it can be," says Karen. "I heard that too."

"The one thing I knew going into it," says Jenna, "is that if you said world peace, you'd lose."

"It's like a beauty contest," I tell them, "except it takes place in February and the girls are all wearing coats and hats."

"It's not that cold," says Jenna.

"I'm sure the judges got a good look at you," says Ellen.

"So what did you say about changing the world?" Moira asks Jenna.

"Nothing at all—I said that the world was a pretty good place to begin with."

"You said that?" says Moira.

"It was the truth. They asked what I'd change, and I said nothing at all."

"Not a single thing?" Moira stares at Jenna. "I mean, seriously."

"Yes, seriously, that's what I'd still say. I've never wanted to move away," says Jenna. "I like it here, sorry about that."

"It was a gutsy reply," says Ellen, "and the judges liked it."

"They respected me," says Jenna.

"I can see that," says Karen.

"And," says Jenna, "I was pretty hot."

"Everyone is hot at the eighteen," says Ioana.

"But I was really hot," says Jenna. "I'll bring in a picture. We'll see what Jimmy says."

"I'm sure you were hot," I tell her, but then she gets this look on her face. A moment later, I say, "I mean I take your word for it. I bet you were really really hot."

"Take it easy," says Ellen.

"You're fine," Jenna tells me.

"I bet that you would be the real fox," says Ioana.

"I bet you would be," I say, a little too emphatically. I know it, but I can't stop myself and Jenna seems not to mind. "I bet you would be the total fox."

"The Snow King was Brian Coulter," Ellen almost whispers. She's looking in the other direction, at the empty hallway wall.

"Brian Coulter?" says Karen. "I made out with him once."

"You did not," says Jenna.

"I can't think of it now," says Karen, "I mean, I really can't. Sometimes, I have to stop myself."

"He was a good kisser," says Ellen.

"What do you know about it?" Jenna asks.

"Nothing," says Ellen.

"I'd like to meet this Brian Coulter," says Moira. "He sounds like a piece of work."

"He was a piece of work," says Jenna.

"He's dead," says Ellen.

"Of AIDS," says Karen. "I went to the funeral."

"It wasn't AIDS," says Jenna, "and you weren't the only one who went to the funeral. It was a brain tumour."

"They said it was a brain tumour," says Karen, "but really it was AIDS."

"Who told you that?" says Jenna. "Was it his mother? Because his mother always hated me."

"No one actually dies of AIDS," says Moira. "That's the name of the virus. In some cases, it can lead to a brain tumour."

"I think that if Brian Coulter died of AIDS someone would have told me," says Jenna. "I think they have to."

"Once I went out with this guy who got chlamydia," says Moira. "This was back, you know, when I was working in advertising. I guess he didn't know it. Then when he went in, the Public Health Department made him call all the girls he slept with, and I had to go in and get tested."

"Was Brian Coulter gay?" asks Debbie.

"Maybe it was AIDS," says Jenna. "I mean, I guess I don't know. I got tested anyway. I wasn't worried, but I did it anyway."

"I've never been tested," says Karen.

"I think you have to keep getting tested," says Moira. "It's got an incubatory period. You don't have it, but later it shows up."

"I heard that too," says Karen.

Jenna turns to me. "How can you be seventeen," she says, "and not have a girlfriend?"

"Leave the boy alone," says Moira. "There's nothing wrong with taking your time. My husband Paul, you know, didn't even speak to a girl before he was twenty-seven."

Ellen laughs. "Is that even possible?"

"He was that shy, if you can believe it."

"I don't believe it," says Jenna.

"When a guy says something like that," says Ellen, "he's got something to hide."

"He would have to speak to the mother," says Ioana. "Maybe shy, but don't be ridiculous, to not speak to the mother."

"That's right," says Jenna, nodding her head as if to say how right she is, "Ioana's right."

"Even Stalin spoke to the mother," says Ioana.

"Paul is nothing like Stalin," says Moira, "believe me."

"It's not like I've never talked to a girl," I say. "I mean, I've been on a date."

"There you are," says Jenna. "What's her name—the last girl you went out with?"

I tell her Jennifer McKellar, though I don't say anything else. Such as, for starters, she was Mike's girlfriend, not mine. Or that all I did was sit next to her in Geography class. I say her name, though. And just saying it out loud, it makes the world seem as still as a photograph.

THE SEPTEMBER OF JENNIFER

Jennifer moved here last summer, while we were in Canada. She arrived from New Jersey sometime in June, though Mike and I didn't see her until September, until that first day of school when we walked in to find her sitting next to us in homeroom. As in most of my classes, I sat beside my brother in Geography. Though Mike was a year older, we'd always been in the same grade. Because of the weirdness of his birth, it took an extra year before he was big enough to go to school. People assumed we were twins—the non-identical kind, that is—because we'd entered kindergarten together and had been in the same grade ever since. In high school we took all the same classes, so I could help Mike with the work, or so he could at least copy off me. In Geography Mr. Atkinson had arranged us in our desks alphabetically, like books on a library shelf. That meant we were near the back, the three of us: Jennifer, me, then Mike. Her father, we learned, was a lawyer and they lived in a white mansion across town, on Derbyshire, near the Shaker Lakes. After we'd told her our names and she'd said hers, she talked about moving here, how she didn't want to leave Jersey or the Jersey Shore where she and a bunch of kids she knew would drive, every weekend, to some great beach house some other kid owned.

"It was great," she told us. "Like my tan?" She pulled her shirt away from her shoulder to reveal a tan line as thin and pale as a ray of sunlight.

"Do you have a boyfriend back in Jersey?" I asked her.

Mike snorted, as if I'd just asked her to marry me.

"Sort of," she said.

"Was he, like, a lifeguard?" said Mike. "Like in *Grease*?"

I was going to point out no one was a lifeguard in *Grease*, they were on the beach and that was it, but Jennifer laughed. "What did your boyfriend say about you moving?" I asked her instead.

"He's cool with it," she said.

"He's cool with it?" Mike said. "Did he *want* you to move away?"

"He's twenty-two," she replied. "He's got a different perspective."

Neither of us knew what to say to that. To date a girl in her twenties, in college, probably on the pill, able to buy beer without needing a fake I.D. was, for both of us, impossible, a feat so entirely outside of human accomplishment that we could only scoff at it. On Fridays at the library we'd sit out on the front steps and watch the college girls from Case Western walk down Lee Road, looking drunk and happy, like a different species. Going out with a twenty-two-year-old was like claiming you were dating Mallory on *Family Ties,* like walking on water. Sitting there in awestruck silence, I turned and checked Jennifer out, watching as she leaned all the way back in her chair, letting her blue tube top ride up, exposing a tanned belly. While she did, her left eye looked out the window and her right eye didn't.

She caught me looking. "It's dead," she told me. "It died when I was born."

That dead eye never seemed very dead to me, though. It roamed and moved around with a will of its own. Sometimes it would roll all the way back in her head as if it was looking at her brain. Other times, when Mr. Atkinson showed one of his slide shows about glaciers, the eye would dart around like it was watching a tennis game. Most of the time, though, the dead eye looked straight at Mike. I'd lurch forward suddenly in my desk, to see if the eye noticed, hoping I could get its attention. I never could. It wasn't interested in me, no matter what I did. Jennifer McKellar's dead eye, I concluded, was in love with Mike. I should have known right then I didn't have a chance with her. Even though it was me who sat right next to her and it was me who memorized her wardrobe, her dead eye clearly couldn't care less.

The next day I got to homeroom first, while Mike was still out in the smoking area.

"Hey," I said, trying to be nonchalant about it.

"Hey, yourself," she said back. "What's your name again?"

"Jimmy Morrison," I said, "like Jim Morrison, lead singer of the Doors."

"Oh yeah." She half smiled while her dead eye glanced over at me, then away just as quickly. "So are you going to light my fire?"

"I will if you let me," I told her. It was just a joke, but I felt my face getting warm and started to wonder if I was about to pass out.

"We'll see," she said, and winked her good eye at me.

Then the two of us just sat there and waited for class to start.

—

Now in the hallway outside the preschool, Jenna is saying her name. "Jennifer McKellar," she says, turning the two words around in her mouth as though she's tasting them.

"Like that princess in *Star Wars*," says Karen. "The one who turns out to be Luke's sister."

"That's Princess Leia," Moira tells her. "Her name is Leia."

"Are you sure? I could have sworn it was Princess Jennifer. The one who kisses Luke and then finds out she's really his sister. They act like it's nothing afterwards, but you can tell. It's really pretty awkward for all of them."

"What else?" asks Jenna. "Did she dump you? Give us the details."

"After that, things got complicated," I tell her, but not the rest of it. I let her think it was a matter of my being on the brink of a great romance when the library exploded, killed my brother and wrecked my life. That's not true—Jennifer was never that interested in me, it was always Mike—but I let her think it anyway. One of the big advantages of having a brother who's been killed is that you can decide to stop talking about anything just by bringing it up. Nobody asks questions.

QUADRATIC EQUATIONS

The topic tonight at grief therapy is the physical side of the grieving process. The way that, when someone we love dies, our bodies show us they have minds of their own. The woman whose three-year-old fell off her tricycle tells us she works in a bank, as a teller, and had a bad day earlier that week. Right out of the blue, for no reason all. Her first thought was she had a brain tumour, she tells us. She missed her bus, added up four balances wrong, and the whole time there was a killing pain in her forehead. One of her customers forgot to put the date on a deposit slip and it wasn't until she wrote it down herself, until she was *actually* writing it down, that she realized her three-year-old, if she hadn't fallen off that tricycle, would have been four today.

Everyone nods at this. It's the sort of incredible occurrence that has happened to them all at one time or another, in one way or another. The woman with the defective baby inside of her speaks next, saying she and her husband, the same guy who is still refusing to attend the sessions, decided to go to Florida for their anniversary last week, because it would just be too sad to stay at home and do nothing. It was a spur-of-the-moment thing. He said let's do it and she said let's do it, and then they were on their way to the airport with their bags packed. But then when she went to get on the plane, they made her sign a consent form saying that she wouldn't sue them if she lost the baby. And that was the end of that, they didn't speak again for days, not even when the results of the new round of testing came in saying that the rare chromosomal defect that was going to kill her baby almost immediately after it was born was still there, despite the fact that we had all prayed it would disappear.

The man whose sixteen-year-old died on a jet ski says that when they got home from his kid's funeral his wife wanted to have sex with him, right away. His wife isn't there, which I figure is probably why he's saying it.

Dr. Kasoff tells us many couples report similar things, and what we need to understand is it isn't about having your mind in the gutter but about intimacy and about wanting to bridge a gap.

And also, says the woman whose four-year-old died of a viral infection—the woman who Dr. Kasoff told to leave that session with her baby and still seems angry about it—it's about having your mind in the gutter.

She's right, says the man whose kid was in the jet-ski accident, in a tone of voice that makes me think he's maybe starting to hate everyone in the group.

The bottom line, says Dr. Kasoff, is we are human beings and do the best we can.

Now my mother starts speaking, saying she killed Mike by being his mother. It's not the first time I've heard her say this; right after the explosion she would obsess over the idea, even said it to some of the people who came to the funeral home. And it seemed she really believed it. No matter how often my father tried to talk her out of it, or Dr. Kasoff pointed out that this was a way of thinking that got her nowhere, she kept saying it. Now she's doing it again, and it's finally clear to me that there's something about the idea she likes, that she wants someone to agree with her. That it makes sense to her in a way that nothing else does. The blood is on her hands, she is telling the group, for getting Mike that job; she should never have sent us down into that basement or dared him to do the wrong thing that day we found the bomb shelter. What she wants is for someone—my father, maybe, maybe the other members of the group, maybe Dr. Kasoff—to blame her. Or maybe it's more than that; maybe, I begin to think, what she wants is for someone to tell her she should never have had children at all. That where she went wrong was leaving the convent. Maybe that's what she thinks—that she's still married to God, and now he's getting back at her.

Dr. Kasoff points out that if she hadn't been Mike's mother, he'd never have been born.

She tells him, "Give, and it shall be given you."

"That's from Luke," I say, "from the Gospel."

"I'm not sure what that means," Dr. Kasoff tells her.

"What my wife is saying," interrupts my father, "is that it's similar to a quadratic equation, where the values on either side cancel each other out, effectively."

There we sit, as an unbreakable silence drifts through the room.

This kind of thing happens in our group with the frequency with which normal people ask each other if it's going to rain tomorrow. And when it does, according to Dr. Kasoff, the important thing is to let the silence break itself, to allow the room to be silent for as long as it needs to be silent. If that's an hour, there's a reason for it. Which is exactly what happens that night. The silence lasts for an hour, and at the end of it everyone gets up and goes home.

Mike used to say: "Cleveland *Hell,* a nicer place to live."

It was definitely cooler to hate living here than love it. Even if he didn't know what he wanted to happen in the rest of his life, he was sure having been born and raised in the suburban calm of Cleveland Heights wasn't a step in the right direction. And that even if he did whatever he could to get out, he'd never be able to. That he really was no Devhan Starway, no matter how many of those books about robots he read, that he'd never do any of the things that Bob Hope had done. If Mike had been our father he would have moved us to somewhere like Beirut, which I've heard is no picnic, or to some Communist country where we would spend our lives fighting the good fight and believing it's all for one and one for all, only to find out that really it's not. Then we'd have to escape in the middle of the night, sleeping out in the open and stealing eggs from the barns of strangers and eventually arriving at Ellis Island. After that, Mike would become a famous movie director who made a movie about his escape. Moviemaking was always his way out. Even if he was lucky enough to escape Cleveland Heights though, it might not mean anything, or make such a good movie.

But in those last few months—after we got back from Canada—Mike started to seem almost desperate, as if being born here had slotted him into some special category of doom. Which was maybe why discovering that bomb shelter had such a strange effect on my brother, like when Peter Parker is bitten by the radioactive spider and finds himself changed forever. I didn't know if we were the only ones who knew it was there, but we didn't ask anyone. It was a secret—*our* secret—and from the look of that abandoned place, it wasn't hard to believe that everyone who had known about it was either too old to remember, or dead. It was a cellar, cool and damp, claustrophobic, no larger than our bedroom, and it looked something like it, too. There was a pair of single beds down there, one against each wall, which had on them thin and probably mouldy mattresses on bare metal frames. Whoever had set the place up—thirty, forty years before—clearly wasn't planning on saving humanity, just himself and someone else. Plus there was no survival equipment, no shortwave radio, no packs of waterproof matches, no Geiger counter to tell you when it was all right to come out and rejoin the world. That made me think it wasn't a bomb shelter at all, that it had all been put together way before anyone started worrying about nuclear war. I thought it was really a hideout, a false basement some Cleveland mobster excavated in the thirties and planned to use if he was ever cornered by the cops. Other than the beds, the only things down there were some random supplies: a box of powdered milk a mouse had gnawed its way into, a bag of old beans, stacks of canned water.

"You think the water in those cans is still good?" Mike asked me, the week after we found the trap door. He was already obsessed.

I was splicing back together an old film that documented the movement of an extinct species of crayfish. "Probably not," I told him. "Who puts water in a can anyway?"

"They did then," he said.

"Who knows if it's even water."

"Why wouldn't it be water?"

I said, "It's probably all rusted out—or else evaporated."

Mike stood up and walked behind the counter, then pulled back the green carpet and a moment later had disappeared down through the trap door. As he closed it behind him, the carpet flapped back over it, so you couldn't tell it was there. This had been Mike's idea, to make it so you could get in and out of the bomb shelter without anyone knowing. A few minutes later, the trap door opened again and Mike came out with one of the cans, which he set down on the desk in front of me.

"It's heavy," he said. "You're wrong about it evaporating."

I picked it up, and knew he was right. Something was still in there. "It's going to be too disgusting to drink," I said. The can was a dull silver colour with a white label upon which someone had written the word *WATER* in a sprawling, spidery hand. "I bet it's beans inside really," I told him. "It looks like a can of beans."

Mike picked up the can and shook it. I could hear the liquid sloshing inside. Then he put it back down.

"I don't care if it is water," I told him. "I'm not going to drink it."

"Fine with me," said Mike.

"You'll get sick as hell."

"Okay," he said. "If you don't want to, I don't care."

I went back to the crayfish film, and we didn't talk about it after that. Still, the can of water sat on the desk in front of me, and that night after our shift was over, Mike talked me into waiting with him across the street for Mary to turn out the lights and lock the library. He had stolen our mother's key to the library and got it copied. We were going to sneak in when the building was closed so we could go down into the bomb shelter and hunt around for clues about who had set it up—and why. That's what he told me we were going to do, anyway. We went in quickly and quietly, got the emergency flashlights from the main floor, pulled the trap door shut behind us and heard the carpet above flap down. It was like a game we were playing, and Mike was in charge. Hiding out in the bowels of the earth, like two moles, two fugitives from justice.

"If we ever had to," said Mike, "we could come here."

"I guess we could," I said. "But there's no bathroom or anything."

He shook his head, as if to say that was beside the point, and produced a can opener, the one from the library break room. I understood this was what he had had in mind all along, he was going to drink the water and I was there as a witness, maybe also to call an ambulance. Setting an old can in the middle of the floor, he got straight to work, and when it was opened, there was a metallic odour that emanated from it, as if someone had been stirring it for a long time with a screwdriver. Even in only the half-light provided by the flashlight, I could see the liquid had turned a weird shade of yellow. It was a toast, or a pledge. Some weird baptism.

"Don't be stupid," I told him.

"Break on through," he told me.

"Are you stoned?"

"People are strange," he said, then took a long drink from the can. When he was done, he set the can down. "It's good," he said after a moment, and handed me the can.

"No way," I said.

Mike shrugged, leaned forward, and took it from me. He took another drink, and handed it back.

What am I doing? I wondered as I tipped the can up to my mouth.

I gagged right away. The water was gritty, full of invisible rusted-out shards of something. A moment later I was throwing up. Mike laughed and held the can out for me to puke into. I began to think I couldn't breathe in there, that I had to get out. But then we heard footsteps above us, a slow, heavy tread we knew to be Mary's. It was a Thursday, about ten thirty at night. She knew we were there, that someone was in the library, and she was up there looking for us. We had to stay where we were, despite the smell of my vomit starting to plume and making me want to throw up more. Each time we'd think she was gone, we'd hear her again, moving slowly, going over every inch of the building. When she was gone Mike eased the door open and climbed out. He crept out first in the darkness and made sure the coast was clear, then we both snuck out. Mary never saw us, though the next day she asked our mother about it, if any of us were in the library the night before, saying that the back door had opened and closed twice, but when she'd come to look no one had been there. But the door had been opened.

"Who was it?" said my father, later that night. "Can she give the cops a description?"

"She didn't see anyone," said my mother. "She saw the door moving."

"Just the door?" said my father.

"She was looking out the window," said Vivian. "It's something that she and Frank do—take turns keeping an eye on the building."

"If I know Frank," said my father, "he's got an alarm in there, hooked up to the back door. He and Mary know whenever anyone's coming in or out. It's not a bad idea. The alarm went off, and she went to see what happened."

The next day at the library, Mike made a point of asking Mary about it before she went up and took her place at the circulation desk.

"What kind of alarm?" Mary replied. "What would it sound like?"

"Maybe it wouldn't make a sound," I said. "Maybe it would be a red light blinking."

Mary shook her head. "If there's an alarm, I didn't hear it," she said, then smiled, almost slyly, to herself.

That was how we knew my father was right—that the doors were rigged with an alarm that was separate from the one that went off if the windows were broken. Any time the door opened, Mary and Frank would know about it.

MRS. DUMME

Petey's teacher at the preschool is Mrs. Dumme, a grandmotherly woman in her sixties with a permanent stoop, probably from bending over so often to talk to the preschool kids, admiring this block tower or that finger painting, putting a Band-Aid on someone's wounded finger. Or maybe it's that I've only ever seen her doing that kind of thing. Maybe outside the classroom she's not a hunchback. It's hard to tell because she's taught at the preschool ever since it first opened its doors and she moves around the classroom as if she owns it. Her first name is Barbara, but she makes everyone, including all of us, call her Mrs. Dumme, as if all that time in a preschool classroom has removed from her any memory of a first name as well as any sense of how things work in the world outside. She first introduced herself to me at the funeral home, during Mike's wake. "I'm Mrs. Dumme," she told me, after she had expressed her condolences, "Petey's teacher."

I didn't laugh, not exactly. At the time I was standing next to my brother's casket feeling stupid and numb, and when Mrs. Dumme told me her name, I smiled weakly and said it was a good one. She replied by informing me her name was actually her name. She didn't chew me out exactly, but almost. It was awkward—every time I drop Petey off it crosses my mind. I haven't said anything about it, but I should.

I don't know what time Mrs. Dumme gets there each morning, but when she arrives she locks the door behind her so no one can drop off a kid early. At exactly nine, the door opens. I know for a fact that none of the Mothers have seen her arrive—and Jenna claims to have heard that Mrs. Dumme lives there, that most nights she sleeps in the classroom. When she said that I imagined her curling up in the sandbox like one of those sea turtles I know so much about from reading Petey's sea creature books with him, laying her giant eggs there the way those turtles do, covering them over with a light dusting of sand and waiting for the waves to come in.

This morning as Petey and I are walking into the classroom, she's over at the goldfish bowl, with a small yellow plastic container of fish food. "A pinch and no more," Mrs. Dumme says when she sees me, as she's putting the cap back on the container. "Maybe tomorrow you can do it."

I tell her no thanks.

"Only if you're here on time."

"I don't want to feed the fish," I try telling her. "But—"

"I'll be with you in a second," she cuts me off. "Why don't you sit on the carpet and I'll come over when I'm finished."

"Sit on the carpet?"

"Maybe do a painting."

"I don't really have time to do a painting."

"Maybe you'll have to learn to be patient."

"But I am," I hear myself saying, "I'm just completely patient."

She's already walking away.

I should storm out of the preschool in an angry huff, but I don't. Mrs. Dumme has a wise and knowing air about her, like that Chinese guy in *The Karate Kid.* Maybe she's going to teach me obscure and important truths about the world, make me catch a fly with chopsticks or wax her car, or hang me upside down and beat me with a stick to toughen me up. So, instead of saying anything, I go and sit down quietly on the carpet like I've been told and by the time she comes over I've made up my mind to apologize for laughing at her name. I blurt out that I know what it's like to have an odd name because most of the time when I tell people I'm Jim Morrison they get this look on their faces like "Light My Fire" or "Break on Through" is going through their heads. I say I bet it's the same thing with her and her name—only it turns out she's never heard of the Doors, has no idea who they are, not even when I sing her a bit of "Light My Fire." "They were really big back in the sixties," I tell her. "And not just to their fans—they were on the front pages of newspapers, of *Time.* And once, for instance, their lead singer—Jim Morrison—got arrested for taking his penis out during a concert."

"Is that right?"

"It's a known fact," I say. It's like I'm testifying.

"I really applaud your use of the word *penis*."

"Thank you," I say.

"You're welcome," she says. "I think we need to use the right names for things, right from the beginning."

I tell her I feel exactly the same way.

"I *much* prefer *penis* to *weenie*."

"Or *schlong*," I hear myself saying. "*Weenie* is better than *schlong*, but *penis* is preferable to *weenie*."

"I haven't heard *schlong*," she tells me. "Is that what the young people are saying now?"

"Some of them," I say. "Not all of them, but some."

"Well," she says, "I much prefer *penis*."

"So do I," I say. It's like we've discovered we were both marching that day with Martin Luther King.

Now Mrs. Dumme leans in and tells me that if I ever want to feed the goldfish, I can. But I have to be careful, because giving him too much food will kill him. Goldfish are like that. They eat and eat and eat and eat—then just explode. The important thing to keep in mind when you're feeding a goldfish is to give them a pinch and no more. "Once a day only," she tells me. "Even if you think he's hungry, even if he looks at you with that hungry look, you mustn't feed him. Even if he comes to the top of the tank, even if you can see him looking right at you."

Then she shakes my hand, which is strange because she does this at the end of our conversation, just when I'm about to walk away.

"Maybe *you're* taking this goldfish thing too seriously," Vivian tells me that night, as she's making dinner. We're having pot roast, a dish that can take as long as four and a half hours in a conventional oven but fewer than seventeen minutes in a microwave. She's standing next to the microwave waiting for those seventeen minutes to be over.

"But why would she make me shake on it, then?"

"Maybe it wasn't that kind of shake."

"It wasn't like I begged her to feed the goldfish. I barely even noticed it there."

"Don't do it," she advises me. "Tell her to feed her own goldfish."

Then the bell on the microwave rings. She takes out the casserole dish, carefully placing it on the counter. Then she takes off the glass lid and turns over the weird-looking bluish meat inside; the pot roast looks like a flattened inner tube that, after being punctured, has not only lost its air but started to bleed. "It's not done yet," she assures me, when she sees me looking at it. "Come back in four minutes and thirty-seven seconds."

MUTINY ON THE BOUNTY

After Jim Morrison the rock star, the next most famous Jim Morrison in the history of the world is the James Morrison who was boatswain's mate on the *Bounty.* Even before Fletcher Christian and the rest of those pissed-off sailors got Captain Bligh out of his cabin in his nightshirt and made him walk the plank, that Jim Morrison, the one who'd turn out to be a mutineer, knew he'd had enough. Maybe you know the story and maybe you don't. Maybe you've seen the movie. Everybody's seen that movie. There was even a copy of it in our library which people were always taking out for their movie nights. What that meant is that we fixed it more often than others, and when we did we had to watch at least a bit of it to make sure it worked.

In it, Clark Gable is Fletcher Christian and Captain Bligh, played by Charles Laughton, is an absolute jerk, a real evil guy. And also, there's a relatively minor character named James Morrison. It's the kind of thing you notice when you're named James Morrison. I read the book, which is how I know James Morrison and the *Bounty* sailed from England to Tahiti to pick up a bunch of breadfruit plants. I have no idea what a breadfruit plant is and I've never been to Tahiti, but that other James Morrison thought it was a great place, because as soon as he got there, he decided he wanted to move in.

Captain Bligh had a diary in which he wrote everything, and this is what he had to say about the mutiny:

> *The Women are handsome . . . and have sufficient delicacy to make them admired and beloved. The chiefs have taken such a liking to our People that they have rather encouraged their stay among them than otherwise, and even made promises of large possessions. Under these and many other attendant circumstances equally desirable it is therefore now not to be Wondered at . . . that a Set of Sailors led by Officers and void of connections . . . should be governed by such powerful inducement . . . to fix themselves in the midst of plenty in the finest Island in the World where they need not labour, and where the allurements of dissipation are more than equal to anything that can be conceived.*

The allurements of dissipation. That's Captain Bligh for you, a tough customer. A guy who, like my father, didn't traffic in ambiguity. When I found that quote, Mike and I were in the library, waiting for the last minute of our shifts to end so we could go home. This was halfway through September, when Mike and I were back in school and therefore not able to spend so much time in either the library or the bomb shelter. I was secretly glad; after puking that night, I didn't want to go back down there again. And somehow Mike was already in trouble in school, having skipped the first two weeks of Functions and Relations. He was still going to Geography and English, but that was because Jennifer McKellar was in those classes with us and he liked her, even though she was his opposite in every way. For all her talk about hanging out on the Jersey beach with college boys, despite her dead eye which made her seem subversive and tough, she was smart and a good student, and always showed up at school with her homework done. She planned on being a lawyer, like her father, and she knew she'd have to have good grades if she was going to get into law school. Maybe that was what she liked about Mike—and what he liked about her—the idea that she could change him, turn him around, maybe get him out of jail one day.

"So," Mike would ask. "What happened this weekend?"

Jennifer would never have anything to say to this, not really. "Hung out, you know," she'd say. "Called my boyfriend."

"How is the lifeguard?" Mike would ask.

"He's not a lifeguard," she said as her dead eye fastened itself on my brother. "And you know that. What about you?"

Usually all we had to report was that we'd had to work. "At the library," I explained, after she asked. I told her about the basement, the cleaning and repair of the films. "It's our mother who got us the job."

Then Mike told her about the movie we were going to make about our lives and times. "Sean Penn would play me," he said.

"What about Jimmy?" she asked.

"I don't know," I said. "Maybe Chris Penn."

"The fat Penn," said Mike. "The fat guy who gets killed halfway through."

"There's no movie where that happens to Chris Penn," I told him.

"You should come visit us sometime," said Mike. "You'd like it down there in the basement, safe from the ravages of time."

"What's that supposed to mean?" Jennifer asked him.

"It's just a joke," I said.

"Not the kind of joke you'd laugh at," said Mike. "It's our mother's idea of a joke."

"She used to be a nun," I informed her.

"A robot nun," said Mike. Jennifer laughed at that. Mike was still mad at our mother for not hating him for being an atheist, but he'd forget it from time to time. I watched him remember it as we sat there, reminding himself inwardly that he needed to find some way to get our mother to disown him.

The rest of the time in Geography—when we were supposed to be drawing the map of Africa or calculating gross national products of countries none of us would ever visit—Mike talked about hitchhiking across the country, actually doing the kind of things other kids just talked about. Gathering material, he started calling it, moving to California and hanging around on the beaches the way Jim Morrison did in those days before he was in the Doors, maybe finding some work in Hollywood. Making contacts and laying the groundwork for the movie he was going to make about our life and times.

At first it seemed like he was joking, that it was all an elaborate prank he was playing on our parents, or that he was trying to make himself seem dangerous and cool to Jennifer. But it went on, and soon our parents were called in for the serious discussion that began the period when they were officially worried about Mike. It became the kind of thing I'd hear them telling other parents. Everything's fine, my father would say, though we're worried about Michael. Most of the time I went to class without him, and was even starting to do well in school—better than I ever had before—but our parents seemed not to care, because there emanated from

Mike a genuine destructiveness that made them think he really needed saving.

Even I began to worry. I was seeing less of Mike, and I didn't have any idea where he was going or what he was doing. One night after asking if I wanted to see something, he drove us out to a part of downtown Cleveland where I'd never been, near 40th Street, to an abandoned pawnshop he'd found. It was a boarded-up place that had been looted and re-looted so many times that all that remained was useless junk, all of it in a massive, wild jumble. Old typewriters, a broken stringless piano, useless lamps with the bulbs in them shattered and the shades caved in. It was like stepping into one of those photos of Pompeii Mr. Linton showed us in History class, that city in Italy that Vesuvius wiped out, like the guy who owned the shop and all of his customers and everyone else had taken off all at once, all got into their cars at the same time and just drove away, leaving everything behind.

"Look at this place," he told me.

I did. Weeds were coming up through the wooden floor, and outside even the trees were dead, snow hanging off bare branches. There was no traffic on the street.

I asked him, "Have you been here before?"

Mike looked out a glassless window at the empty street. "People lived here, you know. They had whole lives."

"Is this what you wanted to show me?" I asked him.

"No one comes here, you know, not anymore."

I had no idea what he was expecting me to see, or what I was supposed to say. I knew that he'd been coming to places like this without me, staying out really late at night and not telling me where he'd been. So when our father eventually sat him down—I was in the next room, pretending to watch TV—to talk to him, I was relieved. Something was going on with my brother and I didn't know what it was, or what I could do about it. The guidance counsellor at Heights High had told my father that Mike was in danger of losing his year if something wasn't done—and it was this threat that my father repeated to Mike that night, putting him on the spot and asking him if he was ready to flush his future down the toilet.

Sure, Mike replied, flush away. My father said fine, trying to make it sound like he really didn't care either. And a moment later Mike was out the door, because it was Friday and Friday meant that Mike and I had to be at the library. This was our job, and we did it together, we *always* worked together. But Mike was leaving without me, and I ran out after him, climbed into the Gremlin just as he was pulling out of the driveway. There was a moment when my hand was on the door handle, when I felt the car start to move away. But then he stopped, let me get in.

By the time we got to the library he was buzzed—we both were, I guess, even though I'd only been listening—at having done the wrong thing. It was like Mike had been waiting for something to happen and it finally had.

As always on Fridays, there were no patrons and we were the only two working. It was raining outside, though, too wet to sit out on the steps and watch the girls. Mike was lying on his back on one of the tables in front of the reference desk staring at the ceiling, like someone contemplating his fate. After our shift ended he locked the door and we went downstairs, opened the trap door and set up one of the projectors in the bomb shelter. Just as we'd do, said Mike, if it was a nuclear war or the feds were on our tail. We ran an extension cord up out of the shelter and into the outlet behind the grey Beast that we cleaned the movies with, running it along the wall so no one could see it without being down on his hands and knees. While Mike threaded *Mutiny on the Bounty* into the projector, I read to him that part about Jim Morrison taking off for the breadfruit plants.

And it seemed exactly right. Mike loved the sound of it. "The allurements of dissipation," he repeated, just as the projector sprung to life. Then he lay down on one of the ancient and thin bomb-shelter beds, and shouted it to the empty library through the open trap door. "Hello, Cleveland!" he announced. "We are the Allurements of Dissipation!" That was the shape of Mike's ambition, to shout something excellent and defiant to an empty library. Then we pulled the trap door shut, and it was like the rest of the world didn't matter, like the bombs had already fallen outside and everyone else was complete history already. Clark Gable's face flared up onto the grey bricks and they made him look even tougher, more prehistoric than he already looked on the deck of the *Bounty.* I felt Mike was forgiving me a little for getting sick, for secretly hating it down there.

"What do you think of Jennifer?" he asked me later, as I was putting on the second reel.

"She's okay," I told him. I didn't know why he was asking me and I didn't want to give away too much.

"You should ask her out."

"She's got a boyfriend."

"That lifeguard? He's history, just watch."

I told him maybe, then lay back down on the thin bomb-shelter bed to watch the movie. And for that moment, everything was fine. The two of us, underground and safe, all those books above us keeping us protected and convincing us there was such a thing as eternity. I didn't know if I was going to ask Jennifer out, but maybe I would. Probably she'd turn me down, I thought, laugh outright at the thought of it. In the movie, it'll be Chris Penn who plays me, and that's okay. That's what I told myself that night, and soon it was like I'd forgotten it completely, and watched the movie. It was like the two of us in our bedroom at home and Mike was whispering a story in the dark, the way he'd done when we were kids. He was the one talking and I was the one listening, and that was exactly as it should be.

ALARMS

Mary DeSilva started calling the police the next week, claiming someone was getting into the library, though she didn't know who it was and had not actually seen anyone inside the building. Nothing was ever missing or out of place in the morning, nothing vandalized or even touched as far as she could tell. All she knew was that the door was opening and closing; not every night, but when it began to move, it kept moving, only stopping when she went out herself to investigate. She told the police about the alarm Frank had installed, and the police came out to test it themselves. They found it working properly, much to my father's surprise. It was really more of a sensor than an alarm, a light that blinked when the door was opened or closed. For whatever reason the sensor was registering the door opening and closing in the middle of the night and it appeared not to be a malfunction. One night, according to Mary, the back door had opened and closed twenty-five times in rapid succession. Exactly twenty-five, she told us. And the night after that it had been thirty. It made Mary think something horrible was about to happen, that there were people in there, maybe crowds of them, all lying in the darkness and invisible.

"So she can't see anyone at all?" Jennifer McKellar asked after Mike told her about it.

"What she sees is the door," he said. "Just the door."

"That is weird."

"I know," said Mike. "It is seriously, authentically weird."

"She doesn't actually see it moving," I said. "There's a sensor. Frank—that's her husband—he put it in."

"I thought she could see the door." Jennifer looked at Mike.

"It just starts off with the sensor," said Mike, "but then she goes to look and that's what she sees, the door opening and closing, moving on its own."

"And then?" asked Jennifer.

"And then nothing," said Mike, as if he was introducing an episode of *The Twilight Zone,* "nothing at all. But the door is always unlocked after."

"It can't be just moving on its own," I pointed out, talking to Jennifer but looking at Mike. "What's going on is that someone is in there, someone's doing it. The door's not moving by itself."

"Still," said Mike, "it's weird." It was like he was daring me to accuse him. "It's weird that even the cops can't find anyone."

"Have you seen *The Exorcist?*" Jennifer asked.

"I love that movie," said Mike.

"It scared me to death," Jennifer told us. "The first time I saw it, I had to shut it off. My dad had the video and I told him to get it out of the house."

"It's a shitty thing to do," I broke in. "Whoever this guy at the library is, Mary never did anything to him, and he's freaking her out." I looked at Jennifer. "Mary stays up all night and waits for it, it's really bad."

"Do you believe in ghosts?" Mike asked.

"I don't know," said Jennifer. "I think there's something out there."

"I do too," said Mike.

"I thought you were an atheist," I said. "If you're an atheist you don't believe anything is out there."

"Are you really an atheist?" said Jennifer. The thought of it seemed to make her dead eye fasten on my brother more completely.

For the next two weeks the library door kept mysteriously moving, though not every night. And the more Mary called the police the more they began to doubt her, thinking she'd become paranoid or was dreaming, or both. Finally, they had to tell her not to call anymore. A detective named Moore, the same man who would drive me to the television studio three days after the explosion so I could tell my brother to come out of hiding, arrived one afternoon to tell Mary the way it was going to be. And if she did call, he said, the police would not respond. They would not send a car, not even answer the phone. Mary replied by saying she was *completely* certain there was somebody getting into the building at night. The detective said he was sorry, but a decision had been made.

This was why that weekend, when Uncle Marco was over for Sunday dinner, my mother asked him to speak to the police about maybe putting a man outside the library at night. As a result of the car recall success and his TV ads, Marco had gained a certain renown. My mother seemed to think that this would carry some weight in the police department—and that hearing from a lawyer would make a difference.

"So you believe there really is someone in there?" he asked my mother.

"Mary thinks so," she replied. "She's going to have a nervous breakdown."

"Maybe they should disconnect that sensor," suggested Uncle Marco. "She's sitting there looking at it and waiting for it to happen. I mean, I'm sure she *thinks* she's telling the truth."

"It's strange that nobody's seen anyone," said my father. "That's what makes me wonder."

"If there is someone," said Uncle Marco, "the guy's a pro, he's good at it. But what's the point of it, what's the guy doing?"

"Why does there have to be a point?" asked Mike.

"Believe me," said my father, "there's always a point."

"For you," said Mike. "For you there's always a point."

"Maybe this guy's got a key," I said. "Probably he stole it from someone and that's how he got in."

"Who would he have stolen it from?" said my mother.

"Maybe you," I said. I could feel Mike looking at me but went on anyway. "Maybe he got it off your key chain, got it copied, and that's how he's getting in."

My mother shook her head. "I don't think so, James James," she told me.

"Jimmy's right," said Uncle Marco. "An old lock like that, even I could make a key from it."

"I wonder if it's not an electrical problem," my father said. "Some kind of malfunction with whatever alarm Frank's installed. Maybe something's tripping it at random. I know it's been inspected but I'd go to look myself. Frank would take it the wrong way, though."

My mother shook her head again. "The police should put a man there."

"They can't," said Marco. "You can't have a cop at the library around the clock just because one person thinks a door is opening."

"It's only a matter of time," said my father. "I don't know what this guy is doing, but he's going to make a mistake."

"He?" said Vivian. "Can we at *least* consider the possibility that this is a woman? I mean, this is 1989."

"Sorry," said my father, ostentatiously, "or *she.*"

"You know something," said Marco, "more than half of the students at Case this year, they're women."

"Maybe it's a ghost," whispered Mike.

"What's a ghost?" Petey wanted to know.

"You want to scare Petey," said my father, "you stay up with him."

"Don't worry," Mike told Petey. "I'll stay up with you."

"How late?" Petey asked.

"Until the witching hour," said Mike.

"The witching hour," repeated Petey.

"Putting the ghost hypothesis aside for a moment," said Marco, "the question remains whether Mary has or hasn't actually seen anything."

"One time," Vivian said, "the door opened really slowly, and Mary saw it. Stood there the whole time, and her blood went cold."

"When she went out to look," added my mother, "there was nothing."

"What she needs to see is an actual person," said Marco. "Or there's no case."

"How can there be no case?" I asked him. The whole time I'd been wondering what I would say when Mike got arrested for breaking and entering, thinking I'd need an alibi.

"What are you going to do," said Marco, "arrest a door?"

"She should wake Frank up," said my father. "He could tell her to go back to bed."

"Poor Frank," said my mother. We all knew that Mary had talked to the cardiologist who treated Frank at the Cleveland Clinic, and his advice had been that Frank should not be exposed to any kind of stress or uncertainty—that he should not be, under any circumstances, woken up in the middle of the night to see if someone was breaking into the library.

"Someone has to do *something,*" Marco told us, like he was giving a summation at a trial. "It can't go on."

My father agreed, and after dinner he went downstairs to his office and called Mary, saying the next time she saw something she should call him. He could be counted on to investigate, no matter what. No matter how often she called.

"You told her what?" was my mother's reaction.

"I'd rather go to a hundred false alarms than miss a real one."

"She'll call, you know. You think she won't, but she will."

My father said he didn't mind. There was something about the idea he liked—the way it seemed he was finishing the job for Frank again, tying up loose ends for the inept Office of Public Safety.

"What makes you think you can catch this guy?" Mike asked my father.

My father smiled, said that line from his hockey-playing days about how people had tried but had never been able to get around Fort Morrison. Mike said nothing back, but I could tell he liked the idea of being chased by our father as much as he liked the idea that he'd successfully eluded the police—and that they'd given up on catching him. Now it was my father. This was the second reel of whatever movie Mike was now imagining himself in, the moment when the case becomes so complicated that not even Sam Spade or Philip Marlowe knows what's going on.

But then, abruptly, the door stopped moving. My father kept the phone by his bed, ready for Mary's call, but there was nothing.

"It just stopped?" Jennifer McKellar asked. "Seriously?"

Mike nodded. "It moved on, I guess. Got interested in other things. Or other people."

"Or maybe it got scared," I said.

"You don't know that," said Mike. "There are a lot of things you don't know."

I pretended not to care. Looked in the direction and acted like I didn't hear what he said. But he was right, I had no idea. Mike was up to something and I didn't know what it was. Only that it had nothing to do with me.

SECRET IDENTITIES

Like my own mother, the undercover ex-nun, the Mothers at the preschool all have secret identities. Moira was a legal secretary on Wall Street, which is where she met her husband. Ellen used to waitress at the Brannigan's in Akron where Rod Stewart showed up one night with Keith Richards—he bought everyone drinks and seemed like a really nice, ordinary guy, except with a British accent. Before they defected from Romania, Ioana's husband sent copies of his college yearbook to relatives who were living in Italy and it was the first thing he had sent to him when he got to the States. Passports, diplomas, all of that can be forged, she tells us, but not pictures of him on the debating team and law society. When she was twenty, Debbie and her amazing breasts appeared in a bra and panties in a Dillard's catalogue, though she now thinks it was a bad move because once you've done that kind of work that's what you're known for. Though when she was pregnant she made some good money on the side by appearing in bra and panties ads for the pregnant. There's a real market for that, and it's different than the straight-out Victoria's Secret stuff, she tells the other Mothers, they should think about it.

Jenna was an English major in college and she had a couple of miscarriages before the twins and so did Ellen. Debbie breastfeeds not just because it's the best thing for the baby—and it *is* the best thing for the baby, according to her pediatrician—but also because she likes the way it feels. She'll latch the baby—*latch,* I have learned, is the word for it—and then feel like doing it, right there, baby or not. It's sort of wild the things they say right in front of me. I wouldn't exactly say they were flirting, that you'd necessarily walk into that hallway and feel the sexual tension, but it's *something* like that, it's *nearly* sexual tension that's in the air.

This is Jenna, this morning while we're sitting there. "Jimmy," she says, "what is it about lesbians that men find so attractive?"

I don't know what I'm supposed to say to this. The fact is that I've not thought about it too much, but then I do start thinking about it and it's difficult to stop. It's like grief therapy, when once you've got something in your head—like it's on sunny days when you have a greater likelihood of getting killed if you're a kid—it's hard to get rid of it.

"Most of the time," says Karen, so I don't have to answer, "the lesbians men get all hot for in movies, they're not really lesbians."

"Too much lipstick," says Debbie.

"Not always," says Moira. "When I was in New York, I knew a couple of lipstick lesbians in Flatbush who were always dressed to the nines."

"Lipstick lesbians," says Karen disapprovingly, shaking her head.

"That's what they call them," says Moira. "I didn't make it up."

"I don't understand it," says Jenna. "What do they do? What do they stick where? What do they stick? Seriously, Jimmy, tell us."

They look at me, waiting.

There's movement inside the classroom and I remember that I'm going to feed Leon the goldfish. That Mrs. Dumme made me shake on it. I make a move toward the door, putting myself in position, pulling Petey along so he's up there with me.

This causes Jenna to stand up. Ellen does the same. Petey's standing in front of me with his diver's mask pulled down and his stuffed hammerhead shark in his hands. Then Karen and Moira stand up as well, and the fact that we're all standing makes it seem as if something important is going to happen. Jenna seems to have made up her mind that if I want to be first inside, she does as well. There's a narrow window in the upper left-hand corner of the classroom door that Mrs. Dumme has covered from the inside with black construction paper—and I can see Jenna's face reflected in it as she smoothes down her blond hair, readying herself. One of the twins runs over to her, then the other, and they bump into the back of my legs.

I turn around and smile in a fake, fatherly way, as if the twins are incredibly cute and I can't look at them often enough, but really it's because I thought it was Jenna, not her kids, pushing herself up against me, pressing into me in a bullying way, like Glenn Close near the end of *Fatal Attraction* when she starts getting it that Michael Douglas is never going to leave his wife, no matter how psycho she acts. And then the thought flashes through my mind that maybe Mrs. Dumme has promised *all* the Mothers that they can feed the goldfish today if they get there early enough—that this is meant to test Jenna's leadership. That if I can manage to do it I'll be head of the Mothers.

"Are you Parent Helper today?" Jenna whispers, standing close behind me.

"No—I'm in a couple of weeks, I think," I whisper back, pretending I don't check the date each time I pass the calendar in the kitchen.

"I didn't think you were."

"Right," I say.

"Because I am." She's still whispering.

"You know," whispers Ellen—I can hear her voice just behind Jenna—and in spite of myself I wonder if she's pressing up into the back of Jenna, "Jimmy's acting strange today."

"People are strange," I say.

"Isn't that a Doors song?" asks Jenna.

"I think you know what I'm saying." Ellen is still whispering.

"I do think you're a little eager to get in there today," Jenna tells me. She's back to whispering herself. "I mean really, really eager."

And then, the sound of the door opening.

"Here we go," I say to Petey, as if we're about to go over the side of a boat and into the Pacific. I rush into the classroom and beeline over to the goldfish bowl. Except Petey's not there. He's gone in the other direction and is taking off his boots. It makes sense—this is what he always does, what he's supposed to do. I should have thought of it, but I haven't, and now it's just me standing there next to the bowl while Petey is on the other side of the room, looking helplessly at his boots.

Leave the boots, I want to scream, but instead I go over and help him take them off as calmly as I can. A moment later we're at the fishbowl, where Mrs. Dumme is just replacing the top of the fish food. I can see the orange flakes floating on the surface of the water. Brittany, the daughter of the badly permed Karen, is wiping her fingers on her skirt.

"I thought that I was—I mean, Petey and me—that *we* were going to feed Leon the fish today."

"I'm sorry," says Mrs. Dumme, a little too ambiguously.

"It's all right, I guess." A moment later, I say, "Isn't it, Petey?"

Petey pretends to swim to the other side of the classroom.

"A pinch and no more," says Mrs. Dumme, and goes over to the carpet where the children are already taking their seats.

After that I head to Dr. Kasoff's for my solo appointment with him. Usually when I get there, the door is open and I go straight in. There's never anyone else in the waiting room, as if he's spaced his patients out so no one runs into anyone else and starts comparing notes, or talks about whether we think he's actually bald or if he shaves his head each morning. Today is a bit different—I'm the only one there but the office door is closed, which means I have to sit there and stare at old copies of *Psychology Today* until he lets me in. It's not long after I've started flipping through those articles about struggling with end-of-life decisions and how to recognize the telltale signs of a nervous breakdown that I find myself wondering if I might actually be crazy, if I've become one of those insane people Jack Nicholson hangs out with in *One Flew Over the Cuckoo's Nest.*

That's another of the movies we had at the library—and it may be the only movie Mike and I ever watched with our father. It was, my father would tell us, his all-time favourite movie. He loved the whole thing, the way Randle McMurphy—that's the name of Jack Nicholson's character—yells at the chief, the way McMurphy moves his freaky eyebrows. My father would kill himself laughing during that scene when the guy who'll later play the scientist in *Back to the Future* starts screaming when he gets a cigarette caught in the cuff of his pants and the orderlies jump on him because they think he's freaking out. Most of all, though, my father loved that moment when McMurphy punches through the glass at the nurses' station and grabs the cigarettes off Nurse Ratched's desk for that guy who's crying because she took them from him. McMurphy gets into a lot of trouble for that—that's what gets him sent to electroshock therapy near the end of the movie—but he does it anyway. And he'd probably do it again.

That was what my father liked about it, the way it showed Randle taking a step and how once he'd taken it, there was no turning back. It seems to me that those letters my father writes—or used to write, anyway—about blood not being on his hands, the ones he would send to Frank DeSilva and to the governor of Ohio and anyone else he thinks might make a difference, are his version of McMurphy smashing his fist through that glass. And it makes me wonder why he isn't writing those letters anymore. Maybe the whole thing is bottling up inside him ready to come out soon, when we least expect it. Or maybe Mike's dying has fried my father's brain the way electroshock therapy turns McMurphy into a zombie at the end of the movie, a guy who only looks like the person he used to be.

This is what's running through my mind when Dr. Kasoff opens the door. "James," he says, "please come in."

I take my usual seat in the chair across from his desk. There's no couch in Dr. Kasoff's office, the way there always is in movies, which came as a bit of a disappointment when

I first started coming here. Once I asked Dr. Kasoff why he didn't have a couch, but instead of answering me, he asked if I would feel more comfortable lying down. I dropped it after that.

"How have you been?" he asks.

I've nothing else to say, so I tell him about McMurphy and Nurse Ratched.

"I don't think smashing the window was crazy," Dr. Kasoff replies. "I think Nurse Ratched is crazy. If I were Jack Nicholson, I'd have done the same thing."

"I doubt it."

Dr. Kasoff slowly raises his eyebrows and then, just as slowly, settles them back into place. This is, I've learned, his version of a shrug. "What would you have done? Would you have done the same thing?"

"I don't know. Probably."

"What do you mean, probably?"

"Maybe, I don't know, it means maybe. Maybe I'd do it."

He nods at this and I nod back and then we just sit there for what feels like forever. It sort of sucks, the way he stays completely still looking at me, but it's better than any alternative. And my advice to you would be to do the same if you ever find yourself having to spend time with a shrink. The thing to do is this: sit there as still as possible. If you just sit there and say nothing, he'll eventually stand up and say it's time to go, and you can leave pretty much intact.

"Fine," I reply. And then a moment later: "Do I have to keep coming back?"

"It's either me or Nurse Ratched," he says, and laughs, but when I don't laugh he stops, slowly, as if it has nothing to do with me.

I tell him: "I'm starting to think this is a waste of your time."

"I don't agree."

"You're getting paid, though."

I think this'll piss him off, but it doesn't. "I get paid," he tells me. "So you don't owe me anything. Unlike the other people in your life, I'm not talking to you for any complicated reason. It's like you get to a hotel, you give a guy five bucks to take your bags up to the room, and that's the end of the story."

"Five bucks," I say and shake my head, as if to say that with a cushy job like his he can afford to throw as much money to the wind as he likes.

"In a hotel," he goes on, "nobody's your friend for any complicated reason. You pay them, and they help you, and then when it's time to move out of the hotel, you can forget about them."

"And you think that's a good thing?"

"I think that's a good thing," he says.

Afterwards, because it feels like I've been banned by Johnny Wang from his Good Food Truck and maybe also to show him I don't really need to eat there at all, I go and sit on the bench in front of Simon's Photography. I don't know who Simon is, whether it's the guy's first name or his last, but mostly the pictures they take there is stuff for catalogues. In the days when there was a library to work at, Mike and I would sit outside on the front steps and watch the models go in and try to guess their names: Tiffany, Mike would say, Claudia, Natasha, Miriam.

Across the street from Simon's Photography, near the back of the fenced-in rubble-filled square where the library once stood, is the hole in the ground that I know to be the opening of the bomb shelter. It's been covered over with a ragged blue tarp, like a neglected waterlogged drum that some kid made at preschool and left out in the rain. But if you sit in a certain way on the bench on the other side of the street, you can tell it's a sizable hole, that something could be down there. There among the twisted pipes and disconnected wires, maybe there's something that'll tell you why the library exploded that night, the real reason why all this had to happen.

The truth is, today isn't the first time I've sat on this bench. It used to be that sitting here was all I would do, after taking Petey to preschool. I'd bring along a camera, sit here with it on my lap. When I told him about the bench, Dr. Kasoff asked me what I'd do if I did manage to take a photo that revealed something about the cause of the explosion, a hidden key piece of evidence. I'd show my father, I said. And then what? Dr. Kasoff wanted to know. Then it would be up to him, if there were letters to write, he'd know who to write them to. Dr. Kasoff seemed skeptical, and it pissed me off. This is going to happen, I told him, Mike is dead and we are going to sue *someone,* just like we sued that car company. Like my uncle Marco says, the innocent should at least get paid. But are we so innocent? This was why I had the camera with me, to get that down on film.

Other days it would be a rosary in my hands instead of a camera. I'd sit there, trying to say it, trying to get all the way through it before it was time to get Petey again. "Hail Mary," I'd whisper, or else I'd just sit there with the beads in my fingers and look out across the street and hope to be moved by the spirit. It's the kind of thing that could happen, the way it does to the Apostle Paul on the road to Damascus, back when he was named Saul and got knocked off his horse. Heaven is not a newspaper, but when it comes it comes. And I'd be ready with my rosary, waiting.

Today I don't have anything with me. Not a rosary and not a camera. Dr. Kasoff told me that grief can be like that, a dirty secret we keep to ourselves. We're ashamed when a loved one dies, as if it's our fault. When he said that I tried to think of something I was ashamed of—of a time when I'd been happy that a terrible thing had happened or hated another person. What came into my mind was the car ride to the hospital the day I broke Mike's arm. I was eight and he was nine, and even though he was older, I was bigger than him. I don't remember who hit who first. Somehow I got Mike's arm behind his back, and I was twisting it. Our father had shown us this: how to bend the elbow a certain way. It was like fighting in hockey, he said, the kind of thing you sometimes have to do. We were not to say anything to our mother about it. It was the sort of thing fathers showed their sons, like the names of the different screwdriver heads. Mike and I practised it, grabbing our father's arm and pressing it behind him into the small of his back. You had to angle the arm at the elbow, but had to be careful, because if you pushed it too far you could break the arm. That's what I was doing to Mike that day, just the way our father had shown us. But I pushed too hard and his arm broke. I knew I could break it and I did. When he heard the pop he went quiet. A second later he started screaming. It was like he had stopped being human. I remember telling God that if Mike lived I'd be a better brother. I wanted to tell Dr. Kasoff that, how it felt like my life had turned suddenly then, though I didn't know how or in what direction.

Now I get up and cross the street and I'm standing right at the fence. It's the first time I've got this close. Even here, I can't see much. It occurs to me I might climb over to the other side, but I know I'd never make it over. Still, maybe I could try, and if the fire department had to come and get me down they'd do it in a really grief-stricken way, having seen me on television that night passing out. Maybe climbing the fence would be good exercise, and if I got good at it I could do it on a daily basis, like Rocky climbing up those white steps while trumpets blare in the background. This is what's going through my mind when I see the guy coming out of the hole near the back of the library. What I see is a gloved hand first, then the rest of him coming up out of the ground. Slowly at first, and not easily. He's wide but not very tall. "Hold on," I call out to him, trying to make my voice sound tough and authoritative. "What do you think you're doing?" He's got a mask over his face, the type of thing you wear when working under ground, where the air could be toxic, and a hard hat on, with protective ear coverings. He's facing the other direction, but when I call to him he turns around to look.

That's when I know it's my father.

He pretends to not recognize me. He taps the hard shells of the things on his ears and acts like he can't hear, and walks off in the opposite direction. I see that he's cut away a small opening in the side of the fence on the other side of the lot. It's not the kind of thing that you can see from a distance, unless you're really looking, unless someone is going through it at the moment when you happen to be watching. He goes down on his stomach so he can slide through it, ferret-like. He does this with practised ease, as though he does it every day. It occurs to me that I no longer have any idea what anyone in my family does during the day, and that I've never given it a thought. Why isn't Dr. Kasoff asking us about *that*? Of course my father's found some way to work the case, and more than that, he's on to something. I don't know why he hasn't said anything to me, but that must be part of his plan. So when they start pulling back my fingernails I won't crack. I've got no idea what they'll ask me, or even who they are, but my father sees them coming for me. This is how it's going to begin.

SHADOWY FIGURE

The night of the explosion, my father and I were the first ones to arrive. This was because Mary had called our house, saying she could see someone in the library—actually *see* him.

"I'm on my way," my father told her, but it took him a minute.

Later he will admit to the police that he didn't know what she was talking about, not at first. Weeks had passed since the last sighting of the moving library door and he'd forgotten about it, more or less. Not completely, of course, but he'd given up thinking that Mary was going to call. And that's why he had no idea at first what she was trying to tell him. When the door had stopped moving, he told himself that it had stopped for good. The only one who had kept watching was Mary, and when she finally got across to him what was happening, he knew he had to do something. The next thing he did was wake my mother up and tell her what was happening. Then he came into Mike's and my room and woke me up. That is how it began for me, that night. "Jimmy," he was saying, "where's your brother?" Then the feeling of coming up, out of sleep, and the surprise of seeing my father standing there.

"Jimmy," he asked me again, "where's your brother?"

"Mike?" I said, incoherently. I sat up, saw Mike's empty bed behind him. The covers pulled back.

"Mary's on the phone, get dressed."

"Who is?"

He told me again. "Someone's in the library," he said.

"Who is it?"

"Let's go," he told me. I could hear it in his voice that he was afraid, didn't know what to expect. This was a person, not an alarm malfunction.

Once he was sure I was awake he went downstairs, and the phone rang again. My mother got it. I remember the sound of her voice, clear and calm, and knew she was talking to Mary, telling her my father was on his way. This was how my mother used to sound always, clear and calm, no matter what the crisis. She was still on the phone when I came into the kitchen. "It's Mary," she whispered, putting her hand over the receiver.

"Does she know who it is yet?" *Yet,* I thought, catching myself too late. I might as well tell her it's Mike.

My mother shook her head. "It's all right, I was talking to Jimmy. Fort got him up."

Then the sound of crying from upstairs. Petey had woken up. Rather than hanging up, my mother handed me the receiver.

"James James," said Mary, when she heard my voice, as if she were my mother.

"You can't see him?"

"I'm looking at him right now," she said. "I can see him right now and I'm scared to death."

"Are you sure someone's there?"

"Don't I sound sure?"

"You've sounded sure before."

"I'm looking at him right now."

"What's Frank say?"

"You know I can't ask Frank."

"What's he doing now?"

"I'm not sure it's a man," said Mary. "I can't see him all that clearly, but he's doing something, it's like he's looking out the window and waiting for someone."

"Do you recognize him?"

"I can't say, it's a shadowy figure."

"*A shadowy figure,*" I repeated, and as I did, I began to worry. I'd been so convinced that it was Mike that I'd never considered any other possibility, but Mary's melodramatic phrase made me wonder if it might actually be someone else, if Mike hadn't been lying to me, if he'd really been as mystified about that moving door as Mary was. But before I could think about it, my father came upstairs with an old sweater of his and said he was ready to go. "Here he is," I told Mary. "We're on our way."

"Tell her to stay where she is," he instructed me.

I told her. It was the last thing I said before I hung up. The last thing I ever said to Mary.

I followed my father outside and into the car, watched as he opened the door and carefully wedged the sweatshirt between the seats. Mike's car—his Gremlin—was there in the driveway, and it seemed to me that this was part of his plan, a tactic to throw my father off, which had been foiled by my father's coming into our bedroom to wake him up. I smiled when I saw it there. Mike was finally going to get in the serious shit he deserved. What he had planned to do, I supposed, was to get my father to come to the library and say that he'd been in bed the whole time—his car, after all, had been in the driveway. What he'd not expected was that my father would refuse to go to the library alone. The thought of what would happen next filled me with foreboding, as though I was watching a horror film where a complete stranger is about to be stabbed. I didn't *want* it to happen, not really, but I couldn't look away either. There was some part of me that wanted to see it, that was looking forward to it. I wondered if my father had already made up his mind to hand Mike over to the cops. Or maybe that was what Mike wanted, what he was daring my father to do. He knew Mary would call our father and so he had let her see him, for once, stood there in plain view. He wanted to be caught and wanted our mother to find out what he'd been doing, wanted to see the look on her face as she struggled to forgive him. I wondered what my father was thinking, if he'd already put it together, and I looked over at him as he backed the car out of the driveway then sped down Yorkshire Road toward Lee Road. He had a coat on, and I remember thinking it strange that he had a sweatshirt with him as well, as if he was going to pull the sweatshirt over his jacket.

"So she can really see him?" I asked.

My father nodded, but didn't speak. As skeptical as he had been before, he didn't hesitate now, driving through the stop sign at Lee then turning sharply. I rocked to one side with the motion, and the balled-up sweater did as well, rolling onto the floor of the car. And out of the sweater fell a gun. It was in a holster, almost touching my leg.

He told me: "I had to get it out of the house somehow without your mother seeing."

I knew my father had a gun, though I'd never seen it. He'd got it during the trial with the car company when someone—we didn't know who—began calling the house.

One of the things I remember most clearly about the trial is those calls—the constant ringing of the phone. Whoever it was would call ten, twelve times a day. If my father forgot to unplug it, the phone would ring in the early morning and wake us up. My mother would insist my father get it or she'd do it herself, even after he'd told her to just let it ring. She'd think it was an emergency or someone calling with really bad news, that there was something urgent happening somewhere we needed to know about. Sometimes, she told us, you could hear him breathing, but other times there was nothing at all. Which made me think of a man with his hand over the receiver, listening to her breathe but not wanting her to hear him breathe. My mother warned us against answering the phone ourselves, but we did it anyway, and then we'd utter threats of our own, like, "I know your name," or, "Come on, make my day." At least Mike did. When I got the phone I worried that whoever was calling—somebody not just in a fedora but in a hockey mask as well, a cross between Freddy Krueger and Don Corleone—was calling from our basement. This made no sense because we had only one phone line, but it still seemed possible because, in horror movies, the caller is always calling from inside the house, the basement or the attic. Usually the killer can see you while he talks to you on the phone.

"Think about it from their point of view," my father told my mother. "They just want to keep their jobs. It's a good sign, it means they're worried."

My mother didn't buy it. "A good sign?"

"Would they call if they weren't worried?"

"Still, Fort," said my uncle, "you should have a gun, just in case."

"I don't *want* a gun" was his reply. "In the country I'm from"—this was one of my father's favourite things to do, to refer to Canada as if it were a distant other world in the far reaches of the galaxy—"we don't have guns."

"I agree with you," said Marco. "But I don't know who's on the other end of the line—and neither do you."

That's what convinced him: the knowledge that he couldn't control—couldn't even *know*—all of the variables involved. Just like he couldn't know or control them tonight.

"I don't know who's in that library," he told me, and I could hear the fear in his voice.

I came out and told him. "It's Mike," I said.

"What?" said my father, still driving. "What did you say?"

"It's been Mike the whole time," I shouted. "He's the one moving the door—it's a prank."

And a split second later, the explosion.

There was a flash, and it blinded us. My father swerved the car and collided with a street lamp. I rocked forward, banging my head against the windshield, and then my father was screaming. A sharp disc of pain was forming in the front of my face.

"Are you there?" he asked me. "Jimmy, can you hear me?"

Slowly my eyes recovered and I was able to see, and then the books began to rain down on the hood of our car. I looked over at my father and saw him holding his eyes, still blinded.

"Okay," he was saying. "Okay, okay, okay, okay."

I got out of the car. I needed to get there before him, to get there first and talk to Mike. Give him the whole story, how Mary had called. What I expected was that I'd walk through the flames and there would be Mike, emerging from the ashes, a little dirty but no worse for wear. As quickly as it had happened, it seems to me now to be unfolding in slow motion, like a replay in a basketball game.

I began to run, and then out of the smoke I saw a figure moving toward me. It's a miracle, I thought, pure luck. He'd been down in the bomb shelter and had made it out alive. But instead of Mike, it was Frank DeSilva. He was dressed in his pyjamas. They were ridiculous; a long, striped nightshirt, a matching striped cap. I thought of Scrooge on the last of his visits, seeing his dead self at the graveside, the world he knew a rumour no one believed in anymore.

"Mary?" he said, stepping toward me.

Then something—a massive dictionary or maybe a complete guide to the wildflowers of Ohio, or that book by Proust about remembering—smashed onto the top of my head.

BIRTHDAY PARTY

Tonight we finish dinner and my mother and I get in the car and go to grief therapy. My father should be with us, but he isn't. I don't know where he is. I go downstairs to his office to tell him it's time to leave, but there's no sign of him. This is what he used to be like when he was working on a case, gone at strange hours to follow up on a hunch, working through the night. It makes me think that he's on to something, that he's that close. So it's just my mother and me who go. I'm the one who drives, and the whole time my mother sits there, not talking. She's thinking of something, though. I don't know what, not until we get there.

Dr. Kasoff tells us the topic tonight is anger, which he says is a necessary stage of grief. There are five stages, he says, but it's wrong to think of it as a pyramid that you're climbing, where at the end of it you get to the place where you're entirely over the loss of your loved one. Sometimes, in the middle of feeling angry (anger being the second stage of grieving) you'll suddenly slip back into denial (the first stage) and wonder if any of it happened, if perhaps none of it ever happened and the kid who died is still alive. And everyone moves at different rates through the grieving process. One man he treated moved quickly through all five stages and landed on acceptance with such rapidity that it made his wife think that maybe he was still back in denial.

The way Dr. Kasoff talks about *landing* on acceptance makes it seem like a gymnastics manoeuvre, that your kid dying isn't all a bad thing. It's an obstacle, for sure, but just like you're a gymnast vaulting at the Olympics, you take a run at it and hit it with such force that it spins you up and into the air. If you're any good, you land on your feet. Just like Dr. Kasoff's patient.

The woman with the defective baby inside of her starts us off by saying that her husband is not even in denial. He isn't even ready to admit she's pregnant. Denial, she says, would be a step in the right direction. He's not even in the air, which means she can't even start to *imagine* what a landing would be like for him. The man whose son died in a jet-ski accident says that he had landed on acceptance, but it was one of those landings you can't stick and so it doesn't matter how beautiful you were when you were in the air. One of those landings where the guy shatters his ankle and can't do gymnastics again. The woman whose four-year-old died of an unnamed viral infection says that she'd taken a run at acceptance but hit the horse—if that's what the thing you jump over is called—and forgot to put up her hands which meant she ran straight into it. She says she imagined the judges standing up and giving her zero right across the board.

Dr. Kasoff tells her there are no judges involved and it's a mistake to take his metaphor too literally. There are plenty of judges, says my mother, don't let them tell you otherwise. She's been sitting there the whole time in silence and when she speaks, her voice is too loud and too brittle and it catches everyone off guard.

There's a moment of silence and then my mother says she's throwing a birthday party for my dead brother Mike.

"A birthday party," repeats Dr. Kasoff. His voice is completely level.

"That's right," she says. "And I hope you'll all come."

She's brought with her a piece of paper on which she wants everyone to write their full names and addresses, and the name of their spouse or significant other. Maybe a parent. Anyone who likes to dance and eat cake.

She hands it to me to pass around, and I do—as if it's something that we've talked about, like I'm not as surprised as everyone else. This is not going to bring him back, I tell her silently, by looking back into her eyes as she hands me the paper. Mike is gone, and this is a fact, he was three pounds, almost, when he was born and he did not die then but now he is dead and this birthday party is not going to bring him back. He will not show up to blow the candles out, no matter what you think. But all I manage to say aloud is: "Do you have a pen?" It's Dr. Kasoff who hands me one and when he does I start to do my silent pleading telekinetic thing with him, asking him to please, as her shrink, do something to make her change her mind about this.

Dr. Kasoff looks back like he's really interested in my reaction, the way he always does. This looking back at you as if to ask what you really think, I'm realizing, is the main thing psychologists do.

"A birthday party?" says Vivian, when we get home.

"The idea is to celebrate Mike's life," my mother tells her. She says it like she isn't completely sure. "And what better way is there to do that than a birthday party? When a person dies, it's like he was never born. But he was, I can tell you that."

I'm going to ask her what she means, but she turns to me then with such a blank look on her face that it makes me think she's suddenly forgotten about it, like the time she said she wanted to put together a radio show and play just songs from Mike's old tapes. That was a great idea. I waited for her to bring it up again, but she never did. That's what I think is going to happen, until she does it again at the preschool, when she comes with me and Petey the next morning.

"We're having a birthday party," she tells all the Mothers. "And I hope you all can come."

There's a certain amount of sneakiness to this, the way she doesn't quite come out and say it's for Mike. She lets the Mothers think whatever they want.

"You should have seen her," I tell Vivian that night, "she didn't even blink."

"Maybe she can see Mike," says Vivian. "Maybe he's here walking around, maybe he's the one calling the shots, telling her to do it."

Vivian is in the process of making Garlic Chicken Surprise for dinner. A dish which, according to my father's microwave cookbook, should take exactly sixteen minutes to prepare, seven of which are to be spent sloshing the chicken around in a large casserole dish and nine of which are to be spent standing impatiently beside the microwave waiting for it to be cooked. Before I can ask her if she's serious about thinking Mom can speak to Mike, she reads to me from the introduction to the cookbook: "'Microwave cooking is not new. Discovered by accident in 1945, when a Raytheon scientist placed a chocolate bar beside a radar vacuum tube he was testing, the microwave was successfully put to use in 1947.'" Then the bell rings and she takes out the chicken. It has turned a pale blue, like a robin's egg.

"What's that smell?" says Petey, coming into the kitchen.

"Garlic Chicken Surprise," says Vivian.

"Is it *supposed* to be blue?" I ask her.

"The microwave doesn't brown the meat," says Vivian. "How many times do we have to go over that?" She puts the dish in the middle of the table.

"Can I have peanut butter and jelly?" says Petey.

"You can use the oven," says my mother. She has a chicken leg on her plate that looks like fossilized remains, the kind of thing you would see on the other side of the glass at the Natural History Museum, a stuffed replica of how chicken legs used to be in prehistoric times.

"You mean the *conventional* oven?" says Vivian. "I don't think so." She cuts a piece of chicken and chews it slowly. "In the future," she tells us, "all food will taste like this."

"Conventional is just the *name* of the kind of heat it supplies," I tell her. "It's not any kind of comment on the kind of person who uses them. Plenty of unconventional people have cooked with conventional ovens."

"Sylvia Plath," observes Vivian, "killed herself by sticking her head into a conventional oven. I learned that in English."

"Jimmy," says my mother. "You're in charge of buying the cake. Vivian is in charge of entertainment and you get to do the cake."

"And what about me?" Petey asks.

"You can help me with the invitations," she says. "You can lick the envelopes."

"What's Dad doing?" asks Vivian.

"I need names from the both of you," my mother goes on, as if she can't hear Vivian. "If there's anyone you want invited to Mike's party, I need the names and the addresses written down and given to me."

"Can I give you a list of people *not* to invite?" says Vivian. "I mean, if anyone from school shows up, I'll stick my *own* head in a conventional oven."

The next afternoon, after I take Petey to preschool, I drop by Dr. Kasoff's office unannounced to tell him what Vivian said about the birthday party, about the possibility of my mother being guided by voices. "But it seems to me that if she really is crazy," I tell him, "she wouldn't be so organized about it. She's got lists of people she's going to invite and we've all got jobs."

"And how does that make you feel?" says Dr. Kasoff.

Which is exactly when I give up on having anything like a normal conversation with him.

SLAB

On Sunday the doorbell rings and Uncle Marco is standing on the veranda, looking exactly the way he looks in his TV ads, same suit and everything. I open the screen door, and right away we're shaking hands. When Mike and I were kids, Marco made a big deal of telling us we needed a firm grip when shaking someone's hand, saying that in his line of work this was crucial. When you shook a client's hand, you watched him make up his mind whether he wanted you to be his lawyer or not. The key, he told us, is the speed with which you approach the other hand. If you came in quickly enough you could get the advantage and do a really impressive handshake, no matter how strong the other guy happens to be. Today, I give it my best shot: when he extends his hand, I grab it as if my life depended on it and squeeze like hell.

"Excellent," he says.

I wish it didn't make me happy.

"It's good to see you," he tells me. "Have you lost weight?"

I've actually put on weight, I tell him.

"You look good, though. Have you been lifting?"

I start to say something about all the walking I've been doing with Petey, but then I realize he doesn't mean it; he's just trying to get on my good side. The fact that he's here in his TV suit is a clear sign to be careful—it means that he's not just here for dinner. Maybe he's just come from a court-room somewhere, doing some legal stuff. Maybe that stuff involves my father. I don't know if they're working together still, if what I saw my father doing that day at the explosion site—the investigation I'm not allowed to know about—is something Marco is in on and that's why he's here, or if it's the sort of thing I'm supposed to keep my uncle from knowing no matter what the cost. Since that day at the fence last week I've been watching my father more closely. As far as I can tell, he spends his days and nights locked in his basement office, not talking to anyone, not to us and not to my mother, poring over the photos he took of the wreckage. Though the fact is I don't really know if he's down there the whole time at all. Standing there this morning, Marco's face gives nothing away. It never does. He's smoking a cigarette and hasn't quite finished it, and a cloud of nearly invisible smoke comes wafting in my direction as he tells me he's here for Sunday lunch. My mother called him and said she wanted him to come by, saying there was something she wanted to talk to him about.

"She called you?"

He gives me a look. "What's wrong? You can talk to me about anything, I want you to know that. I know it hasn't been easy around here."

I tell him okay. Whatever. "Are you coming in, or what?"

He nods, but doesn't move, and goes on finishing his smoke, looking out at Yorkshire Road behind him. It's a typical tree-lined Cleveland Heights street, not that different from the street he grew up on, which is just a couple of blocks away, on Meadowbrook Avenue right here in the Heights. I wonder if his being here makes him nostalgic.

Marco is five years younger than my mother, and both of them graduated from Heights High. Our mother used to walk us all past the house my grandmother lived in until she died. I don't remember her at all, or the funeral, but Mike said he did. I was three and Mike was four and it was the first time Mike had seen a dead person. There was an eerie half-smile on our grandmother's face, he said, and she was wearing a new dress. In front of him was a little girl, the kid of some distant cousin from Boston who we never saw again. She leaned over and kissed our grandmother on the cheek, so when his turn came Mike did the same. He kept his eyes closed the whole time, he told me, and her face was as cool and smooth as a pencil eraser. I wonder if any of this crosses my uncle's mind, and decide it doesn't. His black, slightly greying hair is clipped short and slicked back, and his eyebrows look like they've been plucked. When you see him on TV, you don't know he's from around here: it's as if he sat down in front of the mirror and scoured himself of any and all traces of Cleveland Heights, a stranger who would have to ask for directions to where we live. That was something my brother liked about him, wanted to do himself one day.

Finally Marco flicks his cigarette into the bushes and follows me into the kitchen, where Vivian's standing by the microwave. My mother is on the far side of the room, sitting at the desk in the corner, writing out the invitations for Mike's birthday party. Petey's in the family room watching one of his undersea videos, so completely immersed that he doesn't even glance at Marco when he pokes his head in and tells him hello. When she sees Marco, my mother stands up and kisses him, and is not quite finished kissing him when she starts talking about the birthday party. That's the reason she's asked him over, I can tell, like she's giving him her side of the story right away, so that when the invitations go out and people start thinking she's lost her mind, he can argue her side of things.

"A birthday party?" says my uncle, cautiously. "You mean a memorial service?"

"A birthday party," she says, adding that he should feel perfectly welcome to bring a date, maybe a colleague from his firm.

Marco looks first at me, then at Vivian, and decides not to say anything. Instead, he enthuses about how great the dinner smells.

"Pork chops," says Vivian, just as the bell on the microwave rings. Vivian opens the door and takes a large glass bowl out, setting it down on the counter atop a bricklike pot holder. Instead of ordinary oven mitts, she's wearing thick protective gloves she borrowed from my father. Black and heavy, they're the kind of gloves he'd wear at disaster sites when there's a chance of touching something toxic or slightly radioactive. Vivian doesn't take them off as she reaches into the glass bowl and turns over each pork chop with clinical precision.

"Look at you cooking," says Marco.

"If you can call it that," replies Vivian. Her lack of enthusiasm is complete.

In the next room the voice of Jacques Cousteau is saying that, if handled correctly, moray eels behave like tame dogs.

Vivian puts the bowl back in the microwave and tells us it'll be two minutes and thirty-five seconds until dinner is ready.

"To this party of yours," he asks, "do people bring presents?"

"They can if they want."

"Is that on the invitation?" He speaks quickly, a trained cross-examiner.

"The invitations haven't gone out yet."

He nods. "When do you plan on doing this?"

"When someone dies," my mother tells him, her voice rising, "they still have a birthday."

There's a long moment when the two of them don't say anything to each other. It makes me wonder what they were like when they were kids. If Marco has had to see a shrink like Dr. Kasoff to learn how not to do whatever his sister tells him to do.

"Maybe the presents could go to charity," says Marco.

"We're not going to make them mandatory," my mother replies. It's like she's figuring it out herself and is mad at Marco for making her do it. I wonder how this scene played out in her head when she asked him to come over today. "The important thing is that people are there."

"And candles?" Marco asks.

"Of course candles," she says.

"Who blows them out?" Marco asks her. "You've got the candles on the cake and you light them, but who blows them out?"

"Jimmy is getting the cake," she says, ignoring him. "And we'll also have a band, so people can dance."

"I haven't ordered the cake yet," I say. "This just came up."

"When you do," my mother tells me, "be sure to get a slab."

"A slab?"

"Of cake. What you want to say at the bakery is that you want a slab. Say that and they'll know what you're talking about."

"I'd call it a unit of measurement," Marco tells me. "Slabs," he says, "are what they measure cake in. A unit of cake, if you will. Half a slab is a smaller cake, two or three slabs is a huge one."

"Get that one," says Petey, coming into the room. He sits down at the table, next to my mother.

"There he is," says Marco. "Give your uncle a kiss."

Petey does as he's told, though he lets himself be kissed by Marco instead of the other way around, then moves away from him immediately. It confirms my impression there's something sinister about his being here, as if my little brother is a kind of dog, the kind that can tell the good guys from the bad without having to wonder about it.

"Are you sure it's the best thing, this birthday party?" says Marco. "I mean, from a purely mental health perspective?"

"Dr. Kasoff knows about it, if that's what you're asking," says my mother.

"And he thinks it's all right?"

"He didn't object."

"But did he recommend it?"

"He said it might be exactly what we need," says my mother.

"When did he say that?" I ask her.

"He thinks it's a fine idea," my mother insists. "He said so at one of my own sessions with him." She looks at me and shakes her head.

I want to ask her if she's lying or not. There was once a time when I didn't believe that my mother was capable of lying, when it was one of the things I couldn't imagine her doing. But I'm not sure anymore.

"What does Fort say?" Marco wants to know.

"I have no idea," says my mother. "He works so much. I hardly ever see him."

My uncle is interested, though he pretends not to be. "Is he working on a new case?"

"It's the library," she says. "I heard him say so to Dr. Kasoff. I know that much at least."

"How's it going—has he reached any conclusions?"

My mother shrugs, and sits back down at the desk. "How should I know? I go down there sometimes, and he doesn't even know I'm standing there."

"Sometimes he goes there, you know," says Vivian. "I mean, to the library." The microwave bell rings. Vivian puts on her protective gloves, takes the pork chops out.

"Are you sure they're done?" says Marco, getting up from the table and going over to the counter. "Maybe you should leave them in for a couple of minutes longer."

"A *couple* of minutes?" Vivian shakes her head. "Do you have any idea what a couple of minutes would do to them?"

"You don't know he goes to the library," I say to my sister. "You haven't seen him there."

"Have you?" says Marco.

"Vivian is just guessing," I tell him.

"I understand you can't say anything," Marco says. "That your father has told you not to talk to me, and I want you to know that I respect it."

I don't know anything at all, I tell him, and it's the truth; just as my father would have it, it's actually not possible for me to give anything away.

"So *you* haven't seen him there either?"

"Not that I can remember."

"Not that you can remember?"

It is the wrong thing to say; I know this, though too late. My uncle moves slightly in his chair. "Don't know or can't remember—which is it?"

But right then, as if this is one of those lame Shakespeare plays they make you read in English class where the villain comes in exactly on cue like he's been offstage the whole time listening, the front door opens and my father comes into the kitchen. He's wearing work clothes and is covered in a kind of fine white dust, which I know is the kind of dust that is everywhere at the library ruins. I don't know if Marco has spent enough time there to know what the white dust means. He walks into the kitchen and there's a bolt of hope that passes through me as I think this is the moment I've been waiting for, the turning point. The moment when he cracks the case open and we bring the corporate slime who killed my brother to justice. He's surprised to see Marco, and he stands there for a moment, then sits down at the table, next to me, still in his work clothes. It's about to happen, I'm thinking, now, this is how it starts.

SCARED

Marco is the first to speak. "I'm here for Sunday dinner, so you can relax."

"I'm relaxed," my father says. "You're always welcome."

"I called him," says my mother.

"This a visit," says Marco. A moment later, "I see you've been keeping busy."

"There's something I'm working on," my father replies.

"Can't we just eat like a family?" says my mother. "Vivian worked hard on this dinner."

"Actually I didn't," said Vivian. "That's the beauty of it. You follow the recipe, put it in the microwave and you don't have to do a single thing." With this she pulls on the protective gloves and starts to place pork chops on each of our plates. Instead of brown, the chops are an unearthly grey—exactly the colour pork is *supposed* to be when it's cooked properly in a microwave oven, she tells us, the precise shade of grey that means it's been cooked thoroughly. To break the silence, Vivian says she's been reading the microwave cookbook, and that the authors are sure that it won't be long until there's no need for conventional ovens and the conventions that go along with them—including the idea that all meat, after it's been cooked, has to look just one single way. Kitchens of the future will have one large microwave oven in them and no one will think anything of serving a pork chop that is a silvery-grey colour and has a slightly metallic odour.

Marco bows his head, waiting for my mother to say grace. When she doesn't, he looks up at my father, who's already cutting his meat.

Petey is prodding his pork chop with his fork, like it's a marooned walrus.

"You can eat it," Vivian tells him. "It's not going to hurt you."

"It looks like it's *been* hurt," says Petey.

"One thing I've learned," Marco says, "is don't feel sorry for your dinner." This is a kind of joke, and even if no one laughs, it seems to make my uncle feel more himself, reminds him that he's got his own reasons for being here. "Have you lost weight?" he asks my father. It's the line he used on me, but maybe he's forgotten. It makes me think he's nervous, repeating himself, forgetting who's in the audience.

"Maybe a little," says my father tonelessly.

"He never eats," says my mother. "Maybe he eats on his own, but not with us."

"You seem well," says my uncle. He's talking to my father.

"That's what's important," says my father. "All you need is your health."

Petey sings "All You Need Is Love," a song he learned from Mike. These are the sorts of horrible things that happen every day. The words hang there in the air.

"The time off has agreed with you, in other words," says my uncle after a moment.

"I suppose you could say that."

"How long has it been?"

"I'm not counting, are you?"

I laugh. "You always count. You count everything." I look up at my father, wanting him to get it over with, to say what he's got to say.

"What I'm wondering, Fort," says my uncle, as if I've not spoken, "is when are you coming back?" He looks at Vivian and my mother, then me. "Do you think you're ready? You've been through a lot—we all have—but is it time to come back to work?"

My father is moving the pork around on his plate. "Let's talk about this later."

"Yes," says my mother. "Let's eat."

All the pork chops sit there, untouched.

"I know people go at their own pace, Fort, I can respect that." Marco has put down his knife and fork and is looking directly at my father. I imagine the two of them have had this conversation before, in private, and it got Marco nowhere. He must think my mother will be on his side, or that in front of me and Vivian my father won't be able to say he's not going back. "The thing is, we need to move forward. It would be good for you, if you tried, just see how it feels. On a trial basis. Get back to work for a couple of weeks."

"I just don't have the time right now."

"I see," Marco says.

"I'm glad you understand," says my father.

"What's so pressing?" asks Marco, still smiling. He still hasn't looked away from my father.

In the next room Petey's video ends and there's the sound of the VCR shutting off. The news comes on automatically, and it's loud. My father gets up out of his chair and goes to shut off the television.

"I hear you're having a birthday party," says my uncle, when my father sits back down.

Watching my father not react, I realize my mother hasn't said anything to him about what she's planning. As far as my father knows, Marco's talking about a party for one of his living kids.

I almost can't watch this. "It's for Mike," I tell him, and my voice is louder than I think it's going to be. "The birthday party, I mean. It's Mike's party."

My father looks at my mother. "I don't think so."

"It's been approved by your shrink, apparently," Marco tells him.

"What is he talking about?"

"I hardly ever see you," says my mother, looking off into the backyard. "I planned to tell you when we ran into each other—if we did."

"This isn't the place for this discussion," says my father.

"See," she says to Marco. "I get the same treatment you do."

My father puts his left hand to his eyes, rubs them violently, and looks at my uncle. "I'm not going to be ambushed."

"I'm here for Sunday dinner," my uncle assures him.

"You expect me to just sit here?" my father asks him suddenly. "You must think I'm an idiot—the both of you."

"Let's go, Petey," says Vivian, pulling his chair out from the table and actually picking him up, carrying him so she can get him out of the room as quickly as possible. It's like there's a bomb about to go off, and she's running for cover, ready at any moment to throw Petey to the ground and cover him herself while the shrapnel flies past. I watch them leave the room and wonder if I should go with them. I start to push my chair back, get ready to leave, and then I sit back down. I know I have to stay, that I'm going to stay no matter what. I'm not going to leave my father here.

"Can we pick a date when you'll be coming back?" asks Marco, leaning forward like he's getting down to business. "I think that in times like these, work can be a refuge."

Before my father can reply to this, my mother hands him one of the invitations for Mike's party. "Here," she tells him, "this is what they look like."

My father holds the bright piece of paper in his hand, opens it wordlessly, closes it a second later. He stares up at Marco. "I can't come back, not right now," he says, almost in a whisper, setting the invitation down on the table in front of him. "This is something I have to do. If I don't take this to where I need to, I'll never be able to look in the mirror."

"What is it that you're working on? Is it the library?" Marco is sitting up very straight now, ready to pounce. "You've got something, I can see that. I want to get in front of a judge as soon as I can, while we still can."

My father takes a breath, and it's like we're on the edge of a giant, shattering revelation. And then we'll all live happily ever after, at least the rest of us will. It's not about the money, it's about something happening that will allow my father to act like a normal human being again. But instead of dropping the bombshell, my father shakes his head.

"I don't think there's going to *be* anything."

But my uncle thinks he's lying. "Don't cut me out of this."

"Cut you out?" says my father.

"Is it that you're scared?" Marco is speaking in his lawyer voice now, looking at my father the way he looks at the camera in his TV ads where he tells the maimed and unjustly treated to pick up the phone and give him a call. My father, I see, is one of them now, one of the innocent whom circumstances have conspired against and who now deserve to be paid well for their suffering. Marco is trying to sell my father on that idea. Any moment now my uncle will extend his hand and give my father a really extraordinarily firm handshake.

But then my father stays silent and Marco loses his patience. He stands up, says that he's going to have to think seriously about their partnership. "I know what it's like to lose your nerve, but I can't be in business with someone like that. You have to stay focused. Make from this miserable situation what you can."

"*Make* something from it?" my father says.

"This explosion, Mike, all of it," Marco tells him, not thinking what he's saying. Caught up in the moment, caught up in making the sale, Marco's forgotten about Mike. Forgotten that any of this has anything to do with us. "We need to do what we can—we owe it to Mike."

I watch as my father makes up his mind to hit him. I see his face change, and then the punch itself happens quickly, as if it has been choreographed in advance by the two of them. Marco is standing next to the table and a moment later my father is standing up, taking a quick step in Marco's direction, catching him in the jaw with a jab. Marco reels backward, surprised as much as anything else, and falls against the side of the table, cutting his lip open. My father goes to hit him again, but I grab his arm. "Don't," I hear myself saying, and all of a sudden I'm dizzy. Before I pass out I know my father has given up on hitting Marco and he's catching me instead.

When I open my eyes, I'm lying on the floor and my

mother is yelling at my father about the birthday party and my uncle is nowhere to be seen.

"I'll do it myself," she's telling him. "I don't care if you're there or not."

"Filomena," my father is saying. "We need to talk about this."

"Go ahead, then," she says.

"All right," I say, interrupting them, "I think I can stand up now."

My father helps me to my feet. "Do you want a glass of water?"

I say I just need to sit down. My mother isn't looking at me at all, not concerned in the least. She's standing near the sink with her arms crossed.

"This party is happening, whether you want it to or not," she tells my father. "No matter how many times you assault my brother."

"I didn't assault him," my father replies, though he's clearly shaken.

"I thought we were going to have to call the police," she says.

My father looks like he needs to go and lie down. "This party is something we have to talk about," he tells her again.

My mother laughs and keeps laughing even when she should stop. "I know you think I'm crazy, but I'm not." And all at once she stops laughing. It's like a faucet being turned off. "I'm not a lunatic, though I suppose that might be easier. 'There she goes, the crazy lady who lives with us.' But I'm sorry to say I have all my faculties." To demonstrate, she steps away from the counter into the middle of the room and does a tiny pirouette. When she's done she takes a bow, and then sits back down at the kitchen table, tucking a single strand of her brown hair behind her ear, as if she's exerted herself more than she'd planned. My father sits down as well, on the other side of the table. His hand is getting swollen now, the knuckles reddened and painful. In the other room Vivian has restarted Petey's shark video and I can hear the voice of Jacques Cousteau telling viewers to prepare themselves, that he's about to take them into the deepest reaches of the ocean.

FALLOUT

I don't know—I *still* don't know—how long I was unconscious after Frank stepped out through the smoke toward me, thinking I was Mary. It must have been six or six thirty in the morning and the sun was coming up. By that time the area around the library had been cordoned off and there were police and firefighters everywhere. I could taste blood, and when I looked at myself in the rear-view mirror I saw my lip was bleeding and there was a cut over my eyebrow. My father must have found me, carried me here to the back seat, then run back and tried to find Mike.

After a moment I got out of the car and started looking for my father. Only in the morning light was it possible to see the devastation, the paper everywhere, the books that had been torn up and cast into the wind, the startling look of the collapsed library. It had been decimated, the walls fallen in, the wires exposed, distant alarms still going off everywhere. It looked like something out of *The Road Warrior*, like Mel Gibson was about to drive up and start siphoning off gas from our tank. Somehow, the phone booth across the street from the library, the one just in front of Simon's Photography, was still intact.

I don't know why I called my mother.

"It's James James," I told her, as if she might not recognize my voice.

"Thank God," she said.

I remember looking at the pay phone, thinking the metal cradle where the receiver had been sitting shone with an odd brilliance and wondering if that meant I had a concussion. "I hit my head," I said. "But I'm all right."

"Who hit you?"

"I don't know," I tried telling her. "It wasn't like that."

"Where's your father? Let me speak to him."

"He's busy," I said. I still had no idea where he was.

"What happened?"

"What happened?" I repeated. The question made no sense. I began to ask her about Mike, but stopped. I'd have to tell her everything, and she'd never forgive me.

I said, "Let me talk to Vivian."

"She's asleep—do you know what time it is?"

I didn't know what else to say.

"James James," she said, "what happened? Is your father hurt?"

I tried telling her to not worry but the words caught in my throat. I began to cry, as quietly as I could, clutching the receiver. Farther down Lee Road, near where the front door of the library had been, I could see my father. He was with a pair of firemen, the three of them standing atop a mound of rubble, an urgent look on his face. He was getting desperate, gesturing toward the rubble, giving instructions.

"He's hurt his head," said my mother, though not to me. "It's James James, and he's fine," she went on, talking to someone else. "Michael," she said, "come and speak to him yourself."

"What did you say?" I asked her. "Who are you talking to?"

"Michael just came in."

"Put him on," I told her, "I need to talk to him."

She called to him.

"Give him the phone!" I shouted.

"Just a second." She put down the receiver. There was the sound of her chair moving, of her walking away and calling to him softly. A minute later she was back on the line. "He was just here," she said. "Let me speak to your father."

"I'll get him," I told her, and I knew this was what I had to do—find my father and tell him that Mike was alive and at home. I hung up the phone and ran down the street, toward where he was standing in the centre of the wreckage. On the way I passed Frank DeSilva, who was trying to move a block of concrete with his bare hands. The sight of Frank made me think of Mary, but I couldn't help him, I had to get at my father. Looking at Frank, a whole story flew together in my mind: I'd maybe bring up Jennifer McKellar even, tell him that's why I'd said it in the first place about him being in the library. I'd take it all back because it wasn't too late.

"Jimmy!" Frank called.

"I have to get my father," I said, falling down and then standing up again.

Finally, I reached my father, who was speaking to the fire chief, starting to get frantic, telling him that they would have to move quickly, that cranes had to be brought in immediately. There were people trapped, he was saying, people he knew who were down there.

"This is bad," he said, when he saw me.

And I just told him. Came right out with it: Mike was at home.

It was like I had kicked my father in the stomach. He bent at the waist and put his hands on his knees, trying to catch his breath.

"What's that?" the fire chief wanted to know. "What's the problem?"

"Give me a second" was all my father could say.

The chief looked at him carefully. "Talk to your son," he said, "and then get back to me. I'm going to want you in on this."

"Where was he?" he asked when the other man was gone.

I began to cry, felt myself starting to shake.

My father took a step back, and leaned over again, hands on his knees. Just then Frank climbed over to us, moving awkwardly over the uneven rubble, and told us he needed us to help him. There was concrete he had to move.

"We'll never do it," my father told Frank. "Only a crane can move this stuff. I'm getting them here as fast as I can."

"You think we have that kind of time?" said Frank. "We don't and you know it. We've got to start now."

"You're not thinking straight," my father told him. "You're in shock."

"What the hell is that supposed to mean?"

"You have to go home, Frank," he said. "You have to see if Mary's there."

"Let's give it a solid try," Frank said. "One time."

"All right," said my father, and we followed Frank over.

On the count of three we tried to push it, but the concrete slab wouldn't move. We couldn't even budge it.

"It's no use," said Frank, and all at once he had to sit down.

"You should go home and see Mary," said my father, and it was as if he believed she might be there. That there was a chance of it. He was saying it to Frank with such a clear look in his eyes.

"What I'm saying," said Frank, almost as if he was talking to the concrete slab we'd been trying to move, "is I doubt a blast like that could come from a bomb." Frank didn't want to go home, and this was how he was going to avoid it. He was going to stand in the middle of a disaster site and talk about the cause with my father. He was trying to act normal. "Gas leak, I'm thinking—this is the conclusion my office is going to draw and I believe it to be the right one. A random occurrence, the sort of thing that could happen anywhere. That's bound to happen. You have your own ideas, I'll bet, and I'm going to look forward to hearing them"—out of the blue Frank let out a sob, a jagged hiccup of a sob that might have begun as a sardonic laugh—"as I'm sure I will. And let me assure you, I'll be taking it into consideration. The blood won't be on your hands the next time a thing like this happens."

"Frank," said my father quietly, "I have to get back."

"It's premature," Frank said, "but the conclusion that is going to be reached is a gas leak that was some distance under the library, near the front of the building. What we are talking about is a slow build. What we are talking about are months, maybe years of leaking gas. A blast like this could have taken several years. What we are talking about is a very slow build."

"Jimmy will go home with you." He didn't look at me. "All right, Jimmy?"

I didn't want to go with him. I wanted Mike to get there so we could go together. But my father turned away, leaving Frank in my hands.

There was the sound of a helicopter in the distance.

"Goddamn it," said Frank. But he followed me. To get to the DeSilva house, we had to walk toward what had been the back of the library, and as we did I realized that we were standing in what had been the basement—the poorly lit AV section where Mike and I had spent so many hours—and that it was now fully exposed, not underground any longer. I could see the heavy metallic shelves on which our 16 mm films had sat, some still standing, though the films themselves were scattered, with yards of footage sprawled out onto the white concrete like an oil spill. And I could see the grey Beast on which I'd cleaned the films, squatting there amidst the wreckage. I walked toward it and then I saw the open door of the bomb shelter.

Frank saw it as well.I followed him down the short flight of stairs.

"What the hell is this?" said Frank.

The ceiling had been caved in by the force of the blast and there was a huge amount of dust everywhere. Both of the beds had been smashed into the floor beneath them by falling concrete. And also, lying there on the floor, a smashed half of a red rose. You couldn't tell if it had been left there or if it had blown in from somewhere amidst the pages.

Frank knelt down and picked it up.

"Someone was down here," he said. "Something happened."

I didn't know what to say, and I tried to tell the truth. Or a version of it. "It was Mike," I said, "he came down here a lot. But not last night," I said. "Last night it was a real break-in." I meant this to make Frank feel better, but it didn't. It made me feel better. I don't think Frank heard a word of what I was saying. He'd turned a deathly white and teetered there, a confused look on his face, and I guessed what was happening because I'd seen it before on *Nineteen Action News*. I ran across the rubble and grabbed one of the paramedics, then rode to the hospital in the ambulance with Frank. When they took him in, I called my mother.

By that time she'd seen the pictures on the news. "I have bad news," I said, and told her about Mary.

"Tell Frank I'm coming," she said. "He should not be alone in a time like this. You stay with him until I get there."

I told her I would.

"You're a good boy, James James," she said.

As I hung up the phone the thought flashed across my mind that Mike had done something to cause the explosion. Maybe this was the test he had planned for my mother—a way of completely giving the finger to both our mother and our father. Using the things our engineer father had taught him to destroy a building our mother thought sacred. Maybe Jennifer was in on it, the two of them like a Bonnie and Clyde team. Maybe they'd get a happy ending despite the broken bones and dead bodies. I found myself imagining it into the shape of a *Family Ties* episode at the end of which Mike, the precocious and misunderstood son, had done something to get sent to jail but just because he wanted to be loved, and nothing more. He hadn't wanted to hurt anybody. At the end of the episode he gets taken away in chains to spend the rest of his life behind bars, and no one feels bad about it.

By the time I got back into Frank's hospital room, he'd been given something to help him sleep and was staring listlessly at the television on the other side of the room. There was a reporter standing near the front of the library ruins and then aerial shots of the devastation. I don't know when I fell asleep, but I did. When I woke up my mother was there as well. It was ten in the morning, but it seemed later. Like I'd been up all night. Frank was snoring and she was sitting at the end of the bed, watching a broadcast of the fire chief saying that he had consulted with my father, who stood there looking out over the rubble with that faraway look on his face. It was only a matter of time, I told myself, before he put together what had happened, and why. And who Marco would sue, for Frank. That is what I thought, as I sat there and Frank snored lightly, what I really believed—that the good guys were going to win and we were the good guys.

INVITATIONS

After I drop off Petey today, I'm headed to the bench in front of Simon's in an attempt to spy on my father, when I see my mother. She's on her way to put the invitations in the mail, carrying them in a plastic bag. When she opens it I see the envelopes, stamped and lined up. It's been a week since she started talking about the birthday party, but it's only now I realize she's serious. This is really going to happen. She smiles at me in an unstable, radioactive way. It's like someone's snuck up behind her and plunged a hypodermic needle into her back containing serum that makes her tell the truth about everything—which, if you're in a James Bond movie, gets injected almost exactly halfway through the movie, though hardly ever into James Bond himself. Looking at her with her plastic bag of envelopes, I can't tell whether she wants me to reassure her about the birthday party or if she's feeling guilty for forcing me to be part of it—or maybe both.

"I'm such a complete mess, Jimmy," she says. We're standing in front of the mailbox.

"No, you're not," I tell her, though the truth is I've been standing there thinking what a mess she's become. "Your hair is looking good."

"You don't even mean that."

I know she wants to hand me the envelopes and have me mail them for her, but I'm not going to do that. "You can call it off, if you want," I tell her.

She shakes her head. "The idea is to celebrate his life."

"Is that really what this is about?"

"I think it is," she says.

"Was Mike really there that morning?" I say, suddenly. I've asked her this before—all of us have—but for some reason I need to ask her again. "I mean right afterwards."

But she knows what I mean.

"I think so," she tells me. "I've been over it all so many times that I don't know now. I don't have a clear memory of any part of it."

"Vivian says you can still see him."

"Last night, I woke up and he was standing right there at the foot of the bed."

"But you were still asleep."

"That's what Dr. Kasoff says, and he's probably right, but it didn't feel like that. I remember opening my eyes and feeling thirsty, then getting out of bed. And there he was."

"Did he say anything?"

"He smiled, in a way, and I looked over at your father, trying to wake him up. When I turned back, Michael was gone."

"That's when you woke up."

She thinks about this. "In the Bible, before Mary finds herself with the Jesus child she has a dream of the Holy Spirit, and it's no less real because it's a dream. That's sometimes the way these things happen."

"Is it Mike who wants to have the party?" I don't know if this would be a good or bad thing, if I want to hear that she thinks she's carrying the message of the birthday party to us like Paul brought the news to the Ephesians. This would be both the most insane thing she could say and the thing that would make the most sense coming from her.

"It's not like that," she says. "The idea, I mean for the party, came to me, and I knew I had to do it—I can't explain it better than that, James James." She takes out a handful of invitations and puts them through the mail slot. One handful after another, and soon they've all been mailed.

"That's that," she tells me.

We start walking back in the direction of the preschool.

She asks, "Have you ordered the cake?"

I lie and say yes.

"What flavour did you decide on?"

"Chocolate."

She mulls this over.

"Everyone loves chocolate," I say.

She stops, turns and looks at me. "Do you think I'm demented?"

"Do you think I am?"

"No," she says. "And that's the truth. Your turn."

No, I want to say. *No way.* But I can't say that because I don't know what to think. So I let the question hang there, let it seem like I haven't quite heard her. Which is better, I think, because it looks like I'm thinking about it, drawing a mental line down a mental piece of paper and doing some actual calculations on the subject. And as I'm doing that, I realize I can't answer the question, so I tell her I wish I'd come up with the idea of the birthday party myself.

"You're a good boy, James James," she tells me. She doesn't believe me, but I'd said what I had to say.

"How's it going with Dr. Kasoff?" I ask her.

She shrugs. "How's it going with you?"

"Good," I tell her. "I mean, who knows? He's got me writing things down."

"What kind of things?"

"Anything, I don't know. Everything that happens. A history of the present, he calls it. My life and times. It's supposed to be therapeutic. Like that movie Mike and I were going to make, only not a movie."

"Are you going to write about seeing me now?"

"Maybe. I don't know."

"I think Dr. Kasoff looks like Archie Bunker. You remember that old show? Each time I'm in his office I think maybe I'll forget and call him Archie, and he'll call me Edith. Then we'll go and sit down at the piano and sing about the old days."

Before we get very far down the street, she goes back and checks the mailbox, as if she's thinking that maybe the invitations have decided against the whole thing and spit themselves out. When she sees they haven't, she turns to me and smiles, as if to say that the thing has gone, really, unexpectedly well.

GRANT

Vivian tells us at breakfast the next day that her boyfriend Grant is coming over for dinner tonight. She springs this on us out of nowhere, then warns us to be normal, all of us. No bursting into tears without provocation, no throwing up from grief and exhaustion, she says, then leaves to throw up herself.

For the occasion Vivian makes conventional pasta with tomato sauce and meatballs, using conventional pots and a conventional stove. When he arrives, Grant has greenish hair that's gelled so it stands almost straight up. He's small, almost the same size as my sister, and he's dressed more or less like her, wearing a black Depeche Mode T-shirt and black jeans and black Doc Martens that it takes him nearly fifteen minutes to unlace. It's the first time I've met Grant, but I find out pretty quickly that all his most deeply held convictions have to do with fashion or music. Vince Clarke, Grant says, even before he starts to take off his boots, is the only member of Depeche Mode with any talent; the Pet Shop Boys are the most important duo in the twentieth century, next to Batman and Robin. This is something he says to my father, as if he's trying to convince him his daughter's in good hands. It's better to have your eyebrow pierced, says Grant, than your ear. It would be best to do both, but if you can't, the eyebrow is definitely cooler. My father listens to him intently, as though he can't wait to go downstairs and write it down for future reference.

Whether it's the sight of the spaghetti or the presence of a genuine suitor at the dinner table, my mother gets nostalgic and starts telling the story of how she and my father met. It's a story all of us, including Petey, have heard a hundred times before, like the story of the Garden of Eden, or Noah's ark. It's like sitting there in Geography listening to Atkinson go on about the moving of tectonic plates, how North America one day floated away from Europe. You know it must have happened—it's not the sort of thing anyone would get up in front of his Geography class and lie about. But at the same it's impossible to really imagine it, to have a realistic picture of the world being a single continent in the middle of an almost endless sea.

Back then, in the prehistoric times of our family, it was my father who, not being a nun, made the first move. This first move happened in a classroom at Case Western University, not far from where we live now, right where Cleveland ends and Cleveland Heights begins. There is in fact a big hill right there that justifies the Heights part of the name. The hill isn't a mountain or anything—it's four hundred feet—but at least it exists, which is not always the case with city names. There's no indication that Nancy Drew lives in a town far above a river in River Heights, for instance. The significance of the hill, though, can't really be overstated; from the way all the places around are named, you'd think it was touching the sun. There's Shaker Heights, Garfield Heights, Maple Heights, Mayfield Heights, University Heights, even Highland Heights, which seems excessive, like it was founded by a bunch of guys who wanted to make it clear they were living *that* far above Cleveland. Case Western is at the bottom of that hill, and at that fateful moment my father was a second-year engineering student who had to take at least one English class to graduate. By the time she got to Case Western, my mother had not only given up her vow of silence but she'd become the kind of nun who didn't look like a nun—she didn't wear a habit—who had gotten special permission from the convent to get a university degree.

The class was Major British Writers, and on that day my father sidled over to the girl who would one day be our mother and tried to ask her out. She was twenty-four and he was nineteen. *Sidled* is the word my mother uses—always—to describe the way my father walked up to her, and that makes me think it must have been exactly like that. A slow, deliberate weave, a man in hip boots stepping gingerly into a river.

"Miss," he asked her, "what can't you do with a rope?" This was his idea of a pickup line.

My mother didn't answer. This was supposed to put him off.

"Push it," he told her after a moment. Then he stood there, looking at her and smiling. Dressed in some kind of absurd fifties garb even though it was the sixties, a white shirt with a fistful of pens crammed into the pocket, along with something that looked like a slide ruler. There aren't any pictures of him from that day, but I can guess. I've seen a ton of pictures of my father in the 1960s and in each of them, he's wearing the same inexcusably nerdy garb, the kind of science geek costume you'd have to put on if you were playing one of the NASA engineers in *The Right Stuff*—a costume that says you are absolutely not, under any circumstance, actually going into space yourself. You'll stay on Earth, do the math, and that's *it.*

Again, my mother didn't reply.

"That's the answer," he told her. "I mean to the question of what you can't do with a rope. Answer, push it. Try and you'll see for yourself, it *can't* be done. People say the world's a complicated place, but it's not. There are only two natural laws, and that's the first."

My mother, reportedly, nodded in his general direction. Not right at him, but near him.

She demonstrates this for Grant's benefit as she's sitting at the table. It's a tiny movement, a barely perceptible bobbing of her head, the kind of movement that, if you were fishing and saw your bobber making a similar movement, would mean you do not have a fish on your line.

It was enough for my father.

"I'm in engineering," he told her, "mechanical. Which, by the way, I define as the study of the world as it really is."

My mother got up and walked to the other side of the classroom.

"Was that nice?" says Vivian.

"Do you blame me?" asks our mother.

"I don't blame you," says Grant.

"I thought you were on my side," my father says. It's a kind of corny joke made cornier by the fact that Grant doesn't get it.

"I'd do the same thing," Grant tells my mother.

Vivian looks at me and I roll my eyes.

"Fort was a nerd." My mother smiles, as if to sum up the issue. "He's still a nerd."

"How am I a nerd?" my father says.

"All the same," says Vivian, trying to bring my mother back to the story, "I would have at least *talked* to him. You must have liked *something* about him. I bet he was good looking."

Like the rest of us, Grant turns and looks at my father, which is what you're supposed to do at this point in the story. If you were making the movie Mike and I talked about in the library basement you'd get Bob Hoskins to play my father, because that's what he looks like, short and heavily built, not fat, but also because my father can move like Bob Hoskins, who in one of his early movies plays a thug who breaks another thug's nose by smashing it in with the heel of his hand. This is how my father can move when he wants to: decisively and fast, a little like a dancer, though my father never had much time for dancing. In the same way he thought flowers were a waste of money and would say to the girls he dated that if what they were looking for was the kind of guy who bought flowers, they were out of luck.

"Never mind," says my father, mostly to Grant. "I gave it another shot."

That second shot happened a month later.

Again he sidled over to her. "I'm Fort," he told her, "Fort Morrison."

My mother shook her head, and motioned for him to have a seat, more friendly than she had been the time before. This was because in the time between, she'd been to confession and come to the conclusion that the cause of her rudeness that first time had been not his forwardness but her own vanity. She had formed what she came to believe was the unwarranted conviction that my father's attempt at starting a conversation with her had been romantic in nature. Therefore, she had spurned him. Thrown the first stone. Accordingly, she had resolved that if he ever approached her again—it was, she realized, another mark of her vanity that she believed he *would* approach her again—to treat him in a more civil manner.

"Nice to meet you," she told him.

"Actually," said my father, encouraged, "Fort is my *middle* name. Fortitude. If you look at my birth certificate, you'll see it says James Fortitude Morrison. But I go by Fort. You can try, but there's no getting by Fort Morrison. That's what I tell people. It's a joke, but it's also true. It also lets them know who they're dealing with."

"I get it," replied my mother. "You're named after a building."

"Well, not exactly. It's more like an imaginary building, like it could be the name of a building. There's no actual Fort Morrison."

"I don't know much about history," she said.

"Actually," he told her—just as he tells everyone—"I'm Canadian, from way up north in the wilds of the province of Ontario."

"I've never been there."

"We should go," he said brazenly. "I'll take you." When she didn't reply to that, he felt encouraged and so he tried to keep their game going. He'd asked her a question and now, he said, it was her turn. "Ask me something."

"Like what?"

"Anything—something you know and think I won't."

She said: "What are the seven joys of Our Lady?"

"What lady?"

"The Annunciation," she told him, "the Visitation, the Nativity, the Adoration of the Magi, the Finding of the Child in the Temple, the Apparition to His Mother, the Assumption and the Coronation of the Blessed Virgin."

"Wow," he said, and waited for her to tell him her name.

She didn't.

THE IMPORTANT PART

Now: this is an important moment, maybe the *most* important moment in the whole story. But you have to know it, sort of, in advance. You sort of have to have heard the story about a million times before you get it. Not only do you have to have heard the story a million times before, you need footnotes. If that story were in the kind of book they make you read in English class, the moment when my mother doesn't say anything about her name is the kind of moment the teacher would be sure to ask about. If she introduced herself as Sister Mary Damian of the Infant Jesus, the gig would be up. If she'd been straight with my father and let him know she was a betrothed of God, that would have been the end of it. But the fact is she didn't tell him her name. Instead, she let him think she was just some girl who was, just maybe, interested in him. And just like someone who *was* interested, she asked him about the second law of the universe.

"What's next?" she said. "What commandment comes after 'Thou shalt not push a rope'?"

"It's not like that," he tried to tell her. "I'm not forbidding anyone from pushing ropes, it's just you can't do it."

"I see," she said. Though of course she didn't.

"They're not commandments," he told her. "They're laws."

"Same thing," replied my mother.

"What we're talking about are laws," he told her. "I don't know anything about commandments. For commandments you need a commander."

My mother didn't reply.

"And there's no commander," he told her.

"At that point," says Vivian, "I'd have told him to take a hike."

"Your mother doesn't have it in her," observed my father.

"That's what you think," she tells him. "That's what I should have done. It's what I should do now. You think I don't have it in me, you'd be surprised."

"Take it easy," Vivian tells them. "We have a guest. Be normal."

My father told her the second law had to do with heat. "How does heat move?" he asked her.

"Up?" she replied.

"Not quite," he told her.

"Everybody knows heat rises."

"But *after* it rises?"

"Does heat go up your ass?" asked Mike the first and only time that Jennifer McKellar came over to our house for dinner last fall—during that month when the door at the library stopped opening mysteriously—sitting exactly where Grant is sitting now, right beside my father. She was wearing a thin black dress that she told my mother she got at the Gap the night before, silky and transparent; it came down to about the middle of her thigh. My mother began telling that same story, only my father turned to Jennifer and asked *her* the question about how heat moves. And before she could say a thing, Mike asked my father if heat went up his ass.

Jennifer laughed, then so did my mother, which made it all right. "Cover your ears," said my father to little Petey, then laughed himself. The whole time Jennifer's dead eye moved around slowly while my parents told their story, as if it knew, already, how everything was going to change, get just entirely wiped off the earth three weeks later.

"Do you want me to tell you the truth about heat?" asked my father.

"Yes," says Grant.

"No, Grant," says Vivian. "He's not really saying it, it's in the story."

"Sorry," Grant tells my father.

"From hot to cold," he told her. "The truth about heat is that it cools down."

My mother smiled her most ordinary girl smile.

And that, like they say in the Bible, was how it went in the beginning. We were told it was good, and it was. For a while, at least. My father sidled back to his seat on the other side of the classroom and she began to fall for him. Which means, like Julie Andrews in *The Sound of Music,* she began to wonder if she was supposed to be a nun. It didn't hurt that, at least as far as my father was concerned, being an engineer was a lot like being a priest. Particularly back in the days when the Mass was in Latin and the priest kept his back to the congregation the whole time. You didn't know what was going on, what exactly the priest was talking about, but you knew it was important. And you knew the priest was the only one who could do it.

This may have been what made my mother—who probably would have been a lot happier with a priest—want to marry him in the first place. And in just the same way as you can't ask questions in church, the two immutable laws of the universe can't be debated. You could pull on a rope or hang yourself with it. Or cut it in two. But not push it. And hot turns to cold. You can say you've heard otherwise, that you've seen it, but that would be a lie. And as my mother must have known, it's the second law that makes things so tough on this planet. It's heat that matters most in the world, and that moves only in one direction. You can do without ropes.

After dinner, Vivian says that she and Grant are on their way to a movie. But when we're standing there and he's relacing his boots, I ask which one and he doesn't have a clue.

"Is it, maybe, *Back to the Future*?"

"I think so," he says. "Have you seen it?"

"When it came out, like, two and a half years ago."

Grant doesn't know what to say.

"Maybe you're not going to a movie at *all*?" I say. It's like I'm Philip Marlowe and he's some hapless, outwitted villain.

"I'm really sorry," says Grant.

"Don't be sorry," says Vivian, putting her coat on. "It's none of his business."

I sneer at her. "You can go have sex at the top of the Empire State Building for all I care."

"Maybe I will," says Vivian.

"But that's in New York," says Grant.

Vivian yanks Grant out of the house after that, and when I'm sure they're gone I go downstairs to talk to my father. He's looking carefully at what appear to be blueprints of the library, has them spread out in front of him on the table. I tell him that I think Vivian and Grant are having sex. All

I'm saying," I tell him, "is I think maybe you should have a talk with her."

"Dr. Kasoff says that it's been going on for a while," he replies. "He says Vivian's on the pill."

"The pill?"

"She told him, and he told me," says my father.

"Isn't it against the rules for Dr. Kasoff to tell you?"

"Not according to him. I said the same thing, but he told me no. That there's no hard-and-fast rules, there's what works."

"You know I saw you at the library that day," I say, without meaning to exactly.

"I know," he says.

"What were you doing?"

"What were *you* doing?"

There's the sound of my mother coming down the stairs and we both immediately shut up. I'm not sure why, what it is that she can't know or why she can't know it, but we both stand there and look at her.

The next day I confront Dr. Kasoff about Vivian and the pill.

"Isn't it against the rules to tell my father something like that?" I ask him.

He doesn't deny it. "It's not that there are no rules," he tells me, "but in the context of this sort of ordeal, that affects a whole family in such radical ways, things move in unconventional directions. When you come into this office, it's not like entering a confessional."

Then I start to wonder if maybe Dr. Kasoff has told my father about Vivian and Grant sleeping together for the same reason I have—to give him some ordinary fatherly concern to make him stop obsessing about the library and Mike. But it doesn't. When I try to talk to him about it another time, he says I should bring it up with Vivian myself. "Sit her down and give her a real talking-to," he tells me. "Or bring it up with Grant. See if that gets you anywhere."

PARENT HELPING

On Friday I'm scheduled to be Parent Helper, which means I wake up early, shower, and take longer than usual with my hair, even using some of Mike's hair gel. I'm going for a Dennis Quaid look, like a frazzled cop who's ingested a serum that is going to kill him in a few hours, but I don't really know what I'm doing and end up looking like Richie Cunningham in *Happy Days,* whenever he dresses up.

From here things get worse, and not just from a fashion perspective. We're out of Eggos and my mother finished the milk last night. But instead of telling anyone, she put the empty carton back in the fridge.

"How about water for a change?" I ask Petey.

"Water?" says Petey. "For breakfast?"

"It's not my fault," I tell him and look at my mother.

"Calm down," says my father. "I'll go get milk."

"There's no time for that. It's my day to be Parent Helper and that means I've got to be there on time. I've got to be *early.* It's all there in the Parent Handbook." He looks back at me blankly. "We've got to be there ten minutes early, to help with the set-up. If we're late, we get charged ten dollars."

"That seems punitive," says my father.

"It's supposed to be punitive—it's a punishment."

"If we have to pay ten dollars we'll pay it—if we have to

pay twenty because we're twenty minutes late, I'll cover that as well." He goes on to say that it would be a good idea if my mother were feeling well enough to be Parent Helper. That's how he puts it, as if she's getting over stomach flu or a head cold. If she could go with Petey today it would be a big step in the right direction—and maybe she should try.

"I don't know," says my mother.

"No problem," my father says, "maybe next time." It's almost a replay of the conversation he had with Marco. Maybe that's what's behind this: if my father has to go back to work, so does my mother.

"I'm sorry," she tells him. "Maybe next time."

"It's completely fine," says my father.

"Please," asks Petey. It's like I'm not even there.

"I really do think it would do everyone good." My father gets up from the table and goes over to get himself more coffee.

"I suppose I could," hedges my mother. "If Petey thinks it would be okay."

My father states the obvious. "I think Petey would love it."

"I *would* love it," says Petey.

"I really don't know," my mother says a third time.

"If she doesn't want to do it," I tell my father, "you shouldn't make her."

"Look at my hair," she says.

"Your hair is fine," my father replies. He's controlling his voice, telling himself not to shout at her. Not to *demand* she do what he knows—what she knows—is the best thing for her. "If you're a couple of minutes late, Mrs. Dumme will understand."

"I have to get dressed," my mother adds. "If I'm going to go, I can't go looking like this." She gets up from the table and goes upstairs. Petey follows her; he's going to dress himself, it looks like, something he's never attempted before and which I have asked him to do every day for the last two months.

"I thought you'd be happy to get out of it," my father says when she's gone.

"Sure I'm happy. Come on, seriously, it's just that Petey's sort of counting on it. We talked about it a lot." I take my plate over to the sink.

"Don't worry about the dishes," my father says, in the same the tone he'd use if he were about to give a complete stranger a bone marrow transplant. "I'll take care of them."

"I just hope she doesn't make us too late," I tell him.

"If she does, you'll just have to go, but it's important we let her try."

"It's not the money," I point out. "I just don't know if it'd be the best thing, as far as Petey is concerned, to show up an hour or two late."

"You won't be two hours late. You *might* be five minutes late."

"If you say so."

By now any pretense of cool indifference on my part—of not really caring if I get to be Parent Helper—has gone completely out the window. I hate to admit it, but it's true. Every time I'd pass the calendar I'd see the words written there and do a whole run-through of the day, imagine myself on the carpet beside Petey, watching Mrs. Dumme read a story. If the Mothers are the Mafia, your first day as Parent Helper is when they send you in alone to crack the skull of the guy who owns the variety store for not paying his protection money. Get your bones, they call it. After this, I'm a made guy, I get the tattoo. I've got corn chips for a snack, which I think is sort of excellent. I'll start off by saying they're kind of *corny,* then I'll say they're also amazing, pointing out the *maize* in the middle of *amazing.* It'll be a learning experience for everyone, even for Mrs. Dumme. Maybe she's heard that one before about the corn chips, but I'll bet she hasn't. I'm waiting to see the look on her face. Maybe she'll tell the other Mothers. After that my life will be different. I don't care if my father thinks it's ridiculous.

My mother's still not ready by the time I go upstairs to find Petey, which makes me think she's not going to make it. It's going to be me turning up for Parent Helping, late and without my mother. I'll have to get into the whole thing with Mrs. Dumme about letting her try, that she needed the opportunity, but something came over her and she had to spend the rest of the morning lying on her bed, staring blankly at her ceiling.

Once I think about it like that, it's more or less a race.

I'm hustling Petey into his clothes, pulling on his shirt. Moving fast. I can hear Vivian in the shower, singing along to "Jessie's Girl" at the top of her lungs, and know we have to leave before she gets out. That she'll agree with my father and then I'll never get there.

Once Petey's dressed it's out the door and into the stroller. I'm buckling him in when it occurs to me that I've forgotten the corn chips. I don't want to go back for them, but I know I have to. The worst thing I could do next to showing up late for Parent Helping would be to show up without the snack. I run inside to the kitchen and am back a moment later, looping the plastic bag with the corn chips around the stroller handles.

"Where's Mommy?"

"We have to go without her."

"She said she was coming."

"I know what she said." I start to push him anyway.

"Wait!" he screams.

There's an old guy down the street doing something with his garden, and he turns to look, thinking that maybe he might be able to prevent a homicide. Petey's scream is like that.

"Do you *want* to be late?" I prod him.

"I don't want to go," he insists.

"So you don't care if you disappoint Mrs. Dumme and the other kids?"

"Mommy's coming."

"I know what she said," I tell him again. "But Mommy is sick, you know that." I know it's wrong to say this to Petey, as if saying it has made it true, like now there's nothing any of us can do about it, but I'm desperate. This isn't my job, I want to tell him. I'm not supposed to be doing *any* of this.

"Maybe she got better."

"Do you want *me* to get in trouble with Mrs. Dumme?"

"What about my diver's mask?" He searches around in the stroller. "It's upstairs."

"Upstairs?"

"I need it."

"You don't really need it. You're not actually going diving."

He tries to get out of the stroller. It's not his usual protest, though; it's like he's made up his mind to escape and is working at pressing the button on the front of the plastic belt that holds him in, getting ready to jump out and run back into the house.

I can't let that happen. "Calm down," I tell him. "Stay there."

I run back inside.

My father's nowhere to be seen, already in the basement. Maybe he's gone, has slipped out the back door, and is now hopping over strangers' fences, making his way to the library by some secret way, maybe a whole system of tunnels. His car is still in the driveway, but it could be that he's pulling a Mike, leaving his vehicle in the driveway so we'll think he's there.

Vivian's in the kitchen. I can hear the microwave fan running.

As quietly as I can, I run upstairs and find the diver's mask on the floor of Petey's room. I race back outside and pretty much throw the mask at Petey. "All right," I say, in this really bitter, totally sarcastic way. "Can we please go now?"

"What about my shark?"

"Oh for fuck's sake," I say.

I try to not swear in front of Petey, but sometimes I can't help it. It just comes out. The Mothers all do it, though they seem to have no clear memory of it afterwards, and never talk about it. I have no memory of my own mother swearing ever, not even when we were old enough to swear in front of her. Maybe that's why I never know what to do when I do it, if it's like radioactive waste that I have to quarantine immediately or if it's better to act like it's the kind of radioactive waste that got dumped into Lake Erie during the 1970s that everyone *knew* was radioactive waste but never said anything about. I take a breath. "You should have told me before is what I mean to say. You saw me going inside, you should have said you forgot the shark too."

"I told you."

I tell him he didn't.

"Did too," he says back.

The door opens and out steps my mother. "I thought you'd left," she tells me.

Petey is happy as hell.

I need to yell at my mother about something, so while we're walking I tell her how completely unfair it is that Vivian gets to do the balloons and I have to do the cake.

"I thought you would like getting the cake."

"Because I'm fat?" I'm freaking out now, and I know it. Actually shouting at my mother right out on the street. "I get it—I order the cake because I'm the fat brother? Thanks a lot." I'm saying that to make her feel bad, but the moment the words are out I realize no one is going to say that about me maybe ever again. I'm done with being the fat brother and not because I'm any less fat but because from here on in the pictures won't have Mike in them. It could be Petey, but with Petey I'm the older brother. It'll be up to me to tell people I was once the fat brother, that I once had a brother and he looked nothing like me. You should have seen him, I'll say.

So I just shut up after that.

"Mommy," says Petey, "is there such a thing as a humpback shark?"

"There is if you want there to be," she tells him.

I don't know why that pisses me off, but it does. "No," I tell them both, "there's no goddamn such thing as the humpback shark."

The three of us walk the rest of the way in silence, pretty quickly as it turns out, and though I'm annoyed that we've got there on time, I'm relieved I don't have to go over and hand ten bucks to Mrs. Dumme or worry about my mother wandering in later like some kind of zombie. But I don't go in with them, or anything like that. I leave my mother and Petey there on the sidewalk. Let them fend for themselves.

I walk away, quickly, past the fenced-in lot where the library was, past the Cedar Lee Theatre, straight into Amy Joy Donuts, where I start ordering. I hand the girl behind the counter a dollar. When she asks me what I want, I tell her to surprise me. I say it like I'm some down-and-out private investigator, caught in a mystery so deep it makes him wonder who he even is. Which is something that happens all the time to detectives in those old movies who have nearly given up on the case by the big third reel and don't know if they're one of the good guys or the villain, if they're solving the mystery or making it impossible to solve. I know I'm no Marlowe, no Bogart, but it's the same kind of completely perplexed despair that washes over me as I stand at the counter of Amy Joy Donuts. Set me up, I tell the girl. She asks me again what kind of donut I want and I tell her again to surprise me, I really insist. Another classic Bogart move. Though he would say it and the girl would know instantly there's nothing she can do with a donut that would surprise him. That, when it comes to donuts, he's seen it all. Somehow you'd get the sense that the girl was really attracted to him for being so sad, the way Jennifer was to Mike when he made up his mind to flush his future down the toilet, and that his sadness has a lot to do with how profound a guy he is. She'd fall in love with him right there. Sleep with him anyway. As I stand at the counter of Amy Joy Donuts, though, it's nothing like that, which is because it's a donut and not some really strong drink I'm ordering. But that's how I say it. I don't care what she gives me, I'm going to eat it and when I'm done I'm going to eat another and there's nothing she or anyone else can do to stop me.

So, then, the girl turns around and looks at the rack of donuts and makes up her mind to give me a chocolate one. She gets some waxed paper and picks one out and is about to put it in a bag for me, but I tell her no bag. She turns back to me and hands it over.

I eat it right there. Standing at the counter. There's a guy behind me, waiting, but I don't move. Instead, I order another donut. I push my change toward her on the counter, letting her know how serious I am.

This time she gives me a maple donut. It's my father's favourite kind, I tell her, the number-one-selling donut in the wilds of Canada. And then I eat that too, still standing right there. She watches me the whole time. Like she's never seen anyone eat a donut. Maybe she's never seen anyone eat one so fast. I have to admit I *do* eat it fast. But it's because I'm pissed off, not because I'm starving. I open my mouth and fold the maple donut in, chew a little, or at least try to chew, but it's impossible because my mouth is so full and I have to use my hands, have to stick my fingers into my mouth and push the donut farther back so I can get it with my teeth.

Finally I swallow it, and I feel good. Euphoric.

I'm not talking about the kind of peaceful good feeling you get from cheap carbohydrates and icing sugar. I'm talking ecstasy, the unstable buzz you feel when everything in the world seems possible, all the worst stuff and all the best stuff too—the type of electricity that courses through you after you've kissed civilization goodbye.

I feel like Jim Morrison.

But not Jim Morrison the dead rock star.

I feel like James Morrison the mutineer, and those donuts are breadfruit plants that I'm going to stuff into me as fast as I can, no matter what Captain Bligh has to say about it.

AMY JOY

These two things—stuffing chocolate and maple donuts into my mouth and the high treason mutineer James Morrison committed by taking off to Tahiti despite the freaking out of Captain Bligh—don't really have anything in common. But these are the insights that flash into your mind in those brief moments before you lose consciousness. I've fainted enough times to know when it's coming, to recognize that falling away from the world, the brief flash of insight before the enfolding darkness. Or maybe it's just the effect donuts have on me. You don't have to be a genius to know that donuts are exactly the sort of thing it would be best for me to stay away from. But right now I don't care. I'm eating them anyway, and that makes me feel invulnerable, like this is the start of a really amazing day. I have no idea what its amazingness could possibly involve, no idea at all of what I want to have happen in it—except that I wouldn't mind having donuts for lunch as well as breakfast.

So I have another. Two more, actually. I can feel the Amy Joy Donuts girl starting to panic, but who cares—I go ahead and order a half-dozen to take with me. "No," I tell her, "a dozen." She starts to say something, like maybe she's going to try and talk me out of it. But I shout, "I said a dozen!" People are looking, all the old folks who spend their days sitting around in

Amy Joy Donuts with their coffees and apple crullers. So this girl fills the box as quickly as she can. I put ten bucks down and tell her to keep the change, and take a couple of steps toward the door but then think, fuck it, and I open the box.

First is the chocolate one near the front. Then the glazed one just behind it. Then a third, with sprinkles. The rest of the Amy Joy customers are staring at me in a worried way, like at any moment I might announce I've got a bomb duct-taped to my chest and they should all stay calm.

Then there's a second Amy Joy Donuts girl there asking me if I'm sure I'm all right. She says it like I'm falling apart, like I've turned into a basket case like the rest of my family.

Except she knows my name.

"Jimmy," she says, "are you *sure* you're all right?"

Suddenly, she's gone. I'm falling backward, and somehow she's behind me, catching me. In the last split second before the world goes black I know it's Jennifer McKellar who's lowering me to the floor, telling everyone she knows me, and this is the sort of thing that happens all the time. There's no need to call an ambulance.

When I open my eyes, I find myself looking up into Jennifer McKellar's dead left eye. She's sitting next to me and her good eye is looking off into the distance. I close my eyes for a second and when I open them again her dead eye is still staring right at me. It's ironic that after all that time trying to get its attention in Atkinson's Geography class it should pick this moment to find me so interesting. Ironic or maybe just mean. But I guess that's the thing about dead eyes. It's really hard to understand their perspective. I find myself thinking of "Jessie's Girl," that cheesy song that Vivian was singing in the shower this morning. It's about this guy who wants to go out with this girl, but she's another guy's girl. I don't know the details. There aren't any details. There's just this guy who's singing the song, saying that Jessie is his friend, and that he's got this girl and that the singer really has the hots for her. For *Jessie's* girl, that is. It's a pretty crappy song, except in the middle, when the singer says he's looking in the mirror all the time, wondering what Jessie's girl doesn't see in him. Looking at Jennifer's dead eye looking back at me, it seems to me that Rick Springfield, no matter how worthless a song he's singing, is right on this one point. And not just right about ordinary eyes. About dead eyes too. If a dead eye isn't going to look at you, it won't. If it decides it will, there's nothing you can do to get it to stop.

Jennifer doesn't yet know I'm awake, which makes it seem like the two of us have stepped out of a black-and-white postcard from the 1950s. She's sitting demurely in her pleated Amy Joy Donuts skirt, which, as demure as it is, still shows me her knees. I notice then that there's a small scar on the knee closest to me, a thin line where she had stitches once. I think about running my finger along it, and that's when she sees I'm awake.

"Hey, Jimmy."

"Hey, Jennifer."

"How're you doing?"

"Okay, I guess."

"You want to sit up?" She puts her arm around my back and helps me into a sitting position, and I see that somebody's carried me out to the patch of grass behind the donut place, next to the Dumpster. "I'm supposed to ask you if you're sure you shouldn't go to the doctor."

I tell her I'm fine.

She hands me a coffee cup with water in it. "I better go in and tell my manager you're all right. Be right back."

When she comes back out and sits beside me again, I tell her I didn't know she worked here.

"It's a part-time thing. I'm doing the rest of my classes at night, downtown."

I mumble a few syllables.

"I mean, I wasn't into going back to Heights High after all that. The job sucks, but it lets me go to school. And besides, I figured if I could make some money, I should. You know, for college."

"I dropped out of school."

"I heard something like that."

I shrug. "Who cares?"

"Are you dropped out for sure, or can you go back?"

I think about lying for a second, then don't. "I guess I can go back," I tell her.

"So you didn't drop out, then?"

"No, I didn't," I admit. A moment later, I explain. "It's more like a leave of absence. Dr. Kasoff—this guy—it was his idea and he called the school, and said I'd get As. So I figured, why not. I'll get the rest of my classes in September."

"Weren't you getting As anyway?" she says, and it seems to me that she's disappointed. Still, her dead eye keeps looking at me, which is something. The sun has come out now, and it's great to be there on the grass. I don't want to move. I really wish she hadn't pointed out the fact that I didn't actually drop out. It seems the opposite of that. Neither of us says anything for a bit. She takes a blade of grass and brings it to her lips, as if she's thinking of whistling with it. But she just holds it there.

"Sorry I didn't come to Mike's funeral."

I act like it's the furthest thing from my mind.

"I wanted to go, but my parents were worried, my father didn't want me mixed up in anything." Her dead eye is looking off now, toward the west. "They saw you on the news. What my father said was that it was better I keep my distance."

I say that's fine with me.

"I'm seeing somebody else now."

"I'm sort of my brother's nanny now," I say, as if the two things are parallel occurrences.

She stands up, and helps me stand up too. I wobble for a minute, but soon I'm steadier, almost normal.

"Here," she says, and presses a folded paper into my hand. "It's my number. You can call me if you want. But you don't have to. Anyway, there it is," she tells me, and then, just as I'm about to walk away, she puts her hand on the back of my neck. Softly, barely touching me, she pulls me toward her. I think she's going to kiss me, which she does. It's like a dream, it happens so easily. Then she turns around and goes back into the store.

I walk back to the preschool, and I realize I don't know what happened. It's not like I don't want to kiss her again. I can feel myself walking more quickly, trying to work it out in my mind what Mike would think. I find my mother and Petey standing on the sidewalk in front of the church still in one piece, looking happy even. While we're standing there Jenna drives by in her station wagon, the window down. She honks when she sees us and it's my mother, not me, who waves back. There's a twinge of something, but that's it.

It's strange to think my life had seemed so ruined this morning, and I feel bad about giving Petey and my mother such a hard time. So I tell them both we're going to Johnny Wang's Good Food Truck for hot dogs. They eat one each, and I sit there with a Diet Pepsi, don't order anything, not even when Johnny asks me what I'm going have. Really, though, I'm replaying the whole morning in my mind, a lot of it in slow motion. When he's done eating, Petey lets me put him in the stroller, and by the time we get home, he's asleep. I carry him upstairs, but instead of putting him into his own bed, I put him down on Mike's old bed. One of the first things I learned when I started being Petey's nanny, or whatever you want to call it, is that it's not as easy as you'd think to get a four-year-old into bed without waking him up. It's like defusing a bomb. One false move, the slightest mistake, it'll set off a chain reaction that wrecks everything.

That night, after everyone's asleep, I go and sit outside in Mike's Gremlin, which is still in our driveway. Parked exactly where he parked it the last time he drove it—the last time it ran. When my father and I came out of the house on the night of the explosion, after Mary called, the car's being there in the driveway seemed part of Mike's plan. But it turned out the car just wouldn't start. This was something my father found out the next day. "Where did he say he was going?" my father kept saying to my mother after we got back that morning. And again she'd tell him what Mike had said, what he'd been wearing, listening all the while for some clue. Michael must be around, insisted my mother, his car is here. Being the crack investigator he is, my father went right out and tried to start the car himself. I stood on the veranda and watched him turning the key fruitlessly, heard the radio come on, but the engine refused to turn over. It's the starter, said my father, almost to himself, Mike couldn't have got that car going if he'd tried.

That made me worry. I wondered what Mike was doing and how far he'd go. Maybe he'd been hanging around the whole time and I just didn't notice him, in a fake beard and dark glasses. Lurking around the ruins of the library, wanting to be declared missing or even dead. The fact that the car wouldn't start made it seem he had a secret plan that was in the process of unfolding, that it was the sort of thing I should have known to expect.

This is what Mike's car smells like: Old Spice and Marlboros and Drakkar Noir, Mike's old leather jacket, pizza and french fries, and Jennifer McKellar's perfume. As I sit there, I think of those perfume molecules leaping off her and onto him the last time she'd pressed up against him, maybe just before getting out of the car, maybe even on the night he died for all I know about it. And then, for just a second, it seems like he's there sitting beside me. A bone-chilling spooky feeling courses through me, and soon it's freaking me out because that smell is abnormally—supernaturally—strong, and maybe the Gremlin has turned into the kind of car you find in Stephen King movies that gets taken over by a dead thing or a dead person. Though in this instance the dead thing would be my brother, and therefore not exactly frightening. It'd be weird at first, but then I'd mellow out and get into it. At least I'd like to believe I'd act that way. I'd turn on the radio, only instead of the radio it'd be his voice, talking about what a drag it was to have come back to earth as the ghostly inhabitant of an old Gremlin.

By the time I get out of the car, though, I'm convinced my dead brother's not about to appear. I feel like an idiot, and start to wonder if I've got to add it to the list of things to confess if my mother ever makes me go to confession again. I don't know if it's blasphemy to want your brother to come back and haunt his old car, but it might be. Being Catholic, as far as I can tell, means believing that if you put your broken arm in Lake Erie on the Feast of the Assumption it will be healed or that if you pray to St. Carmella you'll receive flowers the next day. But thinking that your dead brother is hanging around somewhere, either trapped inside something or in some stranger's body, will get you sent to hell.

If you know anything about Jim Morrison, the dead rock star, you know he claimed this actually happened to him. He was seven or eight and in the back of his father's station wagon in the desert and they'd driven by an accident involving some Native Americans, a couple of whom appeared to be dead. One of those dying, an old chief or something, maybe a witch doctor, I forget, looked right at him when the car went by. And at that moment, or so he said, the spirit of that old chief passed into his body. This was what made him say such profound things.

That's the kind of arrangement I'm hoping for, only instead of some dead native guy, it would be Jim Morrison. He died exactly three days before I was born, which, if you read your bible, you know is exactly the amount of time it would take for him to resurrect himself. Not that I've ever *felt* him there, but I'd like to keep it open as a possibility. It might be the kind of thing you wake up with one day. Like a cold, or cancer. You might be secretly in love with your brother's girlfriend and start feeling really depressed about it, like it might turn out to be the sort of thing that could wreck your entire life, but then the dead rock star inside you would say something about the day destroying the night and the night dividing the day. That would put it into perspective. There's an island in your heart, your inner rock star would tell you, break on through.

BAKER GIRL

The next day, I order Mike's cake. I don't know if this is because I've finally decided that the birthday party is really going to happen or if it's because that kiss from Jennifer has made me feel really guilty. But I wake up and it occurs to me that the thing to do is get that birthday cake ordered. Maybe this is what you do when you're wondering how serious it's going to get between you and your dead brother's girlfriend. He's dead, so you don't know how bad you should be feeling. You can't ask him, so instead you go and order him a birthday cake.

At the grocery store I take a cart even though I have no intention of buying anything. There's something about having a cart that makes me feel legitimate, like I'm supposed to be here. I've just dropped off Petey, and at this hour it's mostly mothers in the store with little kids sitting in the shopping carts with their legs dangling, the carts half full as each mother browses the aisles and waits for her kids to grow up.

I wander around a little like I'm one of them, pretending to plan the imaginary meals I'll cook. I start with spaghetti, checking out each of the sauces really carefully: tomato, tomato and garlic, meat, meat with mushrooms, vegetarian. I take down each of the jars, turning them around in my hands, looking at the ingredients on the back, shaking my head at the sodium contents. Finally, I take two bottles of green pepper and mushroom sauce and four packages of penne and put them into the cart. From there I move to the cereal aisle and throw in a couple of boxes of Pop-Tarts, two boxes of Special K and a big can of wheat germ, then veer over to the edge of the store where the fruits and vegetables are. I'm moving slowly, looking carefully at the soups, contemplating the different kinds of crackers, taking my time with the apples, picking them up, testing them for firmness, bringing them to my nose and inhaling deeply.

Grocery shopping was something my mother liked to do with us along in tow, whenever we'd consent. She barely leaves the house now, but she used to take hours, going down the aisles with a serene wariness, as if the artificial shine the staff put on the apples was a snare, every watermelon was a danger. You could be seduced by fruit in the same way you could fall prey to idleness, she seemed to be teaching us. The peaches and plums must be firm because the store is refrigerated and that means that if they're soft at all, they'll turn out to be rotten when you get them home. The cantaloupes must be squeezed at the north and the south poles and if you can make an indentation, they're overripe, already rotten. For a time she was responsible for doing the shopping for her convent, for planning the meals.

I put two dark green cucumbers into the shopping cart, then a bag of radishes and three medium-sized acorn squash. Then a ten-pound bag of red potatoes from Prince Edward Island, which our Canadian father insisted on buying for patriotic reasons. Two gallons of milk, cream for coffee, three cartons of orange juice. Frozen lemonade, cheddar cheese. All of it goes into the cart as if there's a bunch of really hungry nuns on their knees waiting for me.

Finally I arrive at the bakery.

"Can I help you?" says the girl behind the counter. She's younger than I expect her to be, with red or blond hair that's been dyed black and eyebrows that have been plucked into oblivion. There's a gold stud in the middle of her tongue that glints at me when she speaks.

I tell her I'm just looking at the cakes. She nods and looks at the cakes herself. It's like she's noticing them for the first time. "Actually," I tell her, "I'm going to need to order a birthday cake."

"We have those," she says, and doesn't smile. It seems to me wrong that a baker wouldn't be more excited about birthdays. "You can buy one off the rack, or, like, I can make you a specific one—write shit on it, and that."

"I think I'll need a specific cake," I say.

She doesn't pretend to be interested. "What's it for?" she asks.

"A birthday," I reply. "The birthday cake is for a birthday."

"You'd be surprised," she tells me, but in a way that makes it seem like the experience of being a baker has deprived her of that emotion. "People do a lot of things with birthday cakes."

"Is that right?"

"Don't get me started."

"It's for my brother," I tell her.

"I had a brother," she says.

"Did he die?" I say, a little too eagerly.

"He married this Chinese girl, I don't even know her name. Then he moved there, I mean to China. Just like that. Now he acts like he can't speak English. You call him and he acts like he can't understand what you're saying."

"Maybe you've got the wrong number."

"That's what he wants me to think."

"Why would he want you to think that?"

"You don't know him. If you did, though, I mean, if you'd met him, none of this would come as a surprise. He was like that when we were kids, except for the speaking Chinese part."

"Once I broke my brother's arm," I tell her.

"I can see that," she says. "I can completely see that."

"It wasn't on purpose or anything," I tell her. "And we were kids. They put a cast on it and it was better. I mean, eventually."

She nods, like she's wishing she'd had the foresight to break her own brother's arm.

"This cake," I tell her, "it's for my brother's nineteenth birthday."

"Congrats," she says, though without even pretending to smile. Then she goes into the back and brings out a sheet of cookies. She pushes them into a row of boxes sitting out on the counter. Then she seals the boxes closed with Scotch tape. It's like watching someone put stitches into a dead animal.

"I'm just looking right now," I call over to her. "But I'm seriously interested in a cake."

"When you're ready to make a move, let me know."

"I'll need a slab," I tell her.

"Want a sample?" she asks, still with her back to me.

"You have samples?" I ask, as though I can't believe it.

The baker girl goes into the back and comes out with two Dixie cups with cake inside. She passes one to me, over the counter, and I peer inside it, as if it is not a Dixie cup but a deep well.

"Go ahead," she tells me. "It's not poison."

The thought that it could be poison hadn't occurred to me, and I hesitate for a second. But only a second, and then I tip the cup and down it. All at once, like it's a shot of tequila.

She does the same.

"Are you allowed to do that?"

"They don't care," she says. "What are they going to do? Put me in jail? Let me tell you something, you have to do a lot more than this to get thrown in jail around here. A *whole* lot more, if you know what I mean."

I don't know what she means, but I act like I do. She goes into the back again and comes out with two more shots of cake. Again she hands one to me and again we down them together.

I ask her, "What else do you have?"

She comes back with four more cake shots, two for each of us. I down those as well. I say I might like to try some of the cookies. She reaches under the counter and gives me a handful, then takes a handful herself and we stand there eating them together.

"How did you get to be a baker?"

"I got fired from the meat department. Relocated, they call it. Like you're in the witness protection program. As if. Over there you say too much and you're history, if you know what I mean."

"I might have to come back tomorrow," I tell her.

"Knock yourself out."

"Maybe you think I'm just here for the samples, but I'm not."

"What I'm saying is I don't give a shit."

"You know," I tell her, "you're really nihilistic for a baker."

"Whatever," she says, and turns away.

I go back to pushing my cart, moving down a couple of more aisles, past the ethnic foods, the dried noodles and the special hot sauces, down the aisle where they have garbage bags and paper towels, the aisle where you can buy rat poison and deodorant, and then I leave the cart behind. As if I've just said to hell with it. I think for a moment that someone's coming after me, to tell me to come back. But nothing happens, and then I'm out on the street. I'm sort of sad about leaving those groceries, to have to forget all about those meals I was going to make for those hungry imaginary nuns. It'll be someone else's job to put all that stuff back, and the stock boy who'll have to do it is going to wonder about me. Maybe have a whole composite drawing of me in his head, just from the stuff I put in the cart. Then, tomorrow, I'll show up to order the cake and he'll know. He'll recognize me right away.

STAIRWAY

On my way back to the preschool—worn out by Parent Helping yesterday, my mother didn't even make it downstairs this morning—I pass Amy Joy Donuts and think about maybe going in. Instead I stand there and watch Jennifer from the road. It's before eleven and there's not much mid-morning traffic; it's overcast and the air is still and I have a pretty good view of her behind the counter, putting donuts into boxes, making change. Every so often she looks out the window. I think for a moment that it's me she's looking at, and I wave. But she doesn't see me, doesn't wave back anyway.

Whatever happened between Mike and her started at the Homecoming dance while "Stairway to Heaven" blared in the background. It was the first and last high-school dance my brother attended, a few weeks before Halloween. Like my father, Mike always claimed to have no time for dancing—and certainly he was too cool to go to school dances—but he changed his mind when he heard Jennifer was going.

We were in English class when the question of going to the dance first came up, the three of us working on a group presentation about *The Great Gatsby,* debating the advantages and disadvantages of telling a story from the point of view of a minor character. Almost right away, Jennifer said she'd bought her ticket to the dance and wondered if we were going.

"I'm not much of a dancer," said Mike.

"Me neither," she confided. "But I like dances."

"No way I'm going," I said.

"You going with your lifeguard?" Mike asked her.

When he said this I gave the same kind of derisive snort that I'd given a month earlier when we were meeting Jennifer and I asked her if she had a boyfriend. Only now Mike gave me a look like I was being a jerk.

"Actually," she said, as her dead eye edged sideways, "we broke up." She said this so simply it was hard to know how she felt. She might as well have been describing the irregular orbit of the planet Neptune.

"Wow," said Mike.

"It's been coming for a while—we went in different directions."

"You went east, specifically," I said, trying to be funny.

"Yeah," she said.

"You're better off without him," I told her.

"Still, it's a drag," said Mike.

"Thanks," she said.

"Yeah," I said, "it *is* a drag."

"Thanks," she said again, this time to the both of us, and she picked up her copy of *Gatsby* and turned it around in her hands. No one said anything for what seemed like forever, which made my saying her breakup was a drag seem even more of a lie than it actually was. In my mind what Jennifer is doing at that moment is making up her mind between us, pinning us mentally to the front of the paperback, comparing us like Gatsby and Tom maybe, weighing her options.

"Want to go with me?" said Mike.

"With you?"

"I mean, to the dance." I thought he was joking, going to take it all back a moment later after she agreed—but he didn't. He sat very still and waited to see what she was going to say.

"You don't have to do this," she said.

"Do what?"

"Don't feel sorry for me."

"Then it's a date. I'll come get you at seven." The last word he said as Bogart: "*sheven*."

After school, in the library basement, I asked if he was serious about Jennifer. I was repairing one of the oldest films in the collection, a five-minute black-and-white from the 1930s about an extinct Ohio snake. Mike was there with me, but doing nothing at all. Not jumping in and out of the bomb shelter, not rambling on about aliens, just sitting there.

"What do you mean, serious?"

"You know what I mean."

"It's not like we're getting married or anything."

"I don't really care," I told him. I kept my eyes on the film in front of me.

"You can go if you want," he said.

"I know that."

"I meant to the dance," he said. "You don't have to not come to the dance just because I've got a date."

"Well, I'm not going to go."

"You're the boss," he told me.

I threaded the film through the projector and then flipped the switch and the image of a garden snake, thin as a shoelace in black and white, leapt up onto the library wall. Neither of us spoke again until it was time to leave.

But in the end, I decided to go. I waited until the last minute, but then I went.

Not much happened until the last dance of the night, until "Stairway to Heaven" rolled around. I'd planted myself on the gym wall, watching them in the mirror ball half-light of the gym, and saw Jennifer laugh. Not flirting, exactly, but flicking her hair more than she usually did. I should have known something was up. This was the moment I was waiting for. My plan—when I think of it now, it's ridiculous, straight out of one of those crumbling movies—was to walk across the gym floor and ask to cut in like Fred Astaire. I'd have been kidding, but the mood would have been ruined. I didn't, though, just chickened out, and then watched, my back pressed against the wall, as they moved onto the dance floor. Almost right away they were making out. When the music stopped they kept holding hands and sort of drifted over toward where I was standing. It was a matter of acting cool. I kept thinking I was going to pass out, wishing for it really, but it didn't happen. They were holding hands and I said nothing about it and neither did either of them. When the dance was over the three of us got in Mike's Gremlin and drove to McDonald's and I went up and ordered two Big Macs and when I got back they were kissing in the booth. I gave Mike his fries and Jennifer her vanilla milkshake, then sat there eating one Big Mac after another. It was like it had been that way for a million years. Afterwards we drove by the library to see if we could see the door move, but it didn't. The three of us sat in the car and watched it, waiting, and then Mike said we might as well go home, that nothing was going to happen. He could feel it, he said. And he was right, as it turned out. After that night the library door stopped moving, for a little while at least.

Right then, Mike had less than a month to live.

This is the sort of thing real mourners do, Dr. Kasoff has told me. You count back from the date, as if there's some moment when he might have told you where he was going. Or *that* he was going.

It's not something you can stop, according to Dr. Kasoff, but you can know you're doing it. You can remind yourself that it is the past. That there's nothing you can do now that Mike is gone and you're sitting on that bench and watching Jennifer doing her donut-girl stuff. What there is, Dr. Kasoff is always telling me, is the present. I guess that means I should go in and thank Jennifer for saving my life the other day in a really ironic and at the same time very sincere way.

I'm just about to do that when I see my father walking down Lee Road toward me, looking like he's got something important to say. So I sit back down, and a moment later he's there, asking if that's Mike's Jennifer in the donut store.

I say I guess.

"Go in, talk to her," he says.

"Maybe later."

"You miss one hundred percent of the shots you don't take."

It's actually a wise thing to say. He sounds like Dr. Kasoff, who is always comparing the game of life to the game of basketball—only for my father, it's hockey.

"I don't want it to look like I'm stalking her." I tell him about the other day. I don't say how many donuts I ate exactly before passing out, but he gets the idea.

"If she knew anything about lifesaving," he says after a moment, "the first thing she'd have done is clear the airway.

And that would have meant her getting that donut you were eating out of your mouth to begin with. Any girl who does that and still kisses you is worth holding on to."

I change the subject. "What about you? Is Uncle Marco right, have you found anything?"

"I don't know if *found* is the right word. Nothing conclusive, let's say."

"Anything at all?"

"Why don't you take a look for yourself."

"What do you mean?"

"Come with me tonight, behind the fence."

I can't tell if he's asking me for help or if there's something he wants to show me.

"You mean it?"

"That other day you were looking for something, I could tell. I saw you leaning on the fence. You're still on the case."

"I used to bring a camera, every day. In case I saw something."

"I know."

"How do you know?"

"I saw you. Listen, I'll get you tonight. All right? After everyone's asleep." He's about to get up and go when, inside the Amy Joy Donuts store, Jennifer's new boyfriend, a tall guy who's parked his tow truck outside, goes up and kisses her. "That's not good," he says, "but it's not the end of the world. When I met your mother, she was married to God." He walks back down Lee Road, and I watch him slide under the fence surrounding the library ruins, walk quickly in and then disappear somewhere, like he's burrowed under the rubble.

I go back to the grocery store after that and actually order the cake. The nihilistic baker girl gets out a yellow pad and takes my name and number. She does this with a really grim expression on her face, like she's preparing to take down the details of my last will and testament. I decide she's better looking than I thought, wonder if maybe she's changed the colour of her hair.

She says, "Let's talk cake."

"Chocolate," I tell her. "With chocolate icing, a slab."

"And what on it?"

"Icing?"

"What kind of cake place do you think this is? Of course icing. Icing is a given. I mean in the word department. What do you want me to write on it?"

"Mike," I say. Then, as if I'm changing my mind about it, I say, "Michael Morrison."

"You want your brother's *last* name on the cake too?"

"What do other people do?"

"How about *Happy Birthday*?"

"Maybe not," I tell her.

I think she's going to tell me that I have to have *Happy Birthday* on it, but she doesn't. I can tell she likes the idea, that you'd order a birthday cake and leave that part of it off. And it's then that I invite her to the party.

"You serious?"

"It must be depressing to have to make these cakes all the time, to see the people head out the door and never get to go to the parties."

"I'll think about it," she says. And then looks at me like she's mulling it over. She presses the gold stud in her tongue pensively against the back of her bottom teeth.

The last time I saw my brother it was the Friday after Halloween. Two nights before the explosion.

There was a big party some kid from school was throwing, so we'd brought our costumes with us to change into after we finished our shift at the library. Mike was going as Bogart and I was going as a vampire—something with a cape, anyway. As on every Friday, Mike and I were the only ones working, which meant that instead of being down in the basement we were up on the main floor in case anyone came in and wanted to sign out a book. Outside a wet snow was falling, and because there was no one in the library we were sitting out on the front steps, the two of us smoking. This is Mike the last time I saw him: a high-school senior sick of Cleveland Heights and ready for his life to begin. And because he's waiting, so am I. Whatever we are waiting for, we're waiting together. I see all that differently now, though. Now I think we both found ourselves thrown over the side of the same boat and then had to tread water near each other. Sitting on those library steps that night, I was about to find that out.

He was flicking the ashes of his smoke into an empty Fanta can, turning the head of the cigarette slowly around on its metal top to get off the ash. Smoking was part of Mike's rebellion, his mutineer status, a clear indication to our parents and the rest of the world that he was master of his own destiny. Cigarettes cause cancer and he was hoping to die young, it didn't bother him one bit, he used to say.

Mike already had his Bogart hat on, and was starting to talk like Bogart, which is what he planned to do for the rest of the night. "Here's looking at you, kid," he said, lighting up another.

That's when Jennifer McKellar pulled up in front of the library. She was driving her father's car, some kind of Porsche.

"Hey," she said, getting out of the car. Both her dead eye and her good eye planted themselves on Mike. "Can I bum a smoke?"

"Since when do you smoke?" said Mike.

"Since when do I smoke?" she asked him back. It was a kind of game. They were flirting. "Since now," she told him. Then she winked her dead eye at him. "So," she said, her hand outstretched, "smoke me?"

He tapped one out for her, expertly, with his index finger, the way he had practised it in the library basement using pencils. Then he lit it for her, with his Zippo, opening the lighter up and flashing it into flame in one fluid movement. "Here's looking at you, kid," he told her, the same thing he'd said to me a second earlier, and it seemed so rehearsed, so planned out that it made me wonder if this was what he'd been doing those nights in the library, listening to the footsteps of Mary or the cops right above him. It made me sad to think of him there, wanting that desperately to get out, to be something he wasn't. But as sad as that made me, it made me sadder still to think that, in the end, he'd got the girl. The two of them were already a confirmed couple by that time, had been seen by everyone kissing at the dance, and after that making out in the hallways of Heights High, in the smoking area, before class. I went on thinking that it was all a mistake, the way books in a library sometimes get put back in the wrong place and no one knows for years. I had this idea that Jennifer would eventually take me aside to tell me so. I'd be patient, I was prepared to say, I was willing to wait for as long as it took.

"Nice hat," she said, blowing a thin stream of smoke out from between her teeth.

He introduced himself the way Bogart does it at the beginning of *The Big Sleep.* "I'm a Seamus," he told her. "A private detective."

"Seamus is actually a form of James," I said. "It's the Irish version."

"I'm Tiffany," she told us, standing up, turning around once to curtsy. She was already in costume, dressed as a stewardess with a short blue skirt that ended just above her knees, a blue American Airlines blazer, a white blouse and blue nylons with a line up the back. "Is there anything I can get you?" As she said this, she fluttered her eyelashes, and her dead eye looked out straight toward us, as if it had just received some shocking news.

Mike took a drag on his smoke and exhaled.

"This uniform used to be my mother's," she told us, maybe because she knew we were both checking her out. She didn't mind. "She was a model, and that's how she got it. I've got a copy of one of the magazines that ran it, for American Airlines. She's supposed to be handing out drinks on a transatlantic flight to Paris. That's what the photographer told her, told her the photograph wasn't going to be any good if she didn't think about Paris. I said why Paris, why not Des Moines? That's a good city."

"It's American Airlines, after all," said Mike.

"I guess," she said. "But still, it's just a picture. It's not like anyone knows."

Mike nodded, looked down the street introspectively. "You should be a model," he told her. When she laughed, tried to act like he was just saying that, he went on. "Seriously, you're way too beautiful—too cool—to spend your life in a place like this."

"Who's this?" said Jennifer, still in her stewardess role. Maybe Mike's getting all serious had embarrassed her.

"I'm Tiffany," I replied for some reason. It was out of my mouth before I could stop it.

The two of them nearly killed themselves laughing.

"Tiffany Morrison," said Mike. "He's actually in drag right now. That's really a girl."

"I'll tell you what," Jennifer said. "They've got a *Kate* Morrison in Australia. She's some kind of explorer."

"No kidding," said Mike.

"How can she be an explorer?" I asked. "What does she explore?"

"Caves, things like that."

"I only know about it because one of the girls I went to school with in Jersey is from there. It's all she talked about. How one day she was going to make a million bucks and go be Kate Morrison, go spelunking."

Mike laughed.

"That's actually what they call it."

"Do you like caves?" he asked her, out of nowhere.

"I guess. What do you mean?"

"Just what I said, are you the sort of girl who's into caves?"

"I suppose I am," she said, not knowing what he was asking her, sounding nervous about it. Instead of answering, she flipped back into her stewardess character. "I suppose you could say I don't really have that much experience with caves." Her dead eye glared at the sky.

"Want to see something really freaky?" he asked her.

"How freaky?"

"It's in the basement."

"Where, here?"

He nodded, then put out his smoke in the top of the Fanta can, like he was getting ready to take her inside.

"On a scale of one to ten," she said, "how freaky?"

"Don't do it," I heard myself say. "Don't take her down there."

That stopped her. "Down where?" she asked, looking at me.

"Follow me," Mike told her, standing up. "Right this way."

"Don't do it," I said. "This is wrong."

"What are you talking about?" said Jennifer.

"Nothing's wrong," said Mike smoothly, suddenly not himself but Bogart again. "Tiffany here is on her period, and is having a hissy fit. Maybe she needs to lie down for a bit."

"Maybe *you* need to lie down," I said lamely.

"What's going on?" said Jennifer.

"Shouldn't you be putting on your white powder and lipstick?" Mike said to me.

All at once Jennifer seemed to change her mind about being there at all. She'd got scared, I guess, thinking Mike was going to get her to do something really horrible. "I better go," she said, "I'll catch up with you guys later." She reached over and picked up the can, dropping the rest of her cigarette through the opening at the top and went down and got back in her father's expensive car. She was about to drive away, but then rolled down the automatic window. "I'm going to Grace's, she's having a thing, see you there," she called to Mike, and a moment later she was driving away.

"What is wrong with you?" Mike said to me.

"With me?"

"You acted like a total head case." He flicked his lighter a couple of times. "Like a psycho."

"That's right," I said. "I'm the psycho."

"Are you really that jealous?"

"I never wanted to have anything to do with this, with that bomb shelter or whatever the fucking thing is. Don't you get that? I hate it—I've always hated it."

"There are other ways to be a dickhead than making it sound like I'm a serial killer. She's not going to talk to either of us again."

"I wasn't trying to do anything," I told him.

"You're always such a good boy, James James."

"Seriously," I told him, "shut up."

"Or what, you're going to break my arm again? Give it your best shot, champ, come on." He got up off the step and stood in front of me.

I got up myself. *Breathe*, I told myself, *do not look at him*. "Come on," I said as I stood there unsteadily. "Let's go."

He looked at me and changed his mind. "Forget this," he said, and turned.

"Come on," I said. "Where are you going?"

He was headed around to the back of the building, to where he'd parked his car.

"Go ahead," I told him. "Put on your stupid hat and get out of here."

"Just so you know, Jimmy," Mike said, turning back. His face was red. "There's no one making you be such a complete jerk-off. You're doing it to yourself."

"I hope Dad catches you, I really do," I told him.

"Me too," he said, and after that he disappeared around the corner.

I stayed on the steps and a moment later he drove out of the parking lot, stopping for just a second before turning onto Lee Road. He didn't look back at me. I got up and picked up the Fanta can, about to take it inside, but then I threw it, hard, into the big glass window at the front of the library. I braced for the sound of shattering glass, but there was nothing. The can hit the window and bounced off, nearly soundlessly.

I left it there on the ground and went downstairs, locking the door behind me. I climbed down into the bomb shelter and lay down on one of the beds and thought about how one day, maybe soon, Mike and I were going to stop speaking to each other. "Fine with me," I said out loud to the empty room, and concentrated on the weird pockmarked texture of the old ceiling, white paint on old brick.

That would turn out to be the only time I was ever in there alone. Mike's Walkman was there and like always, it was running out of batteries. I listened to Bryan Adams sing about the summer of '69 at half speed, getting his first real six-string and playing it until his fingers bled, then turned it off. After that I walked home and went to bed. Everyone, even my parents and little Petey, was out at some Halloween thing. I must have fallen asleep because the next thing I knew it was past one in the morning. Mike had come home and I could hear him downstairs flipping channels, getting up finally and going into the kitchen. The fridge door opened and shut. And in the background I could hear *Family Ties* ending, that song by Johnny Mathis they play while the credits roll.

You were supposed to think that everyone on the show—Alex and Mallory and the rest of the Keatons—were all clinging to each other even if they hated each other at some point in every episode. And that it was the same for you. You and your whole family were all tied together, no matter how much you pissed each other off. That's what the song was about—it was about everybody watching, families or parts of them, all parked in front of the TV. Only the show wasn't really asking you to think about it, what you would do without each other, not really. There is no way that you're supposed to hear that song and start thinking what it'd actually be like if your family completely wrecked itself. To think about it actually happening. One thing was for sure about those Keatons, none of them were getting sick or old. Even if one of them managed to die of something, they'd all be there to watch, to say a lot of profound and cool and brave things to each other while holding hands. There'd be no explosions and the cops would not be involved. Maybe a cop would drive someone home, but that's as bad as it could get. And even if the wheels did fall all the way off the way it did for the Morrison family of Cleveland Heights, Ohio, the Keatons would always have those reruns of *Family Ties* to watch and see the way they all looked together.

Mike died two days later. You know the rest, the facts anyway. I don't have the details. Not then, and not now. According to the cops a videotape of him surfaced, buying a six of Rolling Rock on the day of the explosion in a variety store in Garfield Heights, another suburb about ten miles away, where he must have known he could get served. The last time anyone saw him it was Sunday and he was walking down Coventry, buying a tape from a guy at Record Revolution who called *Nineteen Action News* after seeing Mike's picture on television. *Disintegration,* by the Cure. I don't know about Jennifer, if they were together then, but when he bought that album she wasn't with him. The next night Mike must have waited until I was asleep and taken off for the library, leaving his Gremlin in the driveway. I thought it was on purpose, a way of throwing my father off, a thickening of the plot.

That whole time, I hated him completely.

GIVE ME SHELTER

My father and I leave for the explosion site a little after one in the morning. He comes into my room and shakes me awake. It's just like the night of the explosion, an awful replay—like someone's spliced the past onto the present and now I have to watch it all again, caught in a loop. I follow him downstairs and my father and I sneak out of our own house as if it's not ours. As if the two of us have broken into a house that looks exactly like ours but isn't and now, for some reason, have to escape from it.

We get into his station wagon and soon we're at Cedar and Lee, the intersection where we were stopped just before the library exploded, where I told him it was Mike inside the library all those times. We wait for the light to change and I know he's thinking the same thing, because he asks again what we did down there, Mike and I, in the bomb shelter.

I tell him about the canned water, and how it made me sick.

He laughs at that, or pretends to, and then we're pulling onto Lee Road, parking in front of the tall fence. He leads the way, a flashlight in his hand, and shows me how to slip under the fence near where the back of the building used to be. Behind us is the DeSilva house, all of the lights out. I wonder if Frank is inside, watching us, if he's thinking about calling the cops the way Mary did that night. We walk past the decimated remains of the old reference section, past stray and shattered blocks of concrete where the circulation desk used to be, and at last into what's left of the bomb shelter.

It looks nothing like it did, the two beds carted away like trash, along with the stacks of canned water. The only thing that's the same is the cold, cave-like walls. It's like a tomb now, but it was like a tomb before. My father squats down on a fallen beam and picks up some rubble, a few stray stones. He turns them over in his hands as he starts to talk, letting the white dust slip through his fingers. "You know, Jimmy," he tells me, "I was fairly convinced he'd done it—that Mike had blown it up."

I admit I'd wondered the same thing, for a little while. It was impossible not to.

"No," he says, "I didn't wonder, I was sure of it. I've spent months trying to prove it, trying to pin it on Mike—on the both of you—somehow. I had to be the one that found out if it was. I couldn't have some cop coming to tell me it was you and Mike after all. I couldn't have taken that. I searched your room, Mike's car, even called Jennifer, though she didn't know it was me. I came up with nothing, and even then I didn't give up. What kind of bomb would he have been able to make, I wondered, and where would he put it, to do that kind of damage?"

I'm afraid of what he might say next.

"But it wasn't him—it wasn't anyone," he's saying. "It's impossible to produce that kind of explosion with a bomb." He smiles to himself. "No, Frank was right, this was a gas explosion. An old pipe and a slow build—way down deep near the front of the building, directly under the front doors."

"So you found the cause?"

"I narrowed it down to two places, two possibilities, but I'm guessing really. And that's as close as I'm likely to get."

"Is that what you're going to show me?"

"Show you?" he says, confused. "There's nothing down there anymore to see even if we could get down. The explosion took care of that. But that's the thing—even when I figured that was how it happened, I wondered if you, if the two of you, were to blame for being down there all the time. What'd Mike call it, the bomb shelter? That's not what it was. They stored coal there, in the thirties. Someone put beds down there, covered it up. I wondered if you'd done something to set it off by being down there, broken into a pipe, even stolen some, taken them out and sold the copper for extra money, I don't know. I thought a lot of things."

"We watched movies," I say, and then can't think of anything else to tell him.

"It doesn't matter, does it."

"What about the explosion—who caused it?" This is the question I've been wanting to ask my father for months.

He stares up at me and I see he's about to tell me the truth. "When you use gas, this is the sort of thing that can happen."

"So what now?"

"Now, nothing. These were old pipes, down deep. Whose fault is that?"

"Who put the pipes down there?"

"I think your uncle could make a case out of anything."

"So, then, you're done with the investigation?"

"I'm not going to lie to a judge, no matter what your uncle says about the poor and wretched of the earth deserving their pound of flesh."

"Doesn't the gas company have to replace the pipes?"

"You can always go further." He shakes his head. "I could spend the next fifty years doing this, and probably at the end, I'd think the same thing."

I can't tell if that's true or not. "So you're giving up."

And suddenly he wraps his hand around his eyes like a blindfold and his bottom lip begins to tremble. "I'm sorry," he says. "I'm so sorry I thought it was you—I wanted it to be." When I start to speak he gets up and walks back up the bomb shelter stairs. He slips under the fence and crosses the road quickly and I have to almost run to keep up. I want to say something, but I don't know what. We drive home in silence, me watching both of his hands on the wheel, and I wonder if he really believes it, if that's really why he brought me here, because he's trying to bring himself around to the idea that there's no one to blame and nothing anyone could have done.

It took a few days, but eventually the police showed up to ask me about Mike. There were two of them, a uniformed officer and a detective in a cheap brown suit. "I'm Dennis Moore," said the guy in the suit, the detective. He had short reddish hair and glasses that were a little too big for his face. A second later, he corrected himself. "Detective Dennis Moore, I mean to say."

The uniformed cop cleared his throat, like he wanted to get down to business. "What we're doing here," he told me, "is a missing person report."

I didn't know what to say to that.

"Now in police work," said the cop, "when people don't think someone is missing, they're surprised when they get told a missing person report is being filled out."

I said: "My uncle's a lawyer."

Detective Moore said he knew Uncle Marco. "You can involve him if you want, I can't tell you not to."

"Should I?" I felt stupid asking, the kind of thing Bogart would never do. Asking the cop if I should call my lawyer.

"I don't think there's any reason to contact him," said the detective.

"But this is your decision," said the cop. He was looking at me carefully.

I said it was okay.

"What we want to know," said the cop, "is if your brother, Michael Morrison, has communicated with you in any way since the explosion."

The detective watched me not reply.

"We believe he was inside the library at the time of the explosion and that he was the person Mary DeSilva saw inside the building that night, and which prompted her to call your house."

"What we want to know," said the cop, "is has he talked to you since then?"

I shook my head. "I don't know where he is," I said.

"We can pull the phone records," the cop warned. "I can get the phone records right here on this desk in an hour."

"I have nothing to hide," I said. I could feel myself starting to sweat, the moisture on my back creeping under the elastic of my underwear.

"That's good," said the detective. Eventually he went on. "I had the opportunity to talk to your friend Mary quite a bit, as you know, in connection with the break-ins a month before and I wonder if there's any light you can shed on that."

I told them about the bomb shelter, the rest of it. "But not that night," I said, the way I tried to tell Frank the morning after. "That night it was a real break-in."

The detective was taking notes.

"I'm going to ask you one last time," said the cop. "Have you had any contact with your brother?"

"Is he dead?" It seemed impossible, a wild thing to say, and I expected them to tell me that. But they didn't. "He can't be dead," I insisted. "My mother saw him, after."

"We've spoken to your mother," Detective Moore told me, and went on to say they'd recovered from the rubble the remains of someone who they knew was not Mary. A second body. They couldn't say yet if it was Mike or not, but it was a possibility. They had yet to rule it out. Maybe Mike had got out of the building in time and was in hiding. These are the things that kids do all the time, Detective Moore explained, they don't think things out to the end, and then they find themselves in the middle of something.

"What about my mother?"

"We think your mother is telling the truth—she thinks she saw him." But it was strange that only she'd seen him. They'd dealt with parental hallucinations before, of course, Detective Moore said, with parents thinking their dead kids had come back somehow, but my mother had seen Mike before she knew—before she could have known—he was missing. Maybe she knew something else—what that might be they didn't know—and maybe it was that that weighed on her, made her think he'd been there.

"This is why we're talking to you," said the cop. "Anything you can tell us, this is the time."

"She spoke to him," I said, again. "He was there. I was on the phone with her."

"But did you speak to him?" asked Detective Moore.

I said I hadn't. "But there was someone there, I'm sure of it."

"Maybe it was noises in the next room," said the cop. "It could have been anything—"

"The fact is we don't know," Detective Moore said, cutting the cop off. "What we think is that your brother went home after the explosion, and now he's hiding out somewhere. We know there's been a history of that, you said so yourself—and we want you to talk to him."

"You want me to talk to him?"

"We want you to go on television," said the detective. "Try sending him a message."

And so I have my moment on TV, the moment everyone seems to have seen, even though the ratings show hardly anyone watches local news programs.

"I'm Jim Morrison," I told the camera, "from Cleveland Heights, Ohio." And the next moment I crumbled down like a bag of hammers, like the sound of the word *boom.*

A few hours after that, they found my brother. Or at least enough of him to know it was him, under the rubble right at the very front of the library, as if he'd been just opening the door at the time of the explosion. Specifically they found Mike's arm—the right one, the one I'd broken—and that was how they knew. The two breaks were in exactly the same place. They showed up at the house and Detective Moore gave the news to my parents. Sat the two of them down and handed it over like the pure fact it was.

DIVER'S MASK

It's almost eleven thirty and I'm waiting in the hallway with the Mothers. Jenna is asking me about the birthday party. "So," she says, "it's for your *older* brother?"

"It's my mother's idea."

Ellen looks at Jenna, and Jenna looks at me like she's trying to think of how to put it.

"It's a vigil," says Karen. "Am I right? This is your idea of a vigil?"

"A memorial service," says Debbie.

"There's going to be a cake," I point out.

"But your brother is dead," Jenna observes. "I hate to be blunt like that, but it's true. I mean, this is a birthday party for a person who has passed away."

"In some cultures," says Moira, "it's believed that the dead move among the living."

"Not this culture," says Jenna.

"What Jenna's saying is," says Ellen, "are people bringing presents?"

Finally, the door to the classroom opens and Mrs. Dumme sends out the children. As Petey comes out, Brittany, the daughter of badly permed Karen, grabs his diving mask.

"Let go," says Petey.

But she doesn't. Instead, she pulls, and Petey pulls back,

and the strap breaks. The children go careening in opposite directions, and Petey falls backward toward the wall and he stays there, on the ground, slumped, holding the mask and staring at the torn strap.

"Go tell Petey you're sorry," Karen tells Brittany.

Brittany doesn't move.

"She broke it," I say.

"She didn't *mean* to break it," says Karen.

"She grabbed it, and she didn't let go."

"Brittany," says Karen, "tell Petey you're sorry."

Brittany doesn't move.

"Put some tape over the back of it," says Karen. "It'll be good as new."

"I doubt it," I say, though too petulantly, as though it's *my* diver's mask.

"It's just a diver's mask," she says. "You can buy another—I'll buy you another, if that'll make it better."

"Brittany." Mrs. Dumme is kneeling down in front of the little girl. "Now be a good girl and tell Petey you're sorry."

Brittany walks over to Petey, but still doesn't say anything. While she's standing there silently, looking at Petey in morose, stubborn silence, he stands up. It makes me wonder if Mike's death has turned him into a four-year-old with unbelievably sound ethical principles, if he's about to perform some sort of formal rite of absolution. Maybe give her a blessing.

Instead, he hits her with the mask. The whole thing happens in cartoonish slow motion: one moment Petey is standing there serenely, nearly monkish in his composure, and the next he's raising the mask over his head, bringing the glass front of it down, hard, on top of her head. The Mothers collectively let loose with a wail, as if they've just been informed that their families have gone down in a plane crash. Before I can move, Mrs. Dumme has grabbed Petey, pulling him toward her in a straitjacket sort of hug, pinning his arms against his sides.

A hush falls over the room as the Mothers and Mrs. Dumme wait to see what I'm going to do. Even I'm waiting to see what I'm going to do. The fact is, I've seen enough in that preschool hallway to know that the great grey area of parenting, the chapter that has been *completely* left out of every parenting book, is the one about what you should do when another person's kid hits yours—and the other person doesn't do anything. I know that I should chew Petey out, scream my head off, maybe turn him over my knee and beat the crap out of him. That this is what the Mothers would do. In the preschool world of crime and punishment, extenuating circumstances only count for so much: it's one thing to grab another kid's diver's mask and break the strap; it's another thing for the kid with the broken diver's mask to use it in an attempt to bludgeon the first kid. I should be screaming at him, should have done it already, but I haven't. And I'm not going to. Maybe if I'd told my father about Mike and the bomb shelter he'd still be alive, maybe if I'd shown Mary the bomb shelter like I wanted to, we'd all be working our regular shifts this weekend. There are things I could have done, and I know that.

But it's too late. All I can do now is stand up for Petey.

So that's what I do.

"She had it coming," I say. "Brittany should have kept her hands off that mask."

Karen glares at me. "What did you say?"

"I think you heard me."

The Mothers are all watching and now the hallway is silent while I wait to see what Karen will say. From inside the church above us I hear a single chime signalling the half-hour, that it's exactly 11:30 a.m., at least according to God.

"That's it?" says Karen. She's talking to Mrs. Dumme, and to the other Mothers as well. She expects them to do something, to intervene. "Isn't someone going to do something?"

"The Jimmy is right," says Ioana. "The girl, she should not be grabbing the mask. Petey was provoked."

"Pro*voked*?" sputters Karen. "I see. Now I'm the one getting the lecture."

"No one's getting a lecture," says Mrs. Dumme as she lets go of Petey.

"That's right," I tell her. "If this was a lecture, I'd have a blazer and an overhead. I'd be standing at a podium and you'd be taking notes."

Karen looks from Mrs. Dumme to the Mothers, then back to Mrs. Dumme. While she's doing that, I take Petey by the hand and we march out together.

"I don't get the thing about the podium and the overhead," says Vivian that evening. "Were you *trying* to be funny?"

"The important thing," my father tells me, "is you stood up for your brother."

"What is this again?" asks Petey, pushing around his plate a piece of grey meat that smells like dish detergent.

"It's leg of lamb," says Vivian.

"For fuck's sake," says Petey.

"What did he say?" my father asks.

"It's something he picked up at school," I tell him.

"He picked up *that* at school?"

"Was the note-taking a metaphor?" Vivian asks me. "Because even if it was, I still don't get it."

"I hope there's no actual detergent in this recipe," says my father, holding up a forkful of grey meat.

"Can I have a cookie?" asks Petey.

"No," says my father. "Eat your dinner."

"Maybe just one," I tell him.

"I'm the father here," insists my father, but changes his mind almost right away, as if all at once he's realized he doesn't really care. "Go ahead, Petey," he says. "One or two, but that's it."

Then we just sit there with our weird food, like astronauts in our private capsules of sadness.

When dinner's over I walk down Lee Road to Amy Joy Donuts, where I see Jennifer McKellar sitting at one of the picnic tables behind the building with her new boyfriend. They're not far from the grassy spot where Jennifer kissed me. The guy is standing with his arm around her, but really it's just his hand on her neck, like a collar. I don't want to go over and talk to them, but she waves and that means I have no choice. I wonder if what she wants me to do is bring up the fact that she kissed me, if she's trying to get me into some kind of brawl with this other guy. The kind of fight where he almost kills me and she nurses me back to health, and then she either decides to marry me or informs me after my recovery that she's sorry but she loves the guy who beat me up. The parking lot lights are on. There are cars on the street now; kids come up from Case Western to go to the bars, and Jennifer and her new boyfriend look like they're part of the scene, like they belong there and belong together.

"This is Anthony," Jennifer says. Her dead eye is pointed inward, as if it's trying to get a good look at her nose.

"Hey," I say.

He nods, barely looking at me.

"Jimmy's the guy who passed out the other day," Jennifer tells him.

I'm nervous that he knows that, and wonder what else she's told him. But Anthony shrugs, like she's just said it's a national holiday in a country he's never heard of. He looks at least twenty and is a little taller than me, with a dirty peach-fuzz moustache and a lot of random stubble on his chin. He's still in his tow-truck-driver uniform, which has his name embroidered over the right pocket. The big zipper that runs down the middle of it is unzipped, and I can see the upper part of his chest, and from just that I can tell he must work out a lot.

"He's Mike's brother," she tells him. "Mike, my ex, you know."

"That Mike?" says Anthony, and looks at me for the first time. "Sorry about that, kid."

I hate it that he calls me kid.

"Man," Anthony goes on, "that must have been a complete drag."

I say, "Right."

Now we have this moment when he feels all bummed. It's okay, though, because I'm suddenly overcome with gut-wrenching anguish. It makes me feel like a fake because I know he's just pretending. That he doesn't know anything about Mike.

"I mean, if it had been one of my brothers—not that any of them have ever even been in a library—I'd have lost it."

It's starting to piss me off that he's not more of a jerk.

"I heard about how you freaked out at school."

"I didn't freak out."

He gives a half-shrug. "Someone told me that, anyway."

I want to ask him if it's Jennifer who said that. "I'm taking a leave of absence."

"Kid," he says, "I'd have done the same thing." A moment later, he says, "Jesus," except in a really introspective, really intense way.

I continue to stand there. "Anyway," I break the silence, "I've got my own room now."

It takes him a second, but Anthony puts it together I'm joking. It's an awful thing to say, a stupid joke, but Anthony cracks up and so does Jennifer, which is what people do when someone who they know is wrecked with grief says anything even *remotely* funny. When you make a joke, even if it's not funny, everything comes pouring out of them all at once, like you're the most hilarious guy in the world. They're laughing so hard I keep going with it, saying I got his clothes, his video camera, his Walkman, even the dead batteries inside it.

"You know," he says, "you're okay, John, you're all right."

"It's Jim, actually," Jennifer tells him. She looks apologetically at me.

He nods, then shakes his head. He can't speak because he's cracking up so hard, like he really might burst an internal organ if he's not careful. Jennifer's stopped laughing now and is standing there while her good eye looks at me in a worried way. Her dead eye is looking down, in the direction of my feet though not exactly at my feet, as if it can't bring itself to look directly at my sneakers. It's like her dead eye *wants* to look at my sneakers but doesn't want my sneakers to know.

I bring up the birthday party as if it might just be the whole reason I've come over to talk to them. I say I ordered the cake myself, just blurt it out like it's some huge accomplishment. "It'd be great if you came," I tell them, speaking mostly to Anthony. "It'd be just great if we could have the new couple there." And then I feel like I'm falling through myself, a shallow heart-stopping bungee jump of a dive.

The idea of the birthday party makes Anthony laugh even harder. He asks me if I want to hang out. There's a party going on at some kid's place over on Fairmount, and he's got some beers in the back of his tow truck. We could score some weed, really hang out. I tell him no, I've got to get home because my little brother will get me up early the next day, hungover or not. Then I walk into the donut store. I head straight to the bathroom, and just manage to get there before the tears start. Huge, wheezing sobs, and I can't stop it. Jennifer comes into the men's room and she stands there until I'm finished. She puts her hand on my forehead, a cool hand like she's my mother, or thinks she can cure me, and I close my eyes. We stand there for a bit and I don't mind it at all, even if it's a bathroom and she's not my girlfriend. Her dead eye looks at itself in the mirror, or maybe at the two of us standing there. She starts telling me how Anthony isn't a bad guy, how after Mike died she freaked and started hanging out at Parnell's, that Irish pub next to the movie theatre where they'll serve anyone. That's where she met him, she says, and one thing led to another. I stop her from telling me anything else by saying he seems like an all-right guy. She nods like I'm just being nice, like I don't mean it. We're standing there looking at each other, and I'm just about to ask her about that last night at the library with Mike when she says she has to go. She gets straight out of there as quickly as she can.

MORBID

It's the weekend, and Petey's at the zoo with my parents. My mother's going to the zoo is Dr. Kasoff's idea, part of his new campaign to get her—to get both my parents, I suppose—out of the house and back into the world of normal people. It's not easy for my father, who, since our late-night visit to the library ruins, seems to have entered his own listless zombie-like period. Today, just as they were about to leave, my mother made an elaborate show of not being able to find a good enough hat, telling my father and Petey to just go without her. When he heard that, my father sat down on the couch, admitted he didn't want to go himself, and if she felt that way they might as well call it off, no matter what Dr. Kasoff said. If it hadn't been for Petey bursting into tears, they might have stayed home. Five minutes later, they were out the door.

Once they're gone and I remember Vivian is out with Grant, there washes over me the feeling of limitless possibility that comes with being alone in the house. I think of finding some booze, blaring the stereo, going through closets and drawers I'm supposed to stay out of. But only for a second. It's times like these when I miss Mike most, when his being gone hits me like a frigid wave. He'd always have some scheme, some project, some obsession he wanted to drag me into, something else to do.

He owned a copy of *War and Peace* with the pages cut out of the middle, to hide cigarettes where my father wouldn't find them.

Once, he ate a spider.

He knew strange and arcane facts, like that Mozart and Davy Crockett were both alive on the planet at the same time, which suggested he had snuck books from the library and read them in secret.

His favourite animal was the Gila monster.

His favourite movie was *The Wizard of Oz* because of that moment when the Wicked Witch of the West dies. Most people think she dies saying that she's melting, which she sort of does. But at the very end, when she's almost entirely collapsed into a small black puddle, she says, "What a world," as she and her particular fate converge. Mike said that was the best line in any movie, ever, because you thought that you knew the whole story about the Wicked Witch when really you didn't.

I suppose you could say that Mike exerted too much influence on me. When he declared Pink Floyd his favourite band, I sang "Another Brick in the Wall" as loudly as I could, in the shower, in my room, at the breakfast table, at the door, and when my mother asked me what I was singing I repeated the words unflinchingly, telling her plainly that I don't need no education. When Mike took to dressing all in black I did the same, and when he got his left ear pierced I thought about doing it too. But I only went halfway and bought a clip-on stud, a tiny metal fastener that wrapped around the outside of my ear and hurt like hell.

With everyone gone I just sit around the house, turn the TV on and off, and eventually go and sit out in Mike's car again. To make it look like I'm working on the car, I try to pop the hood, pull the lever inside the car, then get out and try to find the latch, reaching under with my fingers. I think I've got it at one point, but it's still latched, so I try again, and that's when Uncle Marco's BMW pulls up in the driveway, like he works for triple-A and is arriving to give me some on-the-spot automotive assistance. He gets out of the car quickly, comes over to me. I'm in the process of fabricating an excuse, about to tell him I've been reading up on automotive repair, when he tells me that they're going to pave over the explosion site and turn it into a parking lot.

I tell him I don't believe it. "We would have heard."

"They don't have to tell us anything. This is a reliable source—they're putting in a goddamn parking lot."

I imagine it: a clean black pool of asphalt, the library gone and the bomb shelter filled in. And I realize I don't want to stop it. I want it to happen, for the last of the rubble to be put into a dump truck and carted away, the whole place levelled. It makes me think of the Mothers at the preschool, leading their happy normal lives, and of my ambition to lead one of my own, to have days that have nothing to do with tragedy or truth, or my dead brother.

"What's your father found out?"

I decide I might as well tell him what I know. Probably he knows it all already. "He's decided it was a gas leak."

"This is the gas company we're taking on?"

"He's not taking anyone on," I tell him. "There's not really a case."

"The fact is that your father is not a lawyer, that's not his side of things."

"He says you can make a case out of anything."

Marco doesn't react to this. Maybe he's heard it too many times. "Let's go down to his office."

"Down to his office?"

"I'm just going to look around," says Marco.

I tell him I don't know.

"You walk away and your father—no one—will know you were here, just leave the door open. You have my word on that, James."

"What are you going to do?"

"Let me tell you something, James," he says. His hand is on my back and he's walking me up the driveway, toward the house, guiding me inside. "I want you to know that this is the sort of thing that happens all the time."

I try to move away from him, but his arm is around me and he holds me there.

"People have shit happen to them, terrible shit, crazy, awful things. I don't need to tell you that. They lose an arm or a leg, an eye, or both eyes. They lose a son, like your father—or a brother. And they just—they just give up, accept it. You see it every day. They go to these shrinks and the shrinks sell them what they've got. And that's what's going on. Your father's caving, thinking it's okay that Mike is gone."

"He doesn't think it's okay, but he can't change it." I feel like Dr. Kasoff when I say this, like the next thing I should do is ask Marco how he feels about that.

"That's a good way to look at it, a healthy perspective," he tells me. "And anyone else, I'd say dust to dust and ashes to ashes. But your father's too good a man to let that happen to him, to give in to the shrinks and accept it. You've got to—*we've* got to—help him see that."

"I don't know."

"Just give me a chance to help him, that's all I'm asking."

I don't know what to do. That's what I tell him.

"I'm only going to look around down there," he assures me. "It's no big deal."

"All right," I say. It's Mike handing me that metallic water all over again.

Now Marco follows me inside, straight downstairs. My father's office takes up most of the basement of our house. There's a line of filing cabinets and a fax machine, and a long white L-shaped desk where his computer sits. In the centre of the room there's a table with three super-bright lights hanging over it, and spread out on the table are a series of photographs of the library, of its foundation, a cluster of pipes circled with a red marker.

Marco moves quickly; he knows where to find what he's looking for. "It's all here," he says, almost right away, though I don't know what he's talking about.

Upstairs, the sound of the door opening.

"They're home," I tell him. And it's the old feeling again of knowing something terrible is going to happen. That it's my fault.

"Don't worry," says Marco with excessive confidence. He walks upstairs, into the kitchen where my parents are. There's a moment when my father sees Marco and stares, as though Marco's a hallucination he can blink away.

"What's going on?" He says it not exactly angry, but in a weird way. Like he's still a bit of a zombie, still not quite awake.

"Nothing," my uncle tells him. "I was downstairs."

"You were downstairs?"

"It was just for a minute," I say.

"You should have called," my mother tells Marco. Even she's not oblivious to what's going on, senses something is wrong. She crosses the room to kiss Marco, then just as quickly seems to retreat, going over to the other side of the kitchen, standing next to the oven as if she wants to keep her distance.

"What were you doing in my office?"

Then Marco starts to talk, and as he does my father begins to move around the room, like he's coming out of his trance. Saying it makes no sense, this news about the parking lot. It does to my father what Marco knew it would—it causes him to wonder if he's given up too quickly on the case. Whoever it is who's bought the lot, says Marco, is moving quickly.

"Things like this don't just happen," says Marco. "I don't need to tell you that."

My father sits down at the table, his head in his hands, and Petey goes over to him, saying he's hungry.

"Petey," says Marco, "leave your father alone, he has to think."

"But I'm hungry," he says.

"Petey," says my father, distracted, "it's time for your bath."

"It's not. I have my bath at night, and after I put my pyjamas on."

"Maybe have your bath earlier," Marco suggests.

"I have dinner," says Petey, "and *then* my bath."

"Where's Vivian?" asks Marco. "Isn't dinner her thing?"

He looks at me, like I'm the manager of this low-end restaurant. I decide to join his protest. "Petey's right, we have to eat something."

My mother makes a sound. "I forgot," she says. "Vivian is at Grant's. She's having dinner with his parents tonight."

"When did this happen?" says my father.

"I told her I would make dinner—I can make spaghetti. How would that be?"

"We had spaghetti last night," says Petey.

"We can order something," says Marco. "I'll call."

"Is that what you were doing downstairs?" asks my father, again. "Trying to find something?"

"You need to let me do my job, Fort."

"Is this your job? Breaking and entering?"

"I hardly broke in," points out Marco.

On the other side of the kitchen, my mother is not listening. She's taking out a big pot and filling it with water, putting it on the stove.

"I don't need specifics at this point," Marco says. "What I need is for you to tell me what you've found and what you're thinking. Or there's nothing we'll be able to do about it. Once this starts, once they pave that place over, it's over. You know that as well as I do."

"I'm not going to lie," he tells my uncle.

Marco says, "You think people don't know you've been there, nosing around? That they've not seen you coming and going. You're making people nervous."

"What people?"

"If I knew that," Marco says, "we wouldn't be having this conversation. I don't have the details, and even if I did, it'd be no use."

"How much material did you take out of my office?"

"I was with him the whole time," I say. "He didn't take anything."

"You're a good boy, Jimmy," says my father, but he looks away. It's like I've just confessed to everything.

"We can take down the gas companies if we need to," Marco is saying. "We've done this sort of thing before and we'll do it again."

"I haven't found a thing," my father admits.

Marco says that doesn't matter. Of course he hasn't found anything—he's had such random, compromised access to the site. "At this stage you don't have to have the whole thing figured out. What I need is something plausible, a cause for further investigation. Let me put the tools in your hands."

"I'd have to lie, in other words."

"It would never come to that. The gas companies would settle before we get anywhere near a courtroom. They won't want any part of this—and the fact of the matter, I mean, you don't need me to tell you this, is that they should be more diligent, this should never have happened."

"Get out of this house," says my father.

Marco throws up his hands and goes to leave, but turns around. "I tried," he says, looking past me, at my mother. She doesn't turn around and so he says the same thing to me. "We tried, Jimmy, which is all we can do."

Over at the stove, my mother is putting pasta into the pot, though the water's not boiling yet. "Marco," she says, as he's turning to leave, "I still haven't heard who you'll be bringing to Mike's birthday."

My father bangs his fist down on the table. "Just leave the goddamn party out of it!" he explodes.

"For fuck's sake," Petey calls out. He thinks it's funny, the kind of thing that grown-ups say.

"Petey," says my father, turning on him in his confusion, "if you say that again, I'm taking your sharks away."

"No," he replies, "you can't do that."

"I can, and I will."

"I'm sorry, Daddy," says Petey. "I'm a good boy."

"And let me tell you something," he goes on, like he's going to straighten us all out once and for all, by God. "It's a morbid idea, this birthday party. A sick, horrible idea."

"Is that what you think?" It's like my mother is awake now. "It's not what you said to Dr. Kasoff last week. I don't know what to believe."

"You don't know what to believe? You're one to talk."

"What's that supposed to mean?" she says.

"It was the wrong thing to do, to lie that morning. You knew it was him in the library and you covered it up. I don't know what you thought you were doing, but you did it."

"How could I have known that?"

"You tell me," he says.

"Everyone calm down," Marco tells them both, still thinking there's a way he can talk my father into it. "We need to concentrate."

"Tell the truth," says my father, now standing in front of my mother. "Why don't you just admit it?"

"He was here!" she screams back at him, points at the table. "Right there."

"Do you still expect us to believe that? Do you think anyone ever did?"

My mother is rocking back and forth. "Blessed are the mourners," she says. "They will be comforted."

"See this?" says my father to Marco. "She's still protecting Mike."

"Mike is dead," says Petey, nearly to himself.

"That's right," says my father. "That's the truth. Tell your mother."

"Jesus, Fort," breaks in my uncle. "None of this is going to bring Mike back. What's done is done."

"Blessed are those who hunger and thirst after righteousness," says my mother. "They will be filled." And with that, she takes the uncooked pasta, the olive oil, even the colander, and throws it all into the garbage can under the sink. She doesn't seem angry or even sad, it's just the last straw. It seems my parents are finally having the fight they should have had a long time ago. After it, my mother will give up on the birthday party and my father will give up the idea that he's got to get to the bottom of what caused the explosion. Mike will rest in peace and we'll live happily ever after.

But instead my mother locks herself in the washroom. I can hear the door closing, both taps being turned on.

"I'm still hungry," Petey whines.

My father looks at him. "We'll have toast, then," he says.

"Toast for dinner?" says Petey.

My father gets the bread. He drops a couple of slices into the toaster, and while he's waiting for them to come up, he takes several deep breaths.

"Petey would like waffles better," I say. "He doesn't really eat toast."

"Take the spaghetti out of the garbage," Marco suggests. "Give him that to eat."

"*You* want to take it out?" my father says.

"If I have to."

"Soup," my father decides. "Soup and toast, like we did it back in the mine—Habitant pea soup. Have we got that? We bought a case of it last summer, in Ontario, I know we did. Have we gone through it already? What the hell did your mother do with it?" He goes over to the cupboards and finds soup, a small can of Campbell's chicken noodle, but he opens it anyway then can't find a pot. The toast pops up while he's still rummaging through the cupboard, and he presses it down again, like it's all moving too quickly. He's standing with his hand still on the toaster, pressing the button back down, when my mother comes back into the kitchen.

She's cut her hair. Done it herself when she was in the bathroom. It's a weird, haphazard cut. Somewhere in the vicinity of a lesbian cowgirl who's the lead singer of a Norwegian punk band. She runs her hand over her nearly bald head, and it's like she's noticing it for the first time herself, like she's touching someone else's head.

The sight of her causes Petey to burst into tears and run out of the room.

"You look good," I tell her, because it's the only thing to say.

"Thank you, James James," she says. "You're a good boy."

"What have you—?" my father starts to say, then stops. The sight of her clearly rattles him. It *scares* him. Like the whole time he's been there thinking my mother will snap out of it—that they'll both snap out of it—but now he's not able to believe it. This is real insanity, he decides, something that needs to be defused or else buried so far underground that it won't explode in anyone's face, the kind of manufacturing defect he would find and which Marco would sue over. The blood is on his hands. Something is taking its course and he doesn't know what it is.

"Can I touch it?" asks Petey. He's standing in the doorway, his face still wet from the tears.

"Come here," she tells him.

She lifts him up onto her knees and wipes his face.

"Almost bald," he says, as he runs his hand over her head.

"Bald," repeats my mother. "It's a strange word when you think of it." She says it again and stretches the vowel out all the way, like she's yawning.

GARBAGE BAGS

When I smell the bread burning I realize my father's been standing there the whole time with his finger on the toaster button. When he finally lets go, the toast pops up, blackened and smoking. He takes hold of the slices right away, as though he can't stand the sight of them, and throws them into the garbage. Which is where he maybe gets the idea. All his life he hasn't just been right about everything, hasn't just had an answer before anyone else—it's also been right under everyone's noses all the time. It's like he can't believe he's been sitting around waiting for things to get better over time when direct action has been a viable option. Time to rip the Band-Aid right off.

So he reaches under the sink and takes out a handful of black garbage bags, then seems to reconsider and instead takes out more, stuffing them into his pockets. Then he begins marching around the house picking up everything that's connected in any way with Mike. He takes his obituary off the fridge and stuffs it in the bag, does the same with the longer article in *The Plain Dealer* that reported his death, had the quotes from other kids who were pretending to know him, and the rest of it, all the carefully clipped rectangles that mention him and the explosion in any way, all the cards that people sent and are still, months later, right there on the mantel over the fireplace. When he's filled the first garbage bag, he starts on the next. And when he's done with the main floor he goes upstairs into my room, stuffing Mike's clothes into the bags. Everything from his dresser and desk, all his T-shirts and jeans, his old notebooks, his tapes and CDs, his video camera. All of it, his pencils, his solar calculator, his math set, pushing it into one garbage bag after another.

When he's done, he carries the bags out to the curb, putting them out even though it's a Thursday and garbage day isn't until Tuesday. My mother is shouting at him the whole time, asking him what he thinks he's doing. Petey's running around like crazy, following my father and screaming when he picks up the shark that Mike gave him and tries to put it in a bag. I watch him, follow him as he moves furiously through the house. Then my mother stops making any noise and stands there swaying the way she did at the cemetery as they lowered Mike's casket. None of it makes any sense, not my father rampaging around the house like we're having company over who he doesn't want to know about Mike, not my mother rocking back and forth. Finally Uncle Marco leaves, closing the door quietly behind him. My father doesn't notice.

After he's finished carrying the garbage bags out to the curb, he calls the city sanitation department and says he has a special pickup. The offices are closed for the weekend, but he leaves a long message saying they should get here as soon as they can. Then he goes into his office in the basement, comes out a minute later with his camera. He walks straight past my mother, who now doesn't say a word. He gets in his station wagon and drives away. Then, just as if it's the kind of cheesy movie Mike said he'd never direct no matter how much they paid him, it starts to rain. To pour madly. Now my mother leaves as well, except she's walking, right into the pouring rain. She's carrying an umbrella but it's closed and she uses it like a sword, swinging it in front of her like she's slicing through the rain. Petey runs outside and stands in the rain, watching her go. I start carrying the garbage bags back from the curb. On one of my trips out to the curb, there's a kid—he's my age, maybe a little older—standing there, looking at the garbage bags. He's got Mike's stupid plastic commemorative King Tut salt and pepper shakers, the ones I got him for his birthday, after the exhibit rolled through Cleveland.

"Put them back," I tell him.

"These are cool."

"Yeah, well, they're my brother's."

It's pouring rain and the kid is turning the tiny King Tuts over in his hands.

"I said put them back."

"I was just checking them out."

That's when I see he looks exactly like Sean Penn.

"Hey," I say, "are you Sean Penn?"

Sean Penn shakes his head. "I'm just some kid."

"You look like him."

"This is shitty weather," Sean Penn says.

"Do you live around here?" I ask.

"You could say that."

I'm staring at the King Tut shakers and Sean Penn puts them back into the garbage bag.

"I quit school," I tell him, for some reason. Like I'm that desperate for a friend.

Petey is running around like crazy on the driveway, jumping in puddles.

"Look at that kid," he says.

"That's my brother."

"I'm getting soaked," he says. "You remember that rain in *Stand by Me,* now that was some crazy rain. This is rain like that."

"I'm melting," says Petey.

"What a world," says Sean Penn. "You better get that kid inside."

I pick up the last of the garbage bags and turn around, but Sean Penn is gone. "Where'd he go?" I call out to Petey.

But Petey is nowhere to be seen.

I'm not going to go into the details of what happens next, because I can't go through it again and I'm sure you don't really want to hear it. One minute Petey's there, splashing around in the puddles, and the next he's gone. At first I think that maybe he's just in the backyard, so I sprint around back. But he's not. I call his name a couple of times, then start screaming it, and it's like I'm going to pass out—but somehow I don't. I'm running up and down the street, knocking on doors. Some neighbours know Petey and some don't. Sandy-haired boy with sleepy eyes, I say. Then Grant's car pulls up and Vivian gets out. She looks with me for a bit, running in every direction while the rain falls around us, and says we should call the police.

All along our street you can see people looking out into the night, into the rain.

"I bet it's Sean Penn," I tell her, "I bet Petey is with him."

Vivian looks at me as if I've lost my mind. And maybe I have. Maybe I've imagined that Sean Penn kid, or maybe it was some other Penn brother, maybe a Penn cousin. Finally I go back in the house and pick up the phone and hear the water upstairs. He's in the bathroom, I realize, and I run upstairs and find him in the tub, happy and warm, with his killer whale.

"Jimmy," he says, "are killer whales mean?"

"Petey" is all I can manage to say.

"Mike thought I should have a bath," he tells me.

I run downstairs and yell to Vivian, who comes upstairs and yells at Petey, but can't really get into it because she's so happy to see him.

"He ran his own bath?" says Vivian.

I tell her who cares.

Then Grant calls up to say he's going, and Vivian goes downstairs. I lock the bathroom door and take off my clothes and get into the bath with Petey myself, just as I did once upon a time with Mike.

Later, after Petey's asleep, my father gets home and he sees the garbage bags are gone. Thinking they've been picked up puts him in something like a good mood, a sign that at least someone knows what it means to be responsible, what it means to do a job. When it begins to get dark he comes upstairs and asks me where my mother is. I tell him about her walking off into the rain, and he shrugs, like it happens every day. A little while later he comes up again and asks me again.

I suppose my father thinks he and my mother are having one of their old fights, in a new way. Once upon a time, my mother's main weapon was silence, and now she's trying something different. Now she's pretending to have vanished. It's the kind of thing that happens more often than you'd think, in the Bible. My father hasn't had anything to eat, and neither have I, so he orders a pizza. I should be starving, not having eaten since breakfast, since before the zoo, before Marco came over. I can't believe that all happened today. Still, when it comes I just have two pieces, and then we sit on the couch together in front of the television in the family room watching the Stanley Cup playoffs, and I can feel him waiting for her. Ready to argue her into the ground, to show her how he was again doing the right thing even if everyone thought the opposite. I'm so relieved that Petey wasn't killed or stolen that it's difficult to be mad at my father for anything.

The call from the hospital comes a little after ten.

By the time we get there, she's already in a room. It's on the third floor, at the end of a long hallway. We hear from an ER nurse that she was found making her way toward the middle of one of the Shaker Lakes, about two miles from our house. From her injuries—hypothermia and some cuts on her feet mainly—it was plain she had been walking for some time and then also spent a long time filling her pockets with rocks and stones, even an old soda can that cut the side of her hand. Anything she could find.

We find my mother propped up in a bed, an intravenous tube attached to her arm and something else attached to her chest that keeps track of her heart rate and blood pressure as well as her body temperature.

"There they are," she says, too cheerfully. "You two are a sight for sore eyes."

She waits for my father to say something, but he doesn't. He goes over and sits down next to the bed. He looks smaller there, older.

"How are you?" he asks, speaking quietly.

"Better than when I came in, I can tell you that," she says. She lets out a strange, bad laugh that wells up inside her and bursts out, like a sneeze. After, it takes her a moment to collect herself. Then she looks at my father. "Boy, was I cold. You don't know it at the time, when you're out walking, but then when they bring you in, that's when you feel it."

He says: "You should have called us for a ride."

"I didn't want to bother you."

"Bother? It wouldn't have been a bother."

"You were in the middle of things."

"Who cares if I was?" my father almost yells. And then, more softly, he says it again, "Who cares?" It's nearly a whisper.

The nurse comes in and says my father can stay but I have to leave. Only one family member per night allowed. When I get home I find Petey asleep and Vivian lying beside him on her bed. Both of their faces are peaceful, and in the background Mike's old Kansas tape is playing. Vivian must have dug into one of the garbage bags and found it. Got it out and put it into Mike's old tape deck. I stand there for a second listening to the song, the singer singing about how, if you close your eyes for a moment, the moment's gone, like dust. It makes me laugh, to think how Mike hated that song. Or said he did anyway. Probably he didn't hate it and that was why he'd got the tape. The last time I'd heard it, he was lying on his bed in our room, shaking his head. Saying, Jesus Christ, Kansas, the worst music in the world, then closing his eyes and listening to the rest of it.

WITNESS

In the morning I've got the radio news on when Petey comes downstairs, the weatherman talking about how warm weather is on its way to Cleveland. Petey's Eggo waffle is on the table, already with syrup on it. I've even brewed coffee, like my mother, though I don't drink it; the smell of it suffuses the kitchen.

"Did you have a good sleep?" I ask.

Petey looks back at me with a clear expression of terror. Normally he's the one who wakes up first and has to hit me a few times before I become conscious. Actually, I've not slept at all. I got home from the hospital a few hours ago and figured I'd stay up, had no choice about it actually. Sat there in the front room and waited for the sun.

"Where's Mommy?" These are his first words.

She's out, I tell him. "It's nothing to worry about."

"Where did she go?"

I don't answer his question. "Are you hungry? You must be hungry."

He's not yet sitting down at the table. "Where's Vivian?" he says after a moment.

"Vivian's with Mom."

"They're *both* out?"

"Sure they're both out."

Petey stares back at me, like he's thinking of making a break for it, and I'm wondering if I should have just come out and told him the truth. Not all of it, maybe, but I'm not certain making it sound as if his mother and sister have gone out on an early-morning shoe-buying expedition is the best course of action. There's probably a whole list of dos and don'ts about how to talk with a kid about his mother's failed-and-really-weird-to-begin-with suicide attempt, as well as a whole other list of things you absolutely must not say. These are murky waters. Vivian is taking her turn with my mother at the hospital and I don't know where my father is. Maybe he's lying down in front of the bulldozers, which, for all I know, might be about to flatten everything that remains of the library.

Once I get Petey to the preschool—I'm so late the mothers have already left—he takes his place in the circle. I wait for a bit, hovering around outside the classroom, but as he listens to Mrs. Dumme read a story he looks so unworried that I decide to leave him there, know that I'd only make things worse by being there at the moment he starts to freak out. I make my way to the bench in front of Simon's and watch workers in hard hats taking apart the fence, throwing the parts into the back of a pair of dump trucks parked menacingly on Lee Road. They get the fence down, and then nothing happens. I wonder if Marco has managed to do something, hold things up, but one of the guys in hard hats says there's been an accident on Mayfield Avenue and the bulldozers are tied up in traffic. There's nothing to do but wait, and so I watch the workmen mill about, walking down to Amy Joy for coffee and then walking back, standing around in the new spring sunlight.

Sometime after that, I fall asleep. Right there on the bench.

I wake up just as the bulldozers arrive; it's the noise they make as they're driven off the flatbed truck that wakes me up, a harsh metallic grating, and I look at my watch and see it's one in the afternoon. I'm late—one and a half hours late—for picking up Petey. I start to run back, but then I feel myself starting to pass out and I slow down, try to breathe regularly, feel it again as I reach the preschool stairs and come up them slowly, stopping every couple of stairs. The whole time I'm wondering how mad the Mothers and Mrs. Dumme will be. If there's going to have to be a tribunal wherein everyone decides if they're going to kick me out of the co-op. The gravest of consequences are reserved for just this infraction as outlined in the Parent Handbook. Maybe we're already out. Maybe Petey's been taken away and put into children's services.

When I get there, the Mothers are all waiting for me, still in the classroom.

Jenna stands up, is about to say something, but before she can, I try to explain myself. And these are the words I use to do this: "Jenna," I tell her, "I deserve a break today."

No question: when it comes time to edit my life, this is one of those bits I'd splice out and then creatively reinterpret.

First off, I'd start off by making a more spectacular entrance. I wouldn't take forever to get up those stairs and would instead march in authoritatively like I'm Richard Gere in *An Officer and a Gentleman* on my way to pick up Debra Winger from her place on the assembly line. Only I'd be picking up Petey who's a kid instead of a girl, which means I'd have to pick him up in a way that would impress the other preschoolers, who get picked up by adults all the time. When Richard Gere picks up Debra Winger, it's spectacular because he's doing it in a soul-killing factory where she's been working since before the beginning of the movie. No one expects anyone to be picked up like that in a soul-killing factory, but in a preschool the bar is a little higher. I'd pick Petey up and twirl him over my head, or throw him up in the air and catch him like he's a baton. And then, just as I'm about to leave, Mrs. Dumme would come walking through that sea of Mothers and say something so profound that everybody—and I mean everybody in the movie and out of it—would instantly agree with it. I don't know exactly what she'd say, the actual words she'd use, but it'd be like what that old guy says at the end of *Witness* where Harrison Ford goes and lives with the Amish but ends up punching out this guy who's wrecking their stuff—something that the Amish are totally *not* allowed to do. Punching the guy blows Harrison Ford's cover and he knows it, but he doesn't care. There's a lot more to it, including this sexy Amish girl, and then at the end of the movie the old Amish man—the Mrs. Dumme of the movie—comes up to Harrison Ford, just as he's leaving, and says, "Be careful among them English." This basically means that Harrison Ford is a good guy and they love him, in a weird way.

Also, I would most definitely not tell anyone I really deserved a break today.

No sooner were those words out of my mouth than I could tell, just by looking at the Mothers, that it made most of them start to think about what they were going to have for lunch, and the rest of them think that a Big Mac would not be a bad idea.

I also started thinking a Big Mac might not be a bad idea.

But Jenna wasn't, as it turns out, standing up because she is about to chew me out or expel me from the co-op. What she's doing is coming over to hug me. Which is what all the other the Mothers do, all at once, grabbing me and hugging me in a kind of frantic mass hug that tousles my hair and surrounds me with all their different soapy and perfumy smells.

The Cleveland Clinic keeps my mother for three days while she recovers from hypothermia. That's what they tell her, though we know the whole time they've got her under observation. She's on suicide watch, like they think she's going to make a run for it and try to drown herself again. Or worse. When I go to see her there's this guy—he's dressed in white, like a nurse, though you can tell he isn't one— who lets you in. He presses a button and then the doors to the floor where they've put her open slowly, like the tape deck of a super-expensive stereo.

During the time my mother's in the hospital, my father fixes up the house. The phone rings in his office every so often—I imagine it's Marco—but he never answers. He didn't take any of Marco's calls before, but this is different. Now it's like he's on vacation. He puts a new lock on the back door, fixes Petey's tricycle, then goes around the house repairing the window ropes. It's not easy, putting in those ropes; it means taking out the windows, retying the ropes to the weights that have fallen through to the bottom of the window wells, then threading the ropes back through and nailing the window frame back in place again.

I'm going out the door to the preschool one morning when my father says to come back after I drop off Petey, that he's going to teach me to fix the windows.

I get back just as he's starting on one of the front windows in the living room.

"You fix the rope first," he tells me. "Once you've done that, you put in the window—first one side, then the other." I watch him, and then he gets me to do it myself. "Go ahead, give it a shot," he says, and watches me thread the rope through the top pulley on the right side of the window and try to fish it out the bottom. On my first try, it works.

"See," he says, "there's nothing to it. We could go into business together."

"Maybe this is the future—Morrison and Son Window Ropes."

"You ever stop with Petey at Turtle Park?" he asks me as he's cutting the rope for the other side of the window. "On your way home?"

"Once or twice," I say. "Usually he's having a nap."

"We used to go there, remember? I mean, I used to take you there."

"With Mike and Vivian, when we were kids."

"Remember when Mike broke his teeth?"

"That was Vivian," I tell him. "She was on the monkey bars and fell right through the rungs. You got me and Mike to find them, and then we ran down to the dentist. He put them back in. If you put them in a glass of milk they'd be okay, and that's what we did. Vivian had her bottle—she was, like, three."

"Dr. Reardon," my father says, and shakes his head. "That's the dentist."

I tell him, "We used to have this red wagon and you'd pull us all in it. One time Vivian fell out and hit her head, and after that she had to wear a helmet all the time. She hated that helmet. We'd be on our way out the door and Mom would come after her with that helmet. Vivian would cry every time she saw it."

"Are you sure about the helmet?" For a bit we stand there looking out the screen at the empty street. Then he looks at me. "What happened that night at the library? I mean, really?"

"I don't know. That's the truth. Mike stopped talking to me."

He doesn't know what to say to this. "I'm sorry to hear that," he tells me, then picks the window up off the floor. "Your mother's seen him, you know." He ties the knot twice, pressing it into the groove on the side of the window with his thick fingers. "Mike, I mean," he adds. "She's had a vision, you heard her say it, and not just that morning when she talked to you on the phone. I don't know what she'd call it. She keeps asking me about it, if Mike's come to see me too. Like he's out there making his rounds. Last night at the hospital she said it again, as if it's just a matter of time." He stares out again at the absence of traffic on our street, then he places the window carefully into the opening. I hold it in place and he puts the pieces of frame back and hammers in the delicate nails. Once they're in, he fills in the holes with wood putty, dabbing his thumb into the shallow container and smoothing it over the small nail holes in the window frame. It takes a couple of minutes to dry and then he uses a corner of sandpaper to sand it down, so you can't see the hole left by the nail. "We'll touch it up with a bit of paint tomorrow and it'll be good as new."

He steps back and looks at it. I do the same.

"You know," he tells me, "when we bought this house hardly any of the windows worked. A couple on the second floor, one in the kitchen. Mike was in the hospital still and your mother wanted a real house, and one day we went for a drive. She'd grown up around the corner, and we saw the sign on this place. I wasn't crazy about it, but your mother wanted to take a look. It was like she knew, the way she went right up and looked inside. There were a lot of houses on the market that were empty back then so no one minded. It was an older guy who owned the place before, and he'd let things go. Not all the way, but he'd cut corners, put metal shims in the sides of the windows so they'd stay up, like wedges. You're supposed to have the ropes, but he couldn't be bothered. The windows that *did* work, I had to treat them like they were museum pieces. I'd open them so slowly, but no matter what you did, it was only so long before the rope would break. The next thing you'd hear would be the sound of the weight falling. I'd think, it's gone. Forever, and for good. Like heat. But you've heard that all before. The weights are like that. Either they're there, or kiss them goodbye. You'll never see them again. That's what I used to think, anyway."

After that he walks outside and the two of us sit out on the veranda.

"When my brother got killed," he tells me, "my father saw him. More than once, even. I'd hear him talking and I'd go in and he'd be alone. He'd tell me he was talking to Mike."

"You never said anything about that."

"The point is that it's not really him. It's just the imagination—it felt like he was there, but I know it was just a trick of the mind, not some kind of supernatural force. That's what Dr. Kasoff says, and for once I think he's right."

"I better go get Petey," I tell him. I start walking down the driveway, but then suddenly I turn around, hoping I can catch Mike rematerializing where my father saw him last. A spectral presence in a white lawn chair.

At the preschool, Mrs. Dumme tells me that the kids are making cards for my dead brother Mike's birthday.

DALLAS TUCKBERT

It's Thursday, my mother's first night back from the hospital, and we're having Kentucky Fried Chicken because it's my father's idea of a celebratory meal. He's called my uncle, and though I don't know what's been said, the animosity between the two seems to have evaporated. It's Marco who shows up at the front door with the food, standing there finishing his smoke and almost grinning.

"You ordered Kentucky Fried Chicken?" he asks me.

I tell him to bring it in.

At the kitchen table, I watch him take the cardboard boxes out of the white paper bag with the picture of Colonel Sanders on it, and the smell of the chicken wafts through the kitchen, just as it did through that funeral parlour on Taylor Road when I was on that banana diet, hoping someone would remember and tell me to forget about it and help myself. Live a little. Marco lays everything out on the table so it's ready for my mother's arrival. Plates and plastic spoons, buckets of chicken, bright green coleslaw. When it's all out on the table, we go outside so we can be there when my mother arrives, watch her walk up the front steps.

My mother gets out of the car looking pale and fragile, almost dangerously clean, as though she held herself under a strong stream of water before coming home today. It's disconcerting, her looking so completely sane, so utterly in control. But maybe this is the way it's going to be from here on out. As she walks up the driveway she looks around in bafflement, as if she's surprised to see her old house still standing. It's only been days since she walked out into the rainy night, but it seems somehow longer, as if she's back from the dead—come all the way over from the other side, like some saint out of a Doors song. The kind of person Jim Morrison would have made up. She's wearing a loose-fitting black T-shirt and shapeless black track pants that make me wonder how much weight she's lost. Petey runs and kisses her, almost knocking her down. Then, with Petey on one side and my father on the other, she comes inside.

"James James," she says, touching my face, "what a good boy."

She sits down at the table and Marco makes a big deal of showing her the feast he's set out, saying it's nothing but the best for his sister. She takes some fries and a chicken leg, and spoons some coleslaw out on her plate. Her hands shake a little, and I wonder if she's taking something that's making them do that, or if this is the way it's going to be from now on. When the shaking gets too bad, she holds her hands under the table.

But it's my father who seems to have changed the most. He tells us about Dallas Tuckbert as he's taking his fork and spoon out of their plastic coverings. "She's a birthday party specialist," he explains. "She puts on parties. Helps other people do it, that is. She's an organizer."

"Of parties?" says Vivian. "Is that a real job?"

"She comes highly recommended," Marco assures her. "I asked around."

"Can't we just call it off?" asks my mother. "I'd like to call it off."

"We can't call it off," says my father. "The invitations have gone out already."

"I don't know," says my mother. "I'm not up to it. I really don't think I am."

My father won't hear of it; Marco protests as well. "Whatever needs doing," Marco tells her, "Dallas Tuckbert will get it done."

"Just sit back and enjoy the party," my father says. "I think it could be exactly what we need."

We're putting empty Kentucky Fried containers in the garbage when the doorbell rings. A moment later Dallas Tuckbert strides into the kitchen. She's six feet tall, with bright red hair tied back with a huge scrunchie that matches the light blue of her shoes and purse and the tiny polka dots on her pantsuit. The first thing she does is give us a big fake wink, like we're all old friends and are about to pull off a hilarious caper.

"I'm Dallas," she says, then goes around the table shaking hands. "I'm glad to have you on my team," she tells me before letting go of mine.

"I'm glad to be on your team," I tell her.

"What's the name of the team?" Petey wants to know.

"The name of the team?" Dallas replies. "Team Dallas."

When she gets to Vivian, Vivian says: "I love that suit."

"Well then," replies Dallas, "I can see we're going to be getting along fine." Then she laughs and claps her hands.

"What kind of name is Dallas?" asks my mother.

"Only the name of the greatest city in the world," she says, and then laughs again in such a way as to make it impossible to know if she's kidding or not. "That's right," she tells us, "I'm Dallas but I'm not *from* Dallas, though I wish I was." Now she literally explodes in laugher and it takes her a long moment to recover. We all watch. She takes some deep breaths, followed by a theatrical wiping of her brow, which is not sweaty in the least. And now a final, very deep breath, which makes it seem like she's about to get down to business. "All right," she says. "I don't mind telling you that we have a *lot* of work to do. When I spoke to Fortitude this morning, he said the party was this weekend. Two days from now. I told him that I had to get over here *pronto* and get everyone into high gear. I also told him that if anyone can do it, we can. Am I right?"

No one knows what to say to this.

"Maybe it's too much," says my mother.

"You won't have to do a single thing," my father tells her.

"That's right," chimes in Dallas, who seems to have understood there's something wrong with my mother. Maybe with all of us. "Leave it to me. Leave the whole thing to me."

"Didn't I tell you?" Marco tells us. "Didn't I say she comes highly recommended?"

"Why hello," says Dallas, as if she hadn't quite seen him when he said that he liked the sound of Team Dallas.

He introduces himself.

"Is that an Italian name? Because I have a thing for Italian men. I'm just going to say that right here and now."

Marco shakes her hand again.

"Are you a boxer?"

"Actually," he replies, "it's not the first time someone's said that."

"So, we've got two days," she tells us. Dallas is serious again, as if Marco was trying to distract her from her real purpose. "What *usually* happens to me is that people get me involved a year, perhaps two years in advance. One girl here, you probably know her, Kerry Dray, who lives on Bushnell, she hired me for the first birthday of her little girl Kirsten when she was still in her first *trimester.* That was quite a party. Flawless, and I don't use that word often—*flawless.*"

"Flawless," repeats Petey.

"Are you the birthday boy?"

Petey says he isn't and before he can say anything else, Dallas says how she's already looking forward to it. "I think this will be wonderful," she tells us. "We'll see each other tomorrow and I'll give you a full update. In the meantime"—she puts a finger across her lips—"this is our secret."

Before anyone can ask what she means, she's gone.

"She was nice," says Marco.

"She liked *you,*" says Vivian. "I bet she knows you from TV."

"What did she mean by *secret?*" My mother looks at my father. "What did you tell her?"

"I let her think it was a surprise party."

"We have to tell her." My mother moves her untouched chicken around on her plate. "It's only right she knows."

"Fort's going to tell her," says Marco.

"Of course I will," says my father.

BILLY VALENTINE

That night Jennifer McKellar shows up and the two of us drive out to this big house party. It's strange she's here, but I decide to play it cool, as if I'm wondering what took her so long. I act like her coming by is the most natural thing in the world, as if the whole time she's been sitting around at home thinking about me.

"Hey," I tell her.

"Hey, yourself," she tells me back.

Then we stand there for a bit.

"So," she says. "You doing anything tonight?"

We're like two gunfighters sizing each other up.

The party she takes me to is about a mile away, on the west side of Cleveland Heights, almost at the border where it turns into Cleveland itself, in one of the huge houses at the top of Cedar Hill Road. There's a long line of parked cars stretching around the block, and we have to drive up and down nearby streets looking for a parking spot. It's warm, for April.

I think about telling her she looks pretty but I don't. Maybe that would make it weird. She's wearing a thin white tank top under her cropped leather jacket, and frayed blue jeans. Her blond hair, which is always pinned up so carefully when she's working at the donut place, is hanging down around her shoulders. It's longer, more red than I remember it from our Geography and English classes, and a cool breeze comes in through the open window, blowing her hair toward me. It smells like blueberries, like before she drove over to our house she rubbed a blueberry jelly donut into her hair. Just before we get out of the car her dead eye looks over at me, for just a second, then looks away, focusing instead on something above us, in the night sky. She parks the car and I think she's going to get out but she doesn't.

"Anthony wants me to marry him," she tells me, while we're still sitting there in the car.

"He said that?" I say. A moment later, "Were you and Mike going to get married?"

She laughs at that.

"What's so funny?" I don't know why I want to talk about Mike but I do. It's the last thing I should be doing, if there's any chance of anything ever happening between us, but I can't help it somehow.

"Mike wasn't the sort of guy you marry, not really."

"Not anymore," I say. The words are out of my mouth before I can stop them and I have the feeling that she's about to say this was a bad idea, change her mind, and drive me home. But instead she checks herself out in the rear-view mirror. I can't tell if she's got something in her good eye or wants to see what her dead eye is up to.

"It just wasn't like that between us, you know, we didn't talk about the future. It never came up."

"I thought only the Amish girls got married right out of high school." I can feel myself calming down. "There's no way I'm getting married until I'm forty."

She rolls her good eye. The dead eye is still contemplating the night sky. "I can't imagine being forty."

"Were you, you know, in love with him?"

She laughs again. "We had good sex."

I get out of the car and start walking down the road, as if I'm in a hurry all of a sudden to get to the party.

"Hey," she says, catching up, "sorry."

I tell her not to worry about it.

She wants me to say something profound-sounding, but I don't know what it would be. I actually have no clue what she wants.

The party we're walking to is at the house of a kid named Billy Valentine, who goes to University School. It's an expensive private school east of here in Hunting Valley. Billy is Prescott the Pepper, University School's official mascot; at hockey and football games he wears a hollowed-out Big Boy head, along with a University School blue blazer and school tie. He's an only child, which means he's the sole occupant of the basement floor of his parents' mansion, which is where he grows his own marijuana in a hydroponic set-up fitted out with a complicated speaker system that plays a variety of different tunes twenty-four hours a day to his plants.

I've been to Billy's once before, with Mike, about a year ago. We went there to buy weed—it wasn't long after Mike read that Jim Morrison book, which was what made him decide we at least had to try to get into it. Afterwards Billy took us out back so we could sit around his folks' pool and try some of his Dream On Weed. It was called Dream On Weed, he told us, because it had listened to nothing but Aerosmith while it was being grown. Mike smoked a joint Billy rolled and said he could tell—that the Aerosmith had got into the weed. This was exactly what Billy Valentine wanted to hear, and it made him lean back in the deck chair he was sitting in and close his eyes blissfully. Mike passed me the joint and I passed it right back to him, saying I wasn't into it. Billy and Mike tried to be very cool about it, like they didn't care, but I felt like a loser all the same. Then they smoked some Opus One Weed, which was marijuana that had listened to nothing but big band jazz during the time it was being grown. The truth is I don't smoke up because the one time I did—this was with Mike, one time when our parents were out and we were in our backyard—it gave me a really long weird kind of seizure where I pissed my pants. So I sat there and watched Mike and Billy pass the joint between them. The last time I'd seen Billy Valentine was at Mike's funeral. He'd worn a suit and sat near the back with his father. I saw him as we were carrying Mike's coffin through the front of the church.

Billy's basement looks different than the last time I was here; all of the hydroponic paraphernalia has been cleared away to make room for a makeshift dance floor. It's really loud, and Jennifer and I stand there watching other kids sway back and forth to "Sunday Bloody Sunday," looking thoughtful.

"Where's Billy?" I shout to her over the music.

She shouts back who cares.

Some kid with a mohawk comes over and shouts to me about what a drag it is about my brother being dead. I think we were in History class together two years ago, but I can't say for sure because the kid didn't have a mohawk back then. I shout back yeah, it's a drag, and he says what? and I keep shouting it until he hears.

Jennifer goes and gets us a couple of beers from the keg in the corner.

"Is Billy here?" I shout to the kid with the mohawk.

He looks at me like he doesn't know what I'm talking about.

"Billy Valentine," I tell him, but then he sees somebody on the other side of the room.

I turn around and there's Jennifer with a couple of plastic cups. She hands me one.

"Make a toast," she shouts and raises her cup.

I think about it for a second, and then I shout: "It's a strange and haunting world, reminiscent of a new wild west."

She steps forward and puts her arms around my neck and kisses me, leaning in really close to my ear so I can hear her. "That's a pretty cool thing to say."

I let her think that it's me who came up with it.

"You want to get out of here?"

I say fine and we put down our beers, go back up the stairs, back out the front door. "Where do you want to go?" I ask her when we're out on the street and can hear again.

"I don't know. How about my place?" She smoothes back her already smoothed hair and is very still for a moment.

"Okay," I tell her.

We drive through a maze of streets, a part of Cleveland Heights I've never been to despite living here all my life. The houses are sandstone brick, with both pools and tennis courts in the backyards. Her dead eye is trained on the rear-view mirror the whole time, like it thinks we're being followed, or like it's looking at itself.

"Does Anthony know you came to get me tonight?" I ask her.

"I told him, and he didn't care. He had to work, you know. He sits there, waiting for the accidents. Friday is his big night."

I say that figures.

"He didn't actually propose, not officially. He tried to pretend he could take it or leave it." She lets out a sardonic laugh. "I could tell he meant it, though. I mean, he's that transparent."

"So you're still together, sort of."

"He tried calling me tonight, but I said I didn't want to talk to him."

We pull into a long driveway. At the far end there's three cars, a red old-fashioned Mustang convertible, a pickup truck and a beat-up Mazda. "The wreck's my cousin's, this hippie freak from North Jersey."

We step into the house and she calls out saying that she's home. When there's no reply, Jennifer says she guesses her cousin is out. "Be quiet, though," she tells me. "Just in case."

"Are your parents home?"

"They're in Vegas, some corporate thing."

I nod, as if to say I'd thought as much.

We take off our shoes and I follow her into the living room. It's got a big fireplace and piano, and a coat of arms that she says isn't a real coat of arms, just one they used in some movie about King Arthur. We head upstairs, to her room, which is covered with posters and photographs of the various members of U2. In the centre of the wall over her bed there's a framed life-size picture of Bono at Live Aid, that moment just before he wades into the crowd, stage-diving and singing Lou Reed. She gets out a pack of matches and lights a huge red candle that's next to the bed, then crosses the room and turns off the light. In the darkness, for just a second, I can't see her dead eye at all.

I sort of half sit down on the bed next to her.

"Jimmy," she says, with her hand on the small of my back. "Let's get each other naked."

It's such a lame thing to say—something out of a bad porn movie—I almost laugh and have to turn in the other direction so she can't see me smile. When I do it's like she thinks I'm shy and she gets off the bed, kneeling down on the floor in front of me. "I want you to go first," she says, and starts with my socks, reaching up under my pant leg and peeling back the elastic, taking them off like they're nylons or something. Which they're not, and I start wondering if it was like this for Mike, if this was what it was like that night in the library, before the explosion. Jennifer taking off Mike's socks in this incredibly slow, kind of strange and not very sexy way. It makes me wonder if this was the last thing he did with her. If she went that night, and it was like this, if this was what she told the cops that they kept out of their report. Now she's standing up, taking off her shirt. Standing there in her bra, then taking the bra off, coming up over to the bed and straddling me. I've spent so much time sitting beside her in Atkinson's Geography class imagining this moment that I expect the sight of her in real life—the sight of *any* actually naked actual girl in real life—should be a more completely earth-shattering event. But there's something ordinary about the sight of Jennifer naked, of her dead eye looking at itself in its moonlight reflection in the U2 poster, her small, ghostly breasts in the candlelight.

"What is it?" she says.

"Nothing."

She reaches down, like she's going to unbutton my pants, only instead she puts just the tip of her finger inside the waistband of my jeans.

"Don't," I tell her, and when she keeps going I move away.

She gets off the bed, finds her shirt on the floor near the bed and turns on the lights.

"I'm sorry," I tell her. "It's just one of those things."

"Is it?" she asks, getting dressed.

I put my socks back on, and we sneak out to the car. There's still no sign of her hippie cousin, no sound at all in the gigantic house. Neither of us says a word as she drives me home, and she speeds a little down Lee Road, as though she wants to get past the ruined library as quickly as possible. The bulldozers are still there, I notice, behind the truck that brought them in, the site still untouched, the rubble unmoved.

As I'm getting out of the car, I say, "I like you. I always have, even before."

It's like she can't hear me. "I'm such an idiot," she says, then puts her keys on the dashboard.

"I hope you don't marry that guy."

She lets out a loud sneeze. "We're not going to get married," she says. "I'm not even sure he asked me."

"I better get in there," I say, and then, just as I'm about to get out, she leans over and tells me to wait. "You're right," she tells me. "About me and your brother. It was me that night he was waiting for."

I say I figured it was.

"But I chickened out, I don't know why. Good thing for me, as it turned out."

"I guess so."

She says, "I shouldn't have said that. It was a rotten thing to say."

"It's okay," I tell her.

Then I pause, one leg on the pavement. I want to say something, but nothing comes. I close the car door behind me. "Well," I say to her through the open window, "see you at Mike's party."

She puts the car in gear and I watch her drive down to the end of our street, wait there until she turns. I can still see her hand, hanging out the window with the smoke in it, while she makes the turn.

Inside the house, the preparations for the birthday party are moving along, even though it's nearly eleven. My mother is writing names on name tags and my father is blowing up balloons. The balloons are in the middle of the table, a red and blue and orange and purple rubber mess in a big dish. Like they're the main course, something Vivian has microwaved so thoroughly it has actually turned to rubber.

"So, Jimmy," says my mother, "tell me about this girl."

"She's Mike's old girlfriend," I say, in as matter-of-fact a tone of voice as I can muster.

"Jennifer McKellar," says my father.

"She's already got another boyfriend," I tell them.

"And you're that other boyfriend?" asks my mother.

"If I was," I say, "would I say it like that? Why would I be so coy about it?"

My father says, "Your mother was coy when we met."

I point out that she was a nun.

"Did you know right away?" my mother asks him. She's really asking the question. It's like she's forgotten I'm in the room. "That first time you saw me?"

"Yes," he says. He can't seem to look at her.

"Really? The whole thing, the kids?"

"No," he tells her, after a breath. "Not the whole thing."

Then he blows up a balloon. My mother goes back to her name tags, writing down the names, making sure she's spelling them right. Checking them against the master list when she's finished one, then putting it carefully face down, in alphabetical order. And it's then my father finally looks over at her. Like he's wondering what the hell happened.

Before I go to sleep I get out one of the garbage bags my father carried out to the curb that night he lost his mind. In it there are some photographs of Mike that he took with this camera that used to be my father's, an old Polaroid that spits out the pictures right after you take them. There's a picture of the doorway to our house, then a close-up of the number, then a shot of me, from a distance, looking at nothing. Then some of Mike and kids from Heights High, outside. Then one I took of Mike beside his green Gremlin, that car our father never wanted him to buy in the first place. I sit there for a long time on the floor of our room and look at them. One of the pictures was taken by Johnny Wang himself, in front of the Johnny Wang Good Food Truck. It's of the three of us, me, Mike and Jennifer McKellar. She's in the middle, wearing an orange T-shirt through which you can see her breasts, but not that well. Her dead eye is staring upward, like it's thinking of heaven. I have my arm around her and so does Mike. It's September, before either of us has kissed her, when she was still the new kid. Mike had given Johnny Wang the camera and then said wait, wait a second, and called her over to be in it. At first she didn't, just stood there, but then Mike in that way of his said come on, and she came over and stood first beside him. No, he told her, and then she got in the middle and Johnny Wang snapped the picture.

I spend a long time looking at those faces, looking for some detail that maybe I missed. For a clue, some sign. But then I give up and stuff them under the mattress of Mike's bed. It seems a strange place to put them because of how important they seem suddenly, like the last remnants of an ancient, obliterated civilization.

ROLLING ROCK

Two nights before Mike's party, Vivian and I drive out to Mike's grave. We've got a six-pack of Rolling Rock and the idea is that we're going to open the bottles and pour them out onto his tombstone. Maybe we'll drink a couple. Maybe we'll get a little drunk, sit down and tell stories about Mike. It's the kind of thing Mike would have been totally into. I've got a pack of cigarettes too, though I don't really know how this is going to be part of it. Pouring a beer out in a really mournful way onto your dead brother's grave is one thing; stubbing the end of a smoke out on him is a different thing entirely.

Vivian is dressed for the occasion like Annie Lennox, all in white from head to toe with a brown shawl that she pulls over her head, like a hood. I'm wearing Mike's old Joker shirt, the one he bought at Cedar Point last summer, when my father took us all there to celebrate his big victory over the forces of evil and a massive car company that, not inconceivably, might decide to sue me if they read their name here. According to Mike, the Joker was worth all of Batman's villains put together, worth more than Batman himself. The last time I had it on was that day I went back to school expecting to see Jennifer McKellar and fell apart at the front of the classroom while the "Star-Spangled Banner" played in the background. What I remember most clearly, more clearly even than that day at school, was putting that shirt on in the morning and standing in front of the bathroom mirror, looking at myself with it on. The idea was that kids would see me with it on and know it was his shirt. But not everyone. Only the real fans. The kids who had not just his greatest hits and the box set, but all the albums and maybe even the singles too.

When Petey's asleep we sneak out through the back door. We park my father's car on a side street, and when we're sure the coast is clear, we open the gate and are inside, just like that. The place where Mike is buried is called Lake View Cemetery. It's not hard to get into because it's one of those ancient Cleveland places, huge and old, and we get lost for a bit in the darkness as we look for Mike's grave. Finally, almost by accident, we find it and realize that we forgot a bottle opener for the beer. Vivian picks up one of the bottles, then breaks it open by smashing it against Mike's gravestone. There's glass everywhere, green shards hidden in and amid the grass, and the whole thing seems wrecked, the ritual of it, like we've dropped our communion wafers on the ground but picked them up and put them in our mouths anyway.

But instead of being upset, Vivian tells me that, up until the night before last, she was pregnant.

"With a baby?"

"I think it was a baby. Though it might have been a cat."

"Don't joke around. Jesus, you're sixteen."

"Don't be a dick, Jimmy."

"I'm not being a dick."

"Anyway, you don't have to worry about it."

"That's terrible" is all I can think to say. This is the wrong thing to say even if it feels like the truth. It's not what Mike would have said. He'd have congratulated her on flushing her life down the toilet. Well, *a* life, he'd say. He'd be outrageous and able to say something like that, which would make her laugh, make it okay somehow. And he'd have meant the congratulations part. But I can't.

"It could be worse," she says. "I could have cancer."

"You're right. I know." Though the truth is cancer would have been way better than having a baby. Then I would know what to say. A ton of people have cancer; some of them die and some don't.

She pours out the rest of the beer from the broken bottle onto the gravestone. In the darkness, I can barely make out Mike's name. She says, "I thought it was a great thing at first, I don't know, a replacement for Mike. In the end it was a miscarriage. I guess I was lucky, you know. I don't know what I'd have done. I didn't tell Grant or anyone else, but I feel like I have to tell someone. Otherwise it'd be like it never happened. At the clinic one of the nurses said there's a lot of babies who don't make it out of the first trimester, you know, the first three months. They say when that happens there's something wrong with the baby to begin with, that it never would have survived anyway. She said that at the start, so I wouldn't freak out. That's what they tell you. It happens all the time."

I stand there watching the dampness disappear into the grass over his coffin.

Then she says, "How come you never told me about the bomb shelter?"

"It was Mike's thing," I tell her. "It was up to him."

She's sad, but she's trying not to be. "Dr. Kasoff says it's not our job to second-guess history. There's what happened and there's the rest."

"The turning point is when history refused to turn," I tell her. "I know, I got the lecture."

From somewhere in the direction of the street, the sound of a radio.

"You think it was real that day," I ask her, "that she saw him?"

Vivian shakes her head. "I guess she either imagined it or he came back, actually, you know, from the dead, to say goodbye. Put in one last appearance."

"Do you believe that?"

Vivian stands up and brushes the grass off herself. "We better go."

"When did it stop?" I ask her as we're getting in the car. "I mean, when did you know you'd lost the baby?"

She says, "The thing is, you don't know exactly when you have the miscarriage. It dies on its own and sometime later it all comes out of you, like you're having your period. And just like that you're not pregnant anymore." When she says this, Vivian snaps her fingers in the same way Mary DeSilva did that night when she told us about love, when she tried to tell us how quickly it comes and it goes, how the world can change in the blink of an eye.

It's the sound of that snap that reminds me I've still got Frank DeSilva's invitation to the birthday party in the glove compartment of our car. I saw it near the front door, still un-mailed, and I made up my mind to take it over myself. To make sure that one got to him, no matter what. It's nearly midnight by the time we get there, and I expect the house to be shut up and quiet. Vivian stays in the car and I run up to the front door thinking I'm going to just drop it off. But Frank is sitting out on the dark porch, his eyes gaunt with insomnia. He looks much the same as always, a rake-thin man who may or may not have cast a spell on Mary.

There's a moment when he looks at me and it's like he's trying to decide if he's awake or asleep. "Jimmy?" he says, peering at me.

I hold out the envelope.

All at once, he seems to deflate.

"Peruse this at your earliest convenience," I tell him.

"Peruse?" He opens it, and laughs, almost bitterly. "A birthday party?"

"It's my mother's idea."

"I'll give it a shot," he says. "But I can't promise. I've got no energy these days, I don't know what it is. I should get out more, I know."

I tell him I've got to get going.

"Thanks for coming to Mary's funeral," he says. "I saw you there, even if I didn't say it."

"Who do you think I am, the robot Hart Crane?"

That makes him laugh, even if it's only for a second. "Now where have I heard that before?" he says. "I'm going to try to come," he says. "I really am going to give it my best shot."

Mary DeSilva's funeral was outside, on the shores of Lake Erie. In the big gazebo at Lakewood Park, on the West Side. It was a freezing morning in early November, and an icy wind was blowing up off the lake into our faces as we stood there on the shore. It was the sixth day after the explosion, after Mike was officially declared among the missing. Only

Vivian and I were there because our mother was at home, unable to get out of bed or see how any of this was a blessing and because our father had already locked himself downstairs in his office, with the photos of the wreckage, trying to figure out how Mike had caused such devastation.

Mary had been something called a humanist, and she'd left specific directions about her funeral. She wanted to be cremated and for her ashes to be cast over the waters of Lake Erie. The ceremony began with a brief reading from a Devhan Starway short story called "Moon of the Robot," which is about the funeral of the robot Hart Crane. In it, almost the last thing that happens is the widow of the robot Hart Crane reads a short poem that, if you're from Cleveland, you know is really not by Devhan Starway, but by a human being named Hart Crane, the same guy who the robot is always being mistaken for. It was Mary's wish this poem be read at her funeral. Just in case you're not from Ohio, and even if you are, here's how that poem by the human Hart Crane goes:

Over the greatness of such space
Steps must be gentle.
It is all hung by an invisible white hair.
It trembles as birch limbs webbing the air.
And I ask myself:

"Are your fingers long enough to play
Old keys that are but echoes:
Is the silence strong enough
To carry back the music to its source
And back to you again
As though to her?"

It was read out in a clear voice by the minister, who you could tell was trying her best to sound like a robot. Then there was a eulogy by Mary's brother, who was as rotund as Mary. He talked about how she had loved Lake Erie, about how as children growing up in Lakewood they had played on the beach together. And how, if there was any peace to be found on a day like this, it had to do with the fact that she had not lived to see the decimation of her library, which she and Frank had loved so much and kept such a careful watch over, those many years. By that time everyone knew that Mike had been inside as well, though no one knew the whole story. A lot of people were saying things about how Mike had got inside the library that night and why, but not Mary's brother, who asked everyone to remember Michael Morrison in their prayers. He went on to say that he'd met Mike, had seen the work he was doing with the 16 mm films and knew that it was Frank who had taught him how to do it, and that he had taught him well. The loss, he said, was a great one.

There were about a hundred people there, and in the middle of the crowd stood Frank with Mary's ashes in a simple clay urn.

After Mary's brother had finished speaking, there was a moment of silence and everyone bowed their heads. And then the minister got up and said it was time to let go of Mary, to send her to her final resting place. But when she turned to Frank, he refused to let go of the urn. She tried to take it from him, but he held on. His fingertips were white from the strain.

No one, it seemed, could get Frank to let go.

And that's when I saw him. At first I had no idea who he was despite having studied his author photo, his dissolute beard and interstellar grimace for so many hours, despite having read so many of his books in the desolate silence of a Friday night at an empty public library. I'd imagined him hunched, bent and maimed by life on this planet, but he was nothing of the sort. But there he was, he'd come back to Cleveland. Nearly seven feet tall, with elfin fingers and wire-rimmed glasses that glinted even in the weak November light. Devhan Starway had on a white parka with long sleeves that, unlike any parka I've ever had, billowed in the wind. A silence came over the assembly, and I stepped aside as he moved past me, walking slowly, nearly gingerly, and the crowd parted before him as people understood, like me, that Devhan Starway had returned to say goodbye to his greatest fan.

"Please," said Frank, and handed him the urn.

The tears bubbled up and out of Frank as he watched Devhan Starway lift the urn over his head, seeming for a moment to teeter under the strain. But then, just as he looked like he was about to fall, a great wind came along and lifted Mary's ashes out of the urn like a tiny cyclone, the kind that are said to roam the surface of Jupiter ceaselessly, pulling Mary's ashes up and into the air. They rose improbably like a dark balloon, like a small doorway leading back to light-filled mornings, like a spacecraft moving at the speed of light, bound for a better place.

THE BIG DAY

On the day of the party, Dallas Tuckbert tells me the only thing I have to do is to pick up the cake. Getting the cake is like being best man at a wedding, Dallas says, and goes on to explain that the responsibility of the best man is to make sure that the groom gets there. And in this case, she says, the groom is the cake.

The baker girl brings it out and lifts up the lid of the box so I can take a look. It looks so much like a tombstone that I say: "Mike will love his tombstone."

"And if he doesn't, he can go straight to hell," she says.

"Good luck with your brother," I tell her. "I mean, I hope you guys get back in touch."

"Whatever. And tell your brother happy birthday for me."

"I will."

"I have to say that, actually," she says. "Otherwise I could lose my job."

"He's dead, you know."

"Who is?"

"My brother, the one you made the cake for."

"This is a birthday party for your dead brother?"

"You can still come if you want."

She shrugs and then turns away, like she doesn't want me to know if she's considering it—like she *wants* me to wonder.

There are trays behind her of chocolate-covered cookies, and under those are others trays of cookies with strawberry and vanilla icing. Before I've even walked away she's gone back to what she was doing before. Taping up cardboard boxes, breaking the tape off by bringing it across the tiny jagged teeth at the front of the tape dispenser, like a hacksaw blade.

When I get home Vivian and Dallas are on the veranda, hanging flower baskets. Vivian is on a ladder and Dallas is standing on the front lawn, near the curb, telling my sister to rotate them so the best side faces out. "It's not flawless," I hear Dallas telling Vivian, "but it's not bad." She's excited, and when she sees me, she says, "There's just something about the day of a party, isn't there."

Once it's twelve thirty and there's a possibility that people might arrive, a hush descends over the backyard. We sit there and wait to see if anyone will actually come. Even the giant inflatable bounce house seems couched in expectation. I walk around, afraid to touch anything, looking at the poised trays of carrots and celery, at the nacho chips sitting there in their glass bowl. I watch Dallas walk across the backyard and give my father the thumbs-up, as if to indicate all systems are go. It occurs to me that he and my mother are afraid of the people they've invited, these birthday guests. And I am too. The look of our empty backyard is almost too much to bear, the idea that the afternoon could come and go without anyone showing up. Then it would be like a funeral. More like a funeral than Mike's actual funeral was, where at least there were other people. We'd stand there with the cake and have to eat all the food ourselves, or else gather it all up in garbage bags and take it to the curb.

When he can't stand it any longer my father gets up and moves around the ice in the coolers, asking if maybe we should have mineral water as well. Vivian comes out and tells him to take a Valium. Dr. Kasoff prescribed them to her, she tells him, but she doesn't need them, so there's enough to go around. I say no, but my father thinks about it and takes one from her hand, secreting it away in the breast pocket of his suit jacket. He's still trying to be ready, for anything, despite all those variables out there he knows nothing about.

Vivian is dressed in a dark green cocktail dress that shimmers a little in the spring sunshine. It's elegant and grown-up, and to offset it she's wearing a pair of Mike's old sneakers. They look big on her, like clown shoes, and she trips over them, as though Mike is sticking out his leg every so often.

We've been lucky with the weather and we know it. It's risky to have planned the party outdoors in Cleveland in April, but the weather is warm and sunny. Perfect day to lose a child, I try not to think. Other years in April we've had snow days, the whole city shut down. But not today. The air is smelling sweet and green. It's like someone's up there, says Dallas. The four waiters she's hired stand at the end of the driveway, furtively smoking cigarettes, and the band is tuning up. They're a bunch of older guys, in their forties—a lounge band, a group that uses a drum machine and plays ski resorts and county fairs, taking the requests of senior citizens, the kind of band that plays regular gigs at accounting conventions.

The first of the guests to arrive is Dr. Kasoff, looking dapper. Like he's sent his bald head out to be shined by professionals.

My father goes over to shake his hand, and so does my mother. After that he turns to me and smiles like we're best friends.

"I'm glad you came," I tell him.

"It's not just me, right? You invited other people." He fixes me with his motionless shrink glare.

"How does it work exactly?" I say. "I mean, do I have to keep going to you forever?"

"Why do you keep asking that?"

"Just wondering, I guess."

Now more people are arriving. Some of them from the grief therapy group.

"Look," I tell Dr. Kasoff. "It's your fan club."

Dr. Kasoff laughs a little, though it's not a real laugh. I can tell by now. "I'll tell you something, Jimmy," he says. "You're going to be fine."

"That's good news."

"I mean it, and I can tell. I still worry about your lack of friends"—this is something he's said before, and each time he does, it's like I might not have noticed myself—"but at your age," he goes on, "friends can be as much a hindrance as anything. You'll be fine. It's not everything, you know, being fine. And some would tell you it's overrated."

"I think you're a good shrink," I say. "Even if you're a jerk sometimes."

"Thanks, Jimmy," he replies. Like it's the nicest thing anybody's ever said to him. And for all I know, it might be. He walks across the grass and looks carefully at one of the vegetable trays. Soon he's talking to the couple whose four-year-old died after falling out of a wagon. The kind of thing that four-year-olds do all the time and that hardly ever kills any of them.

Then the Mothers arrive. First are Jenna and Ellen, then Debbie and Moira, all dressed in sundresses with their hair down and makeup on, looking so pretty it takes me a second to realize it's them. I say hello, thinking they're friends of Vivian's who might want to have accidental or sympathy sex with me—and I'm surprised to learn who it is I've been thinking of hitting on. Like she knows what I'm thinking, Jenna observes none of the husbands are there. Hers said he'd come, but she told him he better not, this was a girl's thing. The others, it appears, have told their husbands something along those same lines. It's a kind of compliment, like the Mothers have all decided they're going to be my dates, and maybe it wouldn't be the worst thing in the world if I decided to make a pass at one or two of them. Ellen tells me Karen couldn't make it, that she had a hair appointment, but she says it in a way that makes me wonder if maybe Ellen offed her somehow, fitted her with concrete shoes and dropped her at the bottom of the Hudson. Now they're saying hello to my mother, and the couple arrives whose sixteen-year-old was killed one sunny day on a jet ski.

Mrs. Dumme is behind them, looking smaller than she does within the precincts of the preschool. "This is quite festive," she says. "Did you make these decorations?"

"We bought them," I confess. "My father got a professional party planner."

Mrs. Dumme looks disappointed. Not just in us, but in the entirety of Western civilization.

"Petey's going to be thrilled to see you here," I say.

She gives a short nod, which I take to be a tacit acknowledgement of the fact that it is, indeed, a great honour to have her at any birthday party, that she gets a lot of invitations and cannot possibly go to all of them, no matter what people may think. She joins the Mothers, next to the inflatable house. Most of the kids are inside it now, jumping around, and the Mothers are standing there in a cluster, like a posse not to be messed with. Jenna tells me they brought a present.

"I don't think it's that kind of birthday party," I say.

"It's not for your brother."

"It's for you," says Ellen.

"It's from the all of us," Ioana tells me.

Jenna hands me the box carefully, and when I open it up I see there's a fishbowl inside. With water and a fish.

"Is this Leon?"

"A pinch and no more," Mrs. Dumme says. "No matter how he looks at you."

"Now," says Jenna, deliberately leaning into me so that our shoulders are touching, "which one is this Jennifer?"

She's just arrived and is standing with Anthony, watching the band get ready to play. He's got his arm around her, like they're already married.

"She's okay," remarks Ellen.

"Pleasant looking," says Jenna. "But that's as far as I would go."

"Who's the guy?" says Debbie.

"Her new boyfriend," I tell them. "Maybe they're going to get married."

"Is that what the kids are doing these days?" asks Mrs. Dumme.

"It is," I tell her.

"Is there something wrong with her eye?" Jenna wants to know.

"It's dead," I say. "It died when it was born."

"Now that is sexy," says Moira. "When I worked in advertising I went out with this guy who had his fingers cut off in a lawn mower. Two of them. We were in the same agency and whenever he made a point, he'd wave around those cut-off fingers. It drove me wild."

"This is a completely different thing," Jenna tells her.

"At least she's not the Gorbachev, with that thing on the side of his face," observes Ioana.

"You'd get used to it," Moira tells her. "Believe me, I know what I'm talking about."

"This Jennifer's a little young, if you ask me," says Ellen.

"I think what she's saying," says Jenna, "is that we'd like to see you go out with someone who's just, you know, unbelievably hot."

I tell her I'd like to see that too.

"Let's have a picture." Debbie brings out her camera, and then the rest of the Mothers search through their purses for theirs. She waves over one of the waiters and gets him to take six pictures, one with each camera. I've got Mike's Instamatic, and I give it to him to take one for me. Then six more, with the kids. Petey stands in front of me, like we're actually related. When we're done, he hands me his diver's mask, the strap of which I see my father has fixed, using duct tape. I hold it up to my face so I can see how the world has looked to Petey for the last few months and see it's like the inside of an aquarium, a safe and interesting place that's got nothing to do with us. I need to take Leon and his fishbowl inside, though, so I turn to give the mask back to Petey, but he's forgotten about it and gone back with the other kids into the inflatable house. So I take it in with me and when I come back, Jenna hands me the picture the waiter took with the

Instamatic. I stand there looking at it, checking out the Mothers in their dresses, and me in the middle of it looking like a normal kid. Surrounded by girls who may or may not be going out with me—and somehow, not quite so fat as I used to be. I don't know if it's been all that walking back and forth with Petey from preschool, the endless pacing on the sidewalk in front of Amy Joy Donuts, or if I'm just imagining things and am exactly as fat as before.

There I am: Jim Morrison, of Cleveland Heights, Ohio.

Now the sound of guitars being strummed, of one chord and then another.

Smiling a little, walking toward me almost in time with the beat of the music, my father tells me happy birthday. "Isn't that strange," he says. "The whole time I've been here I've been thinking I should say it to someone. Couldn't bring myself to do it, though."

"Happy birthday, yourself," I tell him back.

"I went to look at the library today," he says. "And it's gone now, completely. They've already done it, levelled the whole thing. The paving crew will probably start Monday." He looks out across our backyard, at the people coming and going, and it's like he's counting them. "We should have had a list at the front. I can't keep straight who's come and who hasn't."

"You can't think of everything."

"No, but you can give it your best shot." He takes a green olive off the tray of a passing waiter. "That's what it was like in the mine. A miserable place, I can tell you that. We worked there, whether we liked it or not. Just like the James Fortitude Morrisons have always done. Until you. You're the first of us to not have to go anywhere near that kind of place. The thing was, we were never safe down there and we knew it. One summer—the summer before the scholarship for me came through—there was a kid who came from Winnipeg, a college kid named Ravvin looking to make money. He couldn't handle it—you'd line up in the morning and see Ravvin checking and rechecking his kit, putting off actually going underground until the very last moment. Finally he had to be let go, and I remember my father telling me it wasn't the first time; it was a hazard of the job. There were men who could do that kind of work and men who couldn't. The thing was, Ravvin didn't need to do it, and he knew it. Everything would be fine, then all of a sudden you'd get too afraid to do anything. When that happened it was time to quit." He looks away. He seems to not have any idea of what he's going to do next, or even what he wants to happen. It seems clear he can't go back to doing what he did before, his old job of getting to the bottom of things. "Who's that?" he says, pointing to a thin man in a fedora. "Is that Frank DeSilva?"

My father gets to Frank just as Frank seems to be changing his mind about having come, as he's about to leave. My father touches his arm, turning him around like they're old friends, the way the governor did on the steps of the courtroom. He and Frank shake hands slowly, and that's when the man whose wife and ten-year-old were killed one snowy day when a tractor-trailer veered out of control on I-270 introduces himself. He brings up the recall, saying he had one of those trucks. He shakes my father's hand, and my father starts to tell the story. Frank stands there listening, shaking his head, looking a little less pale and even smiling as my father goes over the immutable laws of the universe, no pushing ropes, no possibility of hot getting anything but cold.

The band starts playing "Maggie May," which the singer introduces in a fake Rod Stewart accent, saying it's an old folk song some of us might know.

Over by the collage of photos of Mike that my mother put together is Detective Moore, whose idea it was for me to get that photo of Mike and go on television. It's like he's still looking for him, still trying to get an accurate description. He's in uniform now, with his cap on, and when I ask if I can get him something to drink he says no, that he's on duty.

"You ever thought about law enforcement?" he asks me.

"You mean be a cop?" I say not really.

He's looking at the photos. "I can see the resemblance," he says. "You and your brother."

"You really think so?"

"I see it completely."

"People used to think we were twins," I tell him. "The non-identical type, that is."

I leave him there, looking down at the pictures of Mike.

Now the band is playing "Don't You (Forget About Me)" from *The Breakfast Club.* Without a drummer the song is shapeless, an amorphous noise, almost elevator music.

Soon the party is in full swing. Debbie and Ellen are talking to the woman who carried her defective baby to full term. They're eating taco chips and salsa, drinking something green out of clear plastic glasses. The woman's had the baby, it seems, and is already thin again, and she's lost that distraught expression, at least for today. No husband with her, though. Maybe that's a relief, too. Some kids from Heights High have shown up, and I realize I've forgotten their names. Jennifer is over with her possible fiancé talking to Dr. Kasoff, who is swaying to the music and looking like a large bald drumstick. Dallas and her waiters are moving through the crowd, trying to get people to eat things wrapped in bacon.

It's impossible to know if my mother is having a good time or not. She's wearing a black dress, like the one she wore to the funeral, which makes it seem like she wanted to have the party just so she could not be a part of it. So she could show the world that she's not over the death of Mike, not just yet. Detective Moore shakes her hand, says something. From the way they look, I know he must be expressing his condolences, saying how sorry he is. I can almost hear her reminding him, reminding herself, that the idea is to celebrate Mike's life. As I watch her it occurs to me that, of all of us, it's my mother who has the least idea what we're doing throwing this party.

Dallas comes to get me, saying it's time for the cake. I follow her into the kitchen and help her take it out of the box. If Dallas knows anything about Mike not showing up to blow out the candles, she says nothing to me about it. Or maybe she's just decided that a party is a party. She arranges the candles in a colourful half-moon and extracts a lighter from somewhere inside her jacket, a small metal object with an elongated spout made specifically for lighting the candles on a birthday cake.

"Tricks of the trade," she tells me and lights the candles. Then she picks the cake up and hands it to me. I take it from her. "Showtime," she says.

"Showtime," I repeat.

Now we're walking out, very slowly, toward the party. Dallas gives the signal and the middle-aged guys in the band lurch into "Happy Birthday to You."

The cake is in my hands. And Dallas is behind me. I can hear her singing. Everyone moves toward us, singing themselves, and out of the corner of my eye I see another figure in black, a flash of light from her tongue as she smiles at me. It's the baker girl, I realize, she decided to show up after all. I look over at my mother, who is not singing because she's saying the rosary, somehow able to pray again. Her hands are clutching the beads and she is looking at the cake. Then "Happy Birthday to You" ends and a silence descends over the party.

I am holding the cake.

Whatever is going to happen, it is going to happen now.

DON'T BE AFRAID

If this was that movie Mike and I talked about making, here's what would happen: I'd be standing with the cake, with the candles about to burn themselves out into the icing, and Detective Moore would not be able to take it any longer. He'd confess there was a big conspiracy and that the paving of the library lot is part of it. Just like my uncle, and maybe also my father, thought. And then Uncle Marco would sue everyone and my father would use the money he'd got from having his life ruined to buy some very cool apartment in midtown Manhattan, or maybe Paris. Anywhere, as long as my mother wouldn't have to walk these same Cleveland Heights streets, somewhere with the kind of library that stays open twenty-four hours a day, where she could sit any time she wanted.

That would be one kind of ending.

Another kind of ending would be the one where there's this whole big buildup to the party but then, when it's *almost* the end, the audience doesn't get to see the party at all, doesn't even get a glimpse of the cake, because it turns out to be a movie about me—you know this because the camera stays with me at the very end. I turn out not to be the fat kid or the kid with the hat (there's always a nutty kid with a hat in movies) who no one cares about, but the main guy. Instead of going to the party, I take off with Jennifer McKellar because she drags me out to her father's Porsche, pulling me by the hand, and then we drive away, maybe to Niagara Falls.

I'd think she was having second thoughts, but she'd kiss me, and as she did, both her eyes, the good one and the newly resurrected one, would stare at me, at the same time. Then the credits would roll.

But this is what really happens.

First, my knees give way. I feel it coming, the way I always feel it. I fight it, try to pull myself upright, like I can sometimes do, and for a second it almost works. My father comes toward me, then steps back, thinking it's okay but then all at once the different parts of my body are falling asleep. I start to sway and someone announces I'm going down. It's Vivian, and I almost tell her that I'm sad she lost that baby. And that if it had survived I'd have looked after it while she stayed in school. I'm falling face first, into the dark chocolate tombstone of a cake.

I open my eyes to find Dallas Tuckbert breathing into my open mouth. She stops when she sees I'm not about to die, then stands up and announces that the waiters will be coming by with pieces of cake. Next she helps me up—lifts me, actually—and mostly carries me inside, all the way upstairs, and lays me down on my bed. I don't know how she knows where to take me, which of the beds belongs to me, but she doesn't hesitate, like it's one of the things she's made it her business to know. One of the tricks of the trade.

She tells me she's sure I'll feel better in a few minutes and is on her way back to the party. My mother comes in, but Dallas stops her at the door, saying she's got to go back to the party, that if she doesn't appear downstairs in the next thirty seconds people will assume something terrible has happened and will start to leave.

When my father comes in, Dallas tells him the same thing. They ask if I'm all right, and when I say I am, they do as they've been told. Turn around and go back outside where the band is playing a slow, waltzy version of "Blue Monday."

As soon as my parents are gone, Sean Penn walks in.

"Hey," I ask, "are you really Sean Penn?"

"I suppose in a way I'm not," he tells me. "What do you think?"

I'm going to ask him what he means by that, but instead I pretend I'm passing out. I close my eyes for what feels like forever, and when I open them I expect he'll have taken the hint and left. But Sean Penn is still there, next to the bed, like he's standing guard.

"Were you sleeping just then?" he says. "Because you really didn't sell me on it. If you want to make it seem like you're actually sleeping, you have to breathe way more deeply."

Outside the band is playing a Cure song, the one about heaven and being asleep for days.

"I forget your name," I tell him.

"You know, I'm that kid."

"Thanks for your concern and all. But I'm all right."

"Didn't this used to be your brother's room too?"

I look at him. "Did you know him?"

"Sure I knew him," he says, smiling almost. "He was a good guy, I don't care what they say. If you knew what it was like to be down there in that bomb shelter, safe from the ravages of time, with all those books on top of you making you believe in heaven."

"What did you say?"

"Anyway," he says. "I better go."

"No, wait. Did you have a good time at the party?"

"It was all right. I liked how you passed out in the cake."

"I didn't pass out."

"Right."

"I fainted."

"Sure you did."

I'm about to get angry when he smiles this strange smile. It's like he's taken the different parts of me and gathered them together, and is handing them back to me.

And I guess that's when I know it's him.

"Don't be afraid," he tells me.

"Okay," I say, though I am.

"In the movie, you know, I'd end it here though it would be lame. Like it's all right, the whole thing."

"Is it?"

"If you want to know what I think about it, I guess it is. Not much anybody can do about it now. It's a happy ending, though there were parts of it that sucked. I better go."

"Wait. I mean, hang out, or come back."

"This is really more a drop-in kind of thing. It's always that way. You don't want to go and then you get there and you start having fun. That's when you have to go. My ride is here."

"Okay," I tell him.

"Wayward son, carry on," he says. "That's a funny exit line, huh, such a cheesy song. Kansas, dust in the wind, baby. God, the worst music in the world."

There's more I want to say, but he steps through our bedroom door and is gone.

I try to get up and follow him, to say something true, or good, or even that I'm going to miss him. That I already miss him. It should have been me who was in the library that night, not him. He's the real Jim Morrison of the family, the one who should have got out alive. And that I won't make that movie, I never will. But I get up too quickly and lose my balance and bang my head against the corner of the dresser.

My mother comes in and I tell her to get Sean Penn, grab him before he disappears again. But she doesn't know who I'm talking about and I start to shake. Something comes over me, I don't know what. She bundles me up, like she did when I was little. It cheered her up a lot to have someone to look after even if it meant we had to go back to the hospital and have a whole battery of tests done to make sure there wasn't anything interesting or excellent wrong with me.

The official verdict on the explosion, on what caused that bubble of gas to form in the first place, was that it was an act of God. Which seemed to mean it was a pure accident, the kind of thing that could happen anywhere. For no reason at all. Which did make you sort of think that maybe God had been responsible for it. Heaven, like my mother has always said, is no newspaper. You can't just open it up and look at the headlines. There are no headlines. There's this and that, births and deaths, and everything in between.

After the party my father stopped trying to get to the bottom of it. By that time he had written to everyone, to the governor, to the President, to Frank DeSilva's replacement at the Public Safety Office, to the FBI and the CIA and the Army Corps of Engineers. Some replied and some didn't. Most pointed out that the official position of the government, and, for that matter, the official position of everyone who had anything to do with the case, was that it was impossible to really get to the bottom of whatever it was that happened that night. Not that such a bottom didn't exist, but that they were done looking for it. There had been a slow gas leak under the library, and one night it exploded. End of story. The rest of it, the phone calls from Mary DeSilva, Mike and me finding the bomb shelter, even Jennifer McKellar, it's all beside the point. Or else, as the governor said in the letter he sent my father, while it might be *theoretically* true that the bottom my father was looking for exists, it is the sort of bottom that cannot, for various and variously regrettable reasons, be reached by him or anyone else in his employ. It is, therefore, an act of God. For her part, my mother thought it was a good explanation. She believed it and she wanted my father to believe it, though I don't know if he ever did. Not completely.

ACKNOWLEDGEMENTS

Cleveland Heights, Ohio, is, indeed, one of the eastern suburbs of Cleveland, and there is a library there, on Lee Road, and just down the street from that library is the Church of the Saviour where, indeed, you can find one of the very best co-operative preschools any four-year-old could hope to attend. But this is a work of fiction nevertheless; the library never exploded, and any similarities between the parents and the teachers whom I had the good fortune to know there are purely coincidental. Cleveland Heights really is a nicer place to live.

This book was written through a time of momentous change in my life; people from various countries, states, provinces, cities, jobs old and new, playgroups, and writing groups have all had some part in helping me get it done. Too many to thank, but I'm going to thank a lot of them anyway.

Thanks to Peter Kvidera and Melanie Shakarian for your enduring and unstinting friendship, thanks to Dallas, Bill, Barbara and John Schubert for giving us a place to stay and for being among the first audiences of the novel. Thanks also to Nick Santilli, Jim Krukones, Phil Metres, Jimmy and Rique Sollisch, Karen Long, Ho-Fan Lee, Frank Ricci, Norman Ravvin, Alex Cobb, Andrew Biro, Sean Carney, Dennis Moore, Jim and Fran Lissemore, Wendy Simon and Ioana Missits, the last of whom allowed a fictionalized version of herself to appear in these pages.

Thanks to the members of the East Side Writers Group, who read an early draft of the novel and who gave many great suggestions and much encouragement: Sarah Willis, Neal Chandler, Paula McLain, Erin O'Brien, Charlie Oberndorf, Lori Weber, Jim Garrett, and Amy Bracken Sparks.

Thanks also to Dan Chaon and the late Sheila Schwartz, and the members of their writing group who also read the manuscript and gave invaluable advice: Eric Anderson, Erin Gadd, Cynthia Larson, Jason Mullin and Lisa Srisuco.

Thanks to Barbara Day, Jennie Collier, Ellen Barthes, and all my friends at the Church of the Saviour Co-Operative Preschool on Lee Road in Cleveland Heights who inspired so much of this book.

In Colorado Springs, thanks to Dave Mason and Jane Hilberry for your support and expert counsel, thanks to Paula Pyne and Rory Stadler for your patience and assistance, thanks to Adam and Karen Rowe for helping in countless ways, thanks to John Simons, Dan Tynan, and Barry Sarchett, George Butte, Andrew Price-Smith, thanks to Re Evitt for your encouragement and support, thanks to Bonnie Nadzam, Susan Ashley, Patrick Parks, Tim Trunnell, and thanks to Stephen Scott and Victoria Hansen for the soundtrack.

As always, thanks to my students, both at John Carroll University in Cleveland and at Colorado College in Colorado Springs; in addition to commenting thoughtfully and helpfully on parts of the manuscript you have been a continual inspiration.

Thanks, for everything, Vaughan and Kevin McTernan.

Thanks to Miriam Toews and the late Paul Quarrington for talking this book over with me in times of doubt and for both writing novels that led me to write this one.

Thanks to my editor at Knopf, Angelika Glover, for her patience and resolve, and for making this a better book in countless ways.

Thanks to Nino Ricci for reading the novel, and for his wisdom and friendship.

Thanks to Dean Cooke, the very best of agents who stood by this book from the first to the last and who has been a steadfast, supportive, and wise presence throughout.

Thanks to Dick and Fran Carlstrom, who inspired me to write the novel in the first place and who made it possible for me to finish it.

Thanks to my mother, Phyllis Hayward, for making me love stories, and my Uncle Mike and brother Mark.

Thanks to my children, Frances, Eddie and Jimmy, for putting up with so much typing.

And thanks, finally, to my wife, Katherine Carlstrom, who is my first reader, my best editor, and the love of my life.

Steven Hayward was born and raised in Toronto. His first book, *Buddha Stevens and Other Stories,* a collection of short stories, won the Upper Canada Writers' Craft Award and his second, *The Secret Mitzvah of Lucio Burke*, won Italy's Premio Grinzane Cavour Prize. He currently divides his time between Toronto and Colorado Springs, where he is Assistant Professor in the English Department at The Colorado College.